With what dismay Portia would have viewed my dawnings and transformation, her vengeance gone awry! Her sweet, as she'd called me, who should have been soiling himself in abject fear of the barbarians, was himself a barbarian.

I say today I exulted in my rebirth, and I suppose I did. It would, however, be more proper to say I became smug. I was smarter than, and had defeated, Portia. I'd been placed in harms's way and, master player that I was, had with superior wit and intellect once won again. Never had I been more alert, more keenly aware of my surroundings, more alive to possibility. My physical strength increased weekly as the last of the fat laid down in my formerly luxurious life disappeared altogether and was replaced by tough muscles and wiry sinews. Under the rowmaster's tutelage I learned the rudiments of fighting with a dagger, with which weapon, because of my height, I enjoyed a natural advantage. A font of questions, I asked the name of everything new I saw and practiced their language incessantly the more quickly to master its subtleties, which the men said varied from place to place but were similar enough in most for a general understanding.

In this manner, and with no other mishap except a minor encounter with a hungry bear we drove away one night, we poled and rowed and sailed the rest of the distance up the Dnieper to Kiev, which was the most remote Byzantine outpost in those parts, and where I was to be sold.

# WHOSE SONG IS SUNG

Or, A Narrative of the Travels of Musculus Herodes Formosus, Known as Musculus the Dwarf, through Barbarian Territories, Including an Account of His Sojourn with the Northmen, and a True Description of the Demise of a Monster Known as the Grundbur at the Hands of the Hero, Beowulf, and certain other Related Incidents, which elsewhere have been Misrepresented.

A Novel by

FRANK SCHAEFER

A TOM DOHERTY ASSOCIATES BOOK
NEW YORK

This is a work of fiction. All the characters and events portrayed in this book are either products of the author's imagination or are used fictitiously.

WHOSE SONG IS SUNG

Cover art by Gary Ruddell

A Tor Book
Published by Tom Doherty Associates, Inc.
175 Fifth Avenue
New York, NY 10010

Tor Books on the World Wide Web:
http://www.tor.com

Tor® is a registered trademark of Tom Doherty Associates, Inc.

ISBN: 0-812-55012-9
Library of Congress Card Catalog Number: 95-39744

First edition: March 1996
First mass market edition: September 1997

Printed in the United States of America

0  9  8  7  6  5  4  3  2  1

I have pondered at length to which of the rulers I have served in a long life I should dedicate this commentary.

Most of them are dead, after all.

Two, however, it seems to me as I contemplate the empty pages waiting before me, I have served all my days. I might have wearied of them and overthrown them had I been a wiser and more prudent man, but I was not and they rule me still.

It is, then, to those twin lords that I, Musculus Herodes Formosus, the Dwarf, dedicate this account and these meager pages: my mighty and most puissant unwonted Pride, and overweening Vanity.

# 1.    Why A Dwarf Comes to Write an Account of this Nature.

**M**any are the years and long the roads that have led to this rustic cottage nestled in the sundrenched hills overlooking Rome where I spend my final days in peace, quiet, and satisfaction with a long life well lived. One road in particular has led me to quill and parchment in order to set right a fabrication that misrepresents a friend who in death can defend neither his good name nor unimpeachable honor. A fabrication, too, that wrongs me by excluding me. My initial anger has lost its sharp edge over time, but it lingers, ever troubling, like a rotting tooth, and I would set the record straight.

I come to this pass in the employ of His Holiness, Pope Sergius, by grace of God, in the eighth year of his pontificate, which is the year of the incarnation of our Lord 695. Two years ago, though I was leaning toward a feebleness that bade me ill, I bowed my knee to this prince of the Holy Roman Church and set out with his ambassador on a journey to ascertain the state of the Church and the faith in the far northern islands of Britain.

The methods employed on these diplomatic missions are

well known. The ambassador (Bishop Antonius) and his counselors were to parade in full view and confer with priests, princes, and scholars (who are found in surprising numbers there). I, the tripartite dwarf, dunce, and fool, along with a dozen stout Benedictine brothers of some learning but better suited to be bodyguards, which they were, would listen in kitchens, stables, and at the cracks of doors, and concern ourselves with lesser personages whose guards are more relaxed and whose tongues are less discreet. Between the lot of us—those above and those below the salt—we hoped to assemble a well-rounded version of, if not the affairs of the state, the state of our fair Mother, the Church.

We fared exceedingly well. The soldiers who accompanied us kept pirates and barbarian marauders at a distance. We lost only two souls, one a brother who was washed overboard and drowned off the coast of France, the other an elderly priest who died of a bloody flux brought on by tainted pork that, indeed, laid our entire party low for a week. As for the rest, we were protected by certain relics, among which was a finger bone of the blessed Saint Gregory we carried as a sign of His Holiness' favor. No other ill fortune haunting us, and with the winds in our favor, our pilot guided us up the Thames River and we disembarked near the ancient town of London one week before Easter, an expeditious eight and a half months after our departure from Rome.

Britain looked much as I remembered it when I was there some forty and more years earlier. Spring rains had turned London's streets into rivers of mud and offal. I saw three buildings made of stone, one more than I remembered when I left. Only two had leaded roofs, and such glass as could be found was as rare as beauty in a Mongol camp-whore, which is to say it existed, but one had to search long and assiduously, and harbor no great expectations.

London was not Rome, but we didn't complain. Our quarters were commodious and dry, and the food a sybarite's delight after the abuse our palates and guts had suffered during our journey. Aethelbald, the Mercian king who had recently assumed the throne, was a gracious host.

The Church in the southern parts of the Isles was healthy, and though we noted the usual muted whispers and rumors of Arianism, we found no other dangerous or widespread heresies against which the Church must constantly mount guard.

We were less sanguine about the Picts' intransigence in the determination of the true date of Easter. In due course, then, we traveled north to the monasteries at Jarrow and Wearmouth, and thence to Lindisfarne, our northernmost destination.

Lindisfarne is an austere spot even for a monastery. The rough-hewn and heavily thatched oak buildings sit on a windblown headland on the coast of the North Sea, and are isolated from the mainland twice each day by the tides. The wayfarer enjoys few amenities there, but is grateful, as was our party, for shelter from the elements, sanctuary from the depredations of brigands and murderers who abound in the surrounding wild countryside, and simple fare at rude trestle tables. The summer months, with their tangy sea-breezes freshening the air in the dormitories and wafting one to sleep, are pleasant, but woe to the old man with chilblains who's subjected to those breezes transformed into blistering winter gales that bring snow from the nearby highlands and ice from the sea.

Entertainment at a monastery is hardly more common than calves with two heads. Such creatures do exist (I've seen one preserved in brine), though, and, as fate decreed, we were entertained in Lindisfarne. Three days before our arrival, we chanced on a storyteller, called a *scop* in those parts. A poor, half-starved soul, he huddled abjectly close by our campfire, but was sufficiently recovered by the time we arrived at the monastery to offer his services as recompense for his bed and board.

Those were not happy days at Lindisfarne. A plague had swept through there some months earlier and carried off a third part of the brothers. The spring had been so wet they'd had to plant their crops twice, which was an ordeal even for a community sworn to the mortification of the flesh. The good abbot, therefore, with the blessing of Bishop Antonius, ordered the anchorites to sing Compline and, after

Vespers, released the novices and the rest of the brothers from their vows of solemnity for the evening.

The reading that night was from the gospel according to John, wherein Jesus changed water into wine, and the teaching was that merriment, when appropriate, is not a sin. Afterward, instead of the gruel to which the brothers were accustomed, novice, abbot, and ambassador alike feasted on veal, spiced barley, and a pudding made of bread and milk sweetened with honey and berries. Rarely, even in Rome where everything is possible, had I tasted better.

The best, however, was yet to come. No matter how well intentioned, monks are often poor starved creatures, not so much for food, for gruel fills the belly, as for lighter moments. The work of the Lord, however joyful it may be in contemplation of eternal rewards, tends to be dull and plodding when one practices it from day to day: the soul may soar on occasion but, and with distressing frequency, it more often moves at the stultifying pace of a cow caught in a bog.

People regard men of my age as solemn and decaying ancients given either to senile maundering or contemplative wisdom. However right they may be much of the time, such isn't always the case. I, for example, far too frequently yearn for the delicacies of the flesh (luckily, gold will still buy that which is no longer freely given), and I'd as soon live a merry life and help others do the same. To make men laugh is a noble task, and one which, in my vanity, I enjoy to the fullest. Happily, then, I juggled balls and bowls and bones, and plucked coins from cowls and a radish from His Excellency the Abbot's ear (even more than the washing of his novices' feet did his red face make him one with them) and, when I finished, was pleased to accept their applause and be replaced by the *scop*.

Laughter's as heady a tonic as poor wine or humble beer for men whose days and nights are filled with toil and prayer. But laughter may come unbidden, for who hasn't laughed with sheer joy upon beholding the sun emerge after a storm, a chick newly hatched, a calf gamboling wobble-legged next to its dam, or a lark singing the day's praise? Stories, however, especially far from the beaten path in places like Lindisfarne, are stouter fare, and men hunger mightily for them. They're every bit the stuff of life as bread or gruel. At their hearing, the soul shines through the clouds of daily cares, and peeps and gambols in delight of new worlds discovered. I wasn't surprised, therefore, when a hush fell over the hall the moment the *scop* leaped onto the table, sat cross-legged, and tuned his lyre.

I was more than surprised, though, when, no sooner had he begun his song, he mentioned the name of one Hrothgar, who sounded suspiciously like the Hrothgeirr I'd known years earlier, and, shortly thereafter, that of his kinsman, the hero, Beowulf. I was, then, as you may imagine, the very soul of curiosity, and waited with as bated a breath as any story-starved monk for what must surely follow.

Follow it did, that inexorable unfolding, but my initial excitement soon faded, and yielded to disillusionment and disappointment. The tale sung by the *scop* made a mighty tale indeed, but a half-century of telling and retelling had distorted the truth: many names had been changed or given to the wrong people, and so many incidents and events altered, omitted, or added that what remained was as much a web fabricated of lies as the truth.

I know, because I, Musculus the Dwarf, servant and true friend of Einarr, sometimes called Clutcher and, when the time was ripe, Beowulf, was at his side when he slew the Grundbur and, later, his female.

This is what happened.

# 2. *Of My Youth in the Court of the Emperor Heraclius.*

My earliest memories are of overawing splendor surpassing by far any I've known in the years since. I remember many large people adorned in jewelry and dressed in brightly colored clothes. I remember music, and I remember dazzling light inside a building large beyond my comprehension. I retain the dim memory of the odor of an ineffably subtle incense that, to this day when the air is still and humid, I sometimes imagine I can still smell.

Of my parentage, I know nothing, for I was given as a child to the emperor Heraclius upon his ascension to the throne in Constantinople in the year of the incarnation of our Lord 610. I was told that at that time I could barely walk and could not dress myself, so I was perhaps two or three years of age, from which I calculate my present age to be around ninety years. Neither did I know whence I came, although when I was old enough to ponder that mystery, logic dictated certain limits. My skin was more walnut than olive-hued, there was (and to this day is) a heaviness in my speech, and I found strange comfort in dark and wooded places, so I doubted I came from any land to the south or along Aegean or Mediterranean shores. North, was my guess. North of Constantinople, north even of the broad steppes I was told stretched like a grassy sea from the shores of the Baltic until it lapped against the forest lands populated by the barbarians.

I do not pretend to know what children think about the world in which they find themselves. It is enough for me to remember, and to this day dream of, multitudes of people looming over me, poking me, and laughing at me when I tried to flee them. It is enough for me to remember that I thought my name was Dwarf (Heraclius himself gave me my name some years later). It is enough for me to remember hiding under pillows in corners, struck dumb by numbing loneliness, utter confusion, and quaking fear as I pulled on my stubby legs and clubbed fingers in vain attempts to lengthen them so I would look more like other people.

I may be forgiven for not understanding at the time how my early loneliness would be a salvation of sorts in later years. I know only that a more important and timely salvation came when I was five or six years old in the unlikely form of a giant Nubian slave named Amin. Amin came to Heraclius' court after a long, exhausting journey, and was more nearly dead than alive when he arrived. Placed in my quarters, he at first frightened me, but when it became apparent that he was too weak to stand, much less harm me, I found myself bringing him food and doing what small favors I could for him. Before long, we became fast friends.

Amin and I shared a disparate grotesquerie of size, and not much more. He was an adult, I a child. He was as black as onyx, I in comparison nearly snow white. He was twenty hands tall, I but five or six. His voice was deep and resonant, mine high and piping. He spoke but a little Latin, and our conversations at first were halting and limited. He learned rapidly, though, and once he was on his feet again, the sight of us conversing evoked gales of laughter. Infuriated at the time, I too may now smile as I picture myself with head back and shouting up at Amin, and Amin, his head nodding slowly as was his habit, answering me from on high. Sadly, our friendship was not to last. Far too soon, his legs weakened by the unbearable strain placed on them by his weight, Amin tripped, fell, and, from that dizzying height, split open his head like an egg on the sharp edge of a pedestal, and died instantly. Those who were amused by the spectacle were barbarians and, though I received a beating for my troubles, I told them as much and more to their faces.

People seldom pay attention to children, who are man-saplings no more heeded than the mature oak heeds the shaded twig from which another in its image will grow. So, indeed, Heraclius had largely ignored me until the day of Amin's death when, impressed by my loyalty and courage, he later told me, he had me moved into his personal suite. How, then, was my status raised, for an emperor's favorite enjoys unquestionable advantages even if he is a waddling dwarf who's also laughed at. I was, to begin with, seen, which most children aren't. Servants took care to see that I was well fed, clothed, and kept happy. Men and women of high station talked to me and listened to my precocious twaddle when I spoke. I was placed in the charge of the ablest tutors who taught me tricks, and I was soon walking on my hands and turning chariot wheels or back flips, juggling and making other baubles appear or disappear at will. I was taught to play the lyre and the pipes and, more important, to read and write not only Latin, which I learned easily, but also Greek. These arts have served me well, and for all of Heraclius' sins and errors (indeed, he was accused of many), I am grateful to him and will never be his detractor. Hail, Heraclius!

I need say little about Heraclius' fortunes or reign. He was excoriated for being of barbarian birth and for incestuously marrying Martina (his second wife, and by all accounts much nicer than his first, Eudocia, who died before he came to power), who, it's true, was his niece, but those were weakly tailored arguments, the pallid, transparent promotions of men who coveted his power. Try as they might, however, they couldn't gainsay the good he did the empire. His firm grip stemmed the fearful losses after Justinian's grasp had expanded the borders of empire beyond any hope of prolonged defense against the seething hordes pouring out of the east and inundating the lands along our northern borders, not to speak of the ravages suffered in the African south. In the north, he bought off the Avars. In the east, he defeated the Persians. In the south, he restored Egypt, Syria, and Palestine to Byzantine rule. In short, the self-serving and unctuous criticisms against him aside, he put the empire in order again, and warned the barbarian and other nations he wasn't a man to be trifled with. Nor, for the most part and for many years, was he.

I'm not boasting when I say that my value to Heraclius was not solely my size and appearance. More than a mere curiosity to be put on display, I was also his companion. Precociously clever, I amused him in court or on the hunt, and on campaigns carried his maps, slid his sword into its sheath, and, a powerful talisman, rode at his side so, in the moment before battle was joined, he could rub my head for luck.

I wasn't fated to remain only a clever good-luck piece forever, though. I remember the place, setting, and moment when I stepped onto the path that led directly to this place, setting, and moment. Our army was camped on a cramped plain. A river on our left flank ran at spring flood. Low but steeply rising and boulder-strewn hills to our rear precluded escape for cavalry or heavily equipped foot. Soft desert sands on our right flank waited to slow and trap foot and horse. Ahead, a larger, better-fed, and well-rested Persian army lay encamped and, in its confidence, sent an emissary to accept our surrender since we were overwhelmingly disadvantaged and as good as beaten.

I was confused, and didn't understand. Nothing was wrong, yet everything was awry. The day was bright and clear, our army hungry and tired but in good spirits. Heraclius was a proud and capable general, but his confidence had fled him. Upon the announcement of the arrival of the emissary, he retired to his tent, personally extinguished half the candles therein, stationed me behind him in the shadows in the high camp chair he'd had built for me, and summoned his generals to share the dark tidings of imminent defeat.

I'd never seen him act so strangely, and was more alert than usual. Every sense as taut as a bowstring at the mo-

ment before the arrow is loosed, I watched as he seated his
generals to his left, then welcomed the emissary, who he
stood in a place of unnecessary honor to his right.

A triangle is nature's most perfect form next to the circle,
and the wise architect incorporates it for its inherent
strength. Suddenly, but without knowing why, I understood
my master was an architect, and had constructed this triangle for a purpose. The emissary was appropriately smug,
as befits one who expects to prevail. Our generals were
glum and, though they didn't dare say so, angry because
they'd advised against our position in the first place. Heraclius slumped in his camp chair and, his demeanor most
unlike that of an emperor, stared at his feet, sighed, and
asked the emissary's business, which of course he well
knew.

You learn to read a man's back as well as his face when
you've stood behind him for as many hours as I'd stood
behind Heraclius, and I saw, in his back, as the emissary
prattled on about how his lord would slaughter and sell us
into slavery, unmistakable signs of subterfuge and slaughter
of an entirely different sort. Like a trained hound casting
for a scent, I began to sniff them out. And what was a mere
whiff when the emissary took his leave and Heraclius
laughed long and hard became the hot, sweet smell of fresh
blood after he announced his battle plan to his at first crestfallen and then delighted generals.

"So, Stripling," my emperor said as his generals filed
out to dispose his surprises. "A lesson I hope you learn
well. An excess of confidence is a greater danger than a
woman with a pox. A lesson we'll write tomorrow in Persian blood."

I'd never dared be so bold, but never before had I cause,
and even need to be. "And what, Lord," I piped in a voice
that had yet to break, "will the message written in your
confident blood read?"

His brow clouded.

"The emissary gloated, it's true," I said, "to each and
every man in this tent save one."

The cloud darkened. "Who was . . . ?"

"The same, Lord, who most quickly and fervently applauded your true intent." I plucked a coin from my emperor's beard. "And was the most anxious to be out the door to implement his part of it."

He'd noticed, and knew instantly to whom I referred. "You dare accuse..." Lightning flashed in the dark clouds but was quickly replaced by a gray and gloomy look that included, I was sure, the glistening hint of a tear, for Heraclius then still valued and respected friendship, and was capable of trust.

I said nothing.

"I don't want to believe this," he said at last.

There being nothing to add, I again held my tongue.

"Elisaurus? My beloved Elisaurus, alongside whom, bathed in blood, I have fought? Whose life I've saved as he has mine?"

I was frightened, but the truth is its own best argument (I still believed that, then, too), and I stood firm.

Heraclius groaned. His hand, fast enough to pluck flies unharmed from the air, lashed out and sent maps, quills, an ink pot, and a candle flying. "No!" he roared. "I refuse to believe!"

"And are those, Lord," I asked, "the words you'd have written in your blood in Persian sand tomorrow?"

With what contempt he stared at me from under those noble brows! "Your honor," he spat, "is as deformed as your body."

My body had been ridiculed for as long as I could remember, and a ten-year-old boy's honor is no better developed than his testicles, so he might have saved his breath. "Eyes and ears, if they're to see and listen, had best be dispatched immediately," I said, having crossed the Rubicon of my lord's displeasure—and having nothing more to lose if I was wrong. "The sun's going down, and his tent will soon spawn shadows that carry treasonous messages."

I was right, of course. Elisaurus had betrayed us to the Persians and later tried, as I'd predicted, to inform them of the tricks we had up our sleeves that, in the end, slaughtered and enslaved them. You may study our victory the next day in the histories, so I needn't enlarge on it. What you won't read (the *scop* wasn't the first to omit a dwarf from a history) was that the victory, I presume to boast, was as much mine as it was Heraclius'. But of more importance to this particular history was the stronger and more lasting bond established between an emperor and his dwarf, and the swelling of my pride and vanity, which would carry me to great heights, nearly destroy me, and in the end be tempered by a man I wouldn't meet for another quarter of a century.

# 3. On the Dangers of Power.

1 learned early on that the world is dangerous, and believed, however erroneously, a man could control his fate with a keen intellect and boldness of thought and action. In addition, he must mount and maintain a guard as much against his frailties as his enemies, which truth applied equally for an empire as a man. How much more true, then, was it for an emperor, who in one person is both man and empire! An emperor, more than most men, is besieged from many sides. The multitudes who hunger and thirst for power will take advantage of him in multitudinous ways, and dethrone him with no more compunction than a farmer castrates a bull he doesn't want to breed. Lucky, then, was Heraclius, for as clever and careful as he was, two eyes are rarely enough when a throne's at stake, and with me at his side, he had four.

Power, like gold and beautiful women, as has often been remarked, is difficult to win and easy to lose. It's one against many, and rarely can the one count on even one more to protect his flanks. So if I was lucky to be Heraclius' slave, so too was he lucky I was his friend. I say that not because he was without friends—he was surrounded by them—but because their constancy was always suspect. Because of my devotion, and after my role in Elisaurus' exposure became known and I was the proud possessor of my own enemies, both Heraclius and I understood that it was in my interest to bend my efforts, meager though they were, to save his head if I didn't want to lose mine. Luckily (and you'll learn later how I despise luck), I was intelligent enough for the task. I discovered my talent on the day of Elisaurus' perfidy and, recognizing how to further my fortunes with it, immediately set about improving it by closely observing and studying how best to understand and manipulate men. Before my testicles (which I was allowed to keep in the hopes of breeding more of my kind) and my voice dropped and I could call myself a man, I was as cold as a courtesan and utterly confident of my intellectual capabilities. Thus armed, I assured my place as Heraclius' most trusted advisor by my ability to read the motives behind men's deeds and words as easily and without error as the pope reads his psalter.

The metaphor isn't idle. Men are indeed very much like books, and books, as long as they're open, needn't be feared. The book to fear is a closed book, especially if only two or three pages here and there are glued together. Open those pages and the content becomes clear: there's where the heart of the matter lies and therein lay my art, but this isn't a treatise on the art of reading men or books. In any case, I've practiced my art for so long, have seen and read the same dreary lies and half-baked, unimaginative plots so many times, that I now find the subject boring.

Less boring was and remains the difficulty I too frequently experience when trying to read the minds of women, who for me tend to be closed books. I've rarely been able to view them in as detached and unimpassioned a manner as I have men. I never cared what a man thought about me or the body God gave me. With men, it was my intellect, wit, and brawn against whomever I faced: one way or other, I was a match for most I met and capable of giving as much as I got.

With women, however, I was always conscious of my short and bent legs and of my face, which looks as if it's been caved in by a log. Never mind that my mind was (and remains) whole and that I was (and remain, even if, at my age, quiescently) well endowed between my legs. Not that I was a stranger to women. I had, in the first place, my duties with the three females of my kind who Heraclius kept (one could not get pregnant though we tried diligently, one bore three children all of whom were normal, and a fat and imbecilic third was so deformed that she died giving birth to a monstrosity). In the second place, with the exception of Heraclius' concubines whom I was wise enough to avoid, the court was a hotbed of decadent and ambitious women, the vast majority of them as available, however much I repulsed them, as they were beautiful. The line between the two classes blurred, but I can say of the former that decadence has delights I was willing to entertain, and of the latter that their smiles and sweet words didn't deceive me, as I took a certain spiteful delight in helping them indulge themselves with the fiction that the path to the emperor led through my couch. One and all, as they simultaneously desired and were repulsed by me, I similarly idolized and despised them and, with the ear of the emperor my aphrodisiac, lay with them as frequently as I pleased.

If only one had seen past the deformity to the man! I dreamed of finding such a woman. I wasn't lacking in compassion: I was capable of loving greatly, of being a devoted husband and father. But the more desperate my dream and the more women I lay with in my search for the one I sought, the more greatly their secret revulsion stung me to the core. Consequently, though I harmed none of them irreparably, I wasn't above using them spitefully and casting them aside instead of furthering their interest in court, as I often promised I would. One of them, a black-haired and melon-bosomed seductress named Portia, took vengeance on me. She had to wait some score of half-years (as you'll learn the Northmen sometimes reckon time), during which those sweet melons overripened and became dugs nearly as long as my legs, but a measure of vengeance she had.

For which, over the years, I've thanked the many gods I've worshipped because, if she hadn't had her way, I'd have been dead long ago.

# 4. How I Received Three Revelations, and Returned to My Ancestral Home.

**H**eraclius died in the year of our Lord's incarnation 641. Sadly, his death was neither quick nor easy. His body wasted horribly from a disease no one could diagnose or cure, and he was in constant pain. The church fathers, who'd long hated him for his marriage to Martina, took advantage of his growing helplessness and conspired openly against him. His son, Constantine III, with whom, out of love and respect, Heraclius had shared power for the previous ten years, was caught up in the shifting currents of intrigue swirling through the court, and was understandably more concerned with retaining and expanding his power than with defending his father, who'd become more a burden than an asset and was a dead man in any case. I did what I could to protect myself, but at the same time am proud to say I didn't abandon my benefactor and, in fact, was one of the few who remained loyal to him until the end. Constantine gave me a sinecure and a title, neither of which I enjoyed for long because he, too, died (I never did learn how or by whose hands, though I had my suspicions) before we'd finished mourning his father. When that unexpected end came, Constans II, his son and the new emperor, threw me in chains before Constantine was washed and laid out, and neither permitted me to mourn him while he lay in state nor to march in his funeral procession.

I have Portia, who was at last free to disgorge the venom she'd carried in her belly for so long, to thank for that. Having ingratiated herself with Constans (the little shit who, I learned many years later, slit Martina's tongue and banished her) and insinuated herself into a position of power, she had a more wicked fate in store for me.

I can't envision her face, though I thought I'd never forget it, but I can still hear the evil triumph in her low, throaty voice as she purred her vengeance for my having got her with a child—a perfectly normal and even handsome boy, so she had no complaint in that regard—and then having had Heraclius marry her to an oafish lout, one Kouzinos, who made her a slave of his gargantuan phallus and insatiable satyr's appetite, and used her badly until he died on top of another woman, hacked to death by her husband.

"And now," she gloated, "it's your turn to be a slave."

I was terrified, I admit, but couldn't blame her.

"Look at you! Pfaugh!" She spat in my face. "When I think about letting you fuck me, I want to vomit. You disgust me, and always have. You and your short legs and misshapen face. You with your taste for the best of wines and an emperor's cuisine. With skin accustomed to only the finest fabrics. With hands as soft as a child's."

She smiled, and a chill struck my bones.

"And your ass, my pretty. Is it as tender as your hands? As soft and smooth as this silken hair?" She stroked my head, and I'd have bit her had my teeth not been clenched with fear. "Will it, sweet, tender ass, please the forest barbarians? They love oddities like you, I'm told. Some, it's said, tie their prey bottom up over a log, one by one fill him with their filthy seed, and then hang him by his wrists and laugh when the white shit pours out of him. Oh, my pretty, pretty thing, I'm so sorry I won't be there to watch."

Slowly, she raked the nails of her right hand down my chest to my belly and laid open four bleeding furrows, the scars of which can still be seen in my now thin, parchmentlike skin.

"But I will dream of you," she hissed, her eyes not a hand's width from mine. "I'll dream with unbounded pleasure of your adventure, and my wish, which to my great joy you'll grant me, is that you remember who sent you to the barbarian hordes, and dream of me."

And did I fulfill her wish? Oh, yes. In many ways on many nights. During the last two days left to me in Constantinople, I was so beset by dreams of her I hardly slept. I dreamed of her during the storm-tossed crossing of the Black Sea every time I stopped vomiting long enough to sleep. I dreamed of her while I lay in a filthy cell belowdecks on an ancient and reeking fishing boat beached on the Isle of Birches where I was held until a suitable trader was chosen to transport me to the north. I dreamed of her on the riverboat that carried me toward the deep forests in which, I'd been told and later learned was true, men lived more like animals than men.

I dreamed, too, of the barbarians. Truly horrible dreams of horrible men. They came at me in every size, shape, and color. Some carried logs they threw on the ground before seizing me and laying me over them. Some marched in columns of brutish men with brutish laughs, each holding his erect phallus in his hand. Some I fought with and some I slew, but there was no end of them, and I awoke trembling and short of breath, exhausted from my fears.

Portia had been right. For nearly thirty years, I'd lived a soft and pampered life. Comfort had been the watchword of my existence, luxury my handmaiden. Such weapons as I'd needed had been words. My prowess was my wit, my craft intrigue, my art an infallible vision, my armor the love of an emperor. By stripping me of these and leaving me naked against the world, her vengeance was perfectly conceived. Yes, I dreamed of Portia.

But terror thrives on ignorance and is thwarted by understanding, which comes with time. The most frightening aspect of Portia's plot, that I be sold to the forest barbarians for their carnal delight, thus also became its fatal flaw because it took so long to get to where they were. My torpor during the sea voyage and my stay on the fishing boat was so deep I don't count that time. Instead, I reckon from the day I was hauled into the sweet fresh air and blinding light, and thrown like a sack of grain onto a riverboat whose captain had been paid in gold coin to deliver me to the barbarians, and who put me to work the minute Portia's agents lifted anchor and sailed.

Heraclius and others had told me tales about the river Dnieper, but I could never imagine what it looked like until I was on it. Wide with spring rains and treacherous with clawing currents and plunging logs, it was, I thought, truly Satan's river. I was utterly miserable. The days, filled with backbreaking labor, were less distinguishable than birds of a feather lining a roof ridge, so it's difficult to say how long we spent on it. The steppes it ran through were covered with grass deep enough to conceal a tall man standing upright. The world was limited to a wall of grass on either side, ahead, and astern. Only by climbing our mast could I see over it, though why I should have wanted to more than once is difficult to understand because, once above it, the view was of a nightmare void of more and ever more grass, a verdant limbo that stretched to an empty, blurred horizon.

The weather could be execrable. Storms that gave scant warning by day and none by night lashed us mercilessly with howling winds, torrential, cold rain, and ear-splitting thunder. Worst, most dangerous by far, giving the flood its due, was the lightning because it sought the tallest object it could find, which, of course, was our boat. Consequently, we lowered sail and mast when a storm bore down on us, made for shore, tied down, and, as wet and miserable as men can be, cowered in the reeds or grass until it passed. Many was the story I heard of boats struck and burned to the water, and their crews, if lucky enough to escape, left to fend as best they could until another boat or raft happened along to rescue them. Sometimes, too, the lightning set the deep, dry steppe grasses afire, which was especially terrifying if there was a wind, for then the fire could outrun a horse. I saw but one of those fires, and was amazed by the sight of a vast herd of steppe deer leaping into view as they desperately raced the flames to the water, in which false haven we slaughtered them while they swam. We ate well that night and for the next few days, but paid a heavy price: when the wind died, we were wrapped in heavy, choking smoke until, our lungs bursting and no breeze to propel us, we rowed and poled our way up river to clean air.

I've lingered over these details in order to set the scene for three revelations or, I might say, dawnings that were crucial to my survival then and later.

I'd never, even during Heraclius' arduous Persian campaign—the retinue of a victorious emperor lives in comparative luxury—been so miserable or experienced so many difficult aspects of life. A courtier, basically, for whom food, clothing, and shelter were a foregone conclusion, I'd never understood, much less been required to master, the vast hoard of common knowledge and clever tricks other men had to employ and master in order to overcome the hardships they daily endured. So, if I was awed and impressed by the raw and unremitting forces of nature in that inhospitable environment, I was even more awed and impressed, and humbled, by the men with whom I traveled. They were as coarse, crude, and unlettered a lot as I'd seen anywhere, but they'd come to terms with the exigencies of their world and either conquered or bent before them as a matter of course. Living with them on their level nearly drove me to despair until, one night as I watched the stars wheel overhead and listened to the mournful rush of water under the keel, I was struck by my first dawning, that I was no longer the court dwarf.

No longer the court dwarf! The conditions under which Portia had been correct no longer existed. My food, the repulsive slop of peasants and river men, mostly black, wormy bread and a mouldy white cheese of dubious origin, agreed with me and I ate as voraciously as the next man. The fine wines to which I'd been accustomed had been replaced by silty river water. I'd forgotten the smooth caress of silks, and was chafed raw by an evil-smelling pair of badly tanned leather britches and a coarsely spun and woven wool shirt that, I discovered not too many months later, were luxuries when compared to the rancid furs and the crude bark shirts I wove myself.

As for my body, once pale and as delicately sensitive as a child's, I may now laugh. Fat had given way to muscle. My feet, torn and blistered by raw-cut planks, rocks, and sand, and my hands by ropes, oars, and poles, had healed and were growing layers of thick, horny calluses. Sun, wind, and rough, perpetually wet clothes had tanned me so you might have made from my hide a better pair of britches than those I wore. As for my fundament, to speak less commonly than Portia had, I no longer feared for its safety, for it was by then no more desirable than any other filthy, vermin-infested river man's.

My second dawning occurred a few days after my first. Halfway from the mouth of the Dnieper to Kiev, I would guess, some fingers of mountains break the flatness of the steppes. There, famous among river men, are the Seven Devils' Falls. The best time of the year to negotiate them is in the late spring or early summer when there's enough water to cover the rocks but the ice melt and spring rains in the north have yet to sweep south and turn that portion of the river into a raging torrent. We'd come upon the falls a few weeks early, but the captain, who was bullheaded when put to the challenge and didn't want to be late for the spring trading in Kiev, decided to forge through no matter the cost. The first, and easiest, of the seven wasn't much worse than some rapids we'd bulled our way through two days earlier, so we lowered sail and drew close to the bank, where half the crew jumped ashore to haul the boat with ropes while the other half remained aboard to wield the poles.

We were no more than fifty yards from calm water when one of our number, an imbecilic young man who was the son of our rowmaster, was swept overboard. Without hesitation, when the hue and cry arose, his father plunged into the raging current and both were carried astern. The captain vacillated and I think almost decided to continue without them, but the looks on the faces of the crew, which had been partial to the boy, warned of mutiny, so he immediately summoned aboard those on the bank, and put about.

We found father and son beached on a sandy spit some miles downstream, hauled them aboard, and, since it was late in the day, took refuge in a shallow cove and tied up for the night.

The captain had done the right thing. Rejoicing, the crew dispatched three of their best hunters and, when a deer was brought in and dressed, gave the first pieces of liver to the rowmaster and his son, who were greatly fatigued from their ordeal. After they'd eaten, the father, whose eyes were warm and full of gratitude, stroked his son's brow while the poor boy lay shivering on a bed of rags, and the crew, hard men grown as solicitous as a ewe with her lamb, stood in attendance while they gnawed on the barely cooked meat that was our meal that night. In a land where death without compunction is commonplace, it was a touching sight.

Whatever the boy's intellect, he had wits enough to know he'd come close to death, and was still terrified. At last, in an attempt to put his mind on happier matters, I opened for the first time my bag of dwarf's tricks. Standing on one hand, I plucked with the other a small piece of hack-silver from his ear, bit it to show it was solid, and gave it to him. Likewise, I did the Dance of the Fools with the deer's head, and juggled some rocks and pieces of wood.

The boy was transfixed. Evidently never having seen tricks like that before, he sat up, laughed, and clapped his hands. The crew, including the captain, who lived a thankless life with rare surcease from hard labor, was similarly amazed and delighted. The men became like children, and wouldn't let me stop. One played on a crude set of pipes while I taught the others the Fool's Dance, which made, with a bloody deer head being thrown about like a ball, a grotesque sight. Their cracked lips split in gap-toothed smiles, and they made the deck thunder with the stamping of their feet. Their hoots of laughter drew a herd of curious deer, two of which one of the men slipped ashore to bring down for the next day. One by one, each sought me out to read his palm, an art I'd learned from an old woman in Heraclius' court and augmented by my own abilities as an observer of men and how each brings on his own fate.

I lay awake after we crept off to our mats for a few

hours' sleep before the sun rose. My mind seethed as my second dawning budded and burst into bloom. What a fool I'd been! What a pretentious, precious ninny! Thinking myself so much better than they, I'd remained aloof from them and blamed them for not begging for my friendship. But why should they have? I was the intruder in their world, not they in mine, and it was my responsibility to bridge the gap. As proof, they'd accepted me the moment I began to act like one of them, and it took acting like one of them to realize they differed not a jot from more civilized and sophisticated men. Filthy, smelly, and coarse, they weren't courtiers by any stretch of the imagination, but then, I'd had cause to think before, neither were oiled hair and perfumed skin the measure of a man. True, they were animals, but only to the degree their lot in life imposed on them. Conversely, they were as civilized as circumstances permitted.

Portia's vituperation, her absolute certainty of the horrors awaiting me, had blinded me. Heraclius, though great danger threatened anyone who mentioned the stock from which he sprang, had been born a barbarian. A barbarian slave I'd known had been praised, bought, and freed by the church fathers in consideration of the delicately shaped and beautifully colored crucifixes he carved. A slave boy on our boat, a handsome youth as pretty as a girl, had not been violated. A barbarian woman in a nameless settlement we passed mourned her mate's death with the solemn dignity of a queen. More recently, a father had leaped into the flood to save a flawed son, a forceful captain who could have put down a mutiny put his boat about, and as savage a crew as I ever saw rejoiced over a half-wit's rescue.

If the barbarians were then capable of love, they were no less endowed with other human qualities that mitigated in my favor, foremost among them greed and a desire for power, leavened with hot-blooded lust, quick tempers, a propensity for violence, a crude but quick sense of humor, and an almost childlike frankness that could change in a wink into a crafty deviousness as sophisticated as any encountered in an emperor's court and, for me, as easily penetrable. They were, therefore, as manipulable as other men, and I had no more to fear from them than I had from the greedy, jealous, quick-tempered, lustful, violent courtiers with whom I'd dealt for most of my life. I was, in short, back to one-on-one, which is to say that my fundament was doubly safe. And upon that realization, I fell into a deep and satisfying sleep.

My two previous dawnings had come in the dark, and my third came on the darkest night of all, not counting those I spent in the windowless cell after Constantine's death. We'd seen the first tree since the Seven Devils' Falls (which had taken a week to negotiate), and were soon surrounded by them. Before too many more days had passed, I could easily believe, as I'd heard, that the forest stretched to the northern edge of the world.

A dwarf is accustomed to looking *up* at nearly everything, but the trees were so monumentally huge they virtually redefined the word. Never had I seen such trees! Thicker in girth than three of me lying flat on the ground, their tops, when one could see them, sometimes stretched literally into the clouds, and would have given the dwarf's perspective to my long-departed friend Amin, the Nubian giant. When the river narrowed, their lower branches touched overhead and our boat glided under a light green gauze net of budding spring leaves and through a silent, soft rain of falling seed clusters. And then, one morning a week after we'd entered the forest, the water widened into what looked more like a lake than a river.

I'd stood many times in the Hagia Sophia, the great cathedral in Constantinople, and been moved by its beauty and majesty, but the Hagia was a mere building, a clumsy pile of stones and mortar in comparison to the scene that met my eyes as we set our sail and moved out onto the lake. The sight was so spectacular that an awed hush fell over the crew and my senses were overwhelmed. The water, filthy and turbulent downriver, was a deep blue dazzling sheet smoother than a mirror, and reflected an inverted forest around its perimeter. Save for the creak of rope and an occasional distant avian cry, the silence was absolute. The vast scene seemed to shrink our boat to the size of a walnut shell, and we men to vulgar motes of dust.

That night, we tied up under a tent of overarching trees whose leaves, full by then, blocked out the rising moon and the stars. After we ate and bedded our fire, the only light was the dull rust-red glow of coals, and soon the only sounds were of snores and the comforting creak of our hawsers.

I don't know how long I slept before I was awakened by the howl of a wolf. The hair on my neck prickling and my skin rough with fear bumps, I barely breathed. To my surprise, though, the fear quickly drained away and a great calm descended on me, followed by a rush of ecstasy in which I realized I'd returned to my ancestral home.

Earlier, I said I'd surmised I'd come from the north, and in that moment, my blood sang proof that I had. The wolf was no stranger. Neither was the shaggy brown bear I heard snuffling about a safe distance from the men he feared, but would have attacked if he'd been hungry enough. I knew the primeval, pressing darkness through which man moved at his peril. The green smell, the brown smell, the smell of rot and life were familiar, ancient lullabies. I heard, from the dim past, wild oaths and exuberant shouts, screams of death and peals of laughter. My mouth watered as my tongue recalled the taste of hot blood, and of meat freshly slaughtered.

The forest was Father, who laid his net of roots over Mother Earth. From them sprang the abundant life they entwined with secret spells and charms. Mother and Father were mighty forces that tolerated men only because they were amused by them. With those who were brash and bold, they shared their bounty of nuts and honey, furs and meat. On those who were weak or foolhardy, they imposed their judgement of death.

This I knew, and as I, forgetting my Christian faith, thanked Mother and Father for receiving me into their bosom after so long an absence, a great lassitude fell over me and I slept like a child in its mother's arms, and in the morning woke as one reborn.

# 5. *How the Captain Sold Me for a Handsome Profit.*

With what dismay would Portia have viewed my dawnings and transformation, her vengeance gone awry! Her sweet, as she'd called me, who should have been soiling himself in abject fear of the barbarians, was himself a barbarian.

I say today I exulted in my rebirth, and I suppose I did. It would, however, be more proper to say I became smug. I was smarter than, and had defeated, Portia. I'd been placed in harm's way and, master player that I was, had with superior wit and intellect once again won. Never had I been more alert, more keenly aware of my surroundings, more alive to possibility. My physical strength increased weekly as the last of the fat laid down in my formerly luxurious life disappeared altogether and was replaced by tough muscles and wiry sinews. Under the rowmaster's tutelage—his name was Ulo, I now recall—I learned the rudiments of fighting with a dagger, with which weapon, because of my height, I enjoyed a natural advantage. A font of questions, I asked the name of everything new I saw and, a veritable babbling child, practiced their language incessantly the more quickly to master its subtleties, which the men said varied from place to place but were similar enough in most for a general understanding. Likewise, I inquired of their customs so I wouldn't unwittingly give offense or be insulted without knowing it, the latter being as great a danger as the former, for the man who allows himself to be insulted immediately loses respect, and is thereafter lost.

In this manner, and with no other mishap except a minor encounter with a hungry bear we drove away one night, we poled and rowed and sailed the rest of the distance up the Dnieper to Kiev, which was the most remote Byzantine outpost in those parts, and where I was to be sold.

The crew had talked for days about the women and strong drink they'd buy as soon as we tied up at the wharf and they were paid and let off the boat. For my part, my own hand was a fantasy fulfilled compared to the pitiful creatures who made the beggar-whores of Constantinople look like queens, and one taste of the fiery swill and rancid beer they drank there convinced me it was more dangerous than Portia. In any case, I was scheduled for the block in four days and was resolved to go for a high price and thus make myself too valuable to abuse or let come to harm. Further, insofar as I could, I meant to choose a wealthy and powerful master who was of the forest, for I hated the open country of the steppes. With that in mind, I set out to prepare myself as best I could.

The captain was reluctant to let me out of his sight, but relented when I pointed out that escape was impossible because the inhabitants of Kiev tripped over their feet gawking at me and my whereabouts and business were common knowledge. In addition, where would I flee to in that godforsaken place? South to the empty steppes? To the dark forest, inhabited by hungry wolves and bears? My points well taken, he warned me to return to the boat by nightfall, and let me go on my way.

The view of Kiev from the river and the wharf promised little, and that promise was kept. Kiev was filthy, muddy, dusty, and dangerous. From the stench and cloud of flies that enveloped it, a traveler might think it had been built on a bed of dung and offal, and he wouldn't be far from wrong. The inhabitants, whose number was difficult to guess, lived little better than the multitudes of livestock that roamed at will. Drunken, armed men, in town for the spring trading and to get winter out of their blood, strutted the narrow, crooked lanes I could better describe as a maze. Traders bawled the wares and goods of civilization, the vast majority of them of inferior quality, and fights, one I saw to the death, broke out for no discernible reason. Fornication in broad daylight was common, as it was for a man or woman to void either feces or urine in the street with no more modesty than an ox or a horse. My estimation of the barbarians plummeted, I confess, until I recalled some of the villages I'd seen during Heraclius' campaign through Persia, which was supposedly civilized, and took heart anew.

Few men, I think, have been better prepared to be sold. I begged, stole, and otherwise collected a small purseful of trinkets I hung at my waist. I learned the names of the shopkeepers and craftsmen in Kiev, whom I most emphatically did not want to buy me because I couldn't stomach the idea of remaining there to rot. I ferreted out the names of the transient chieftains, warrior princes, and merchants in town for the spring trading, and from them chose three: Azak the Bulgar, Vengo the Slav, and Kapsabelis the Greek. Each was rich and powerful, and hated and feared the other two. One of them, though they didn't know it, I was determined would be my new master.

Portia's agents had paid the captain well to carry me up the river and hand me over to the barbarians. He'd been paid a second time, as it were, by my labor, since he'd made me a slave. My hope to bring a good price was bolstered by the belief that, being far from Constantinople and with no one the wiser, he'd gladly take a third profit from me. In this I was correct, of course, and he furthermore agreed to the plan I proposed in order to increase that profit. On his part, he was to delay putting me on the block for as long as possible unless I gave him the sign, in which case he was to put me up quickly. On my part, I was to wander through the crowd to increase interest in me, and especially among the three men I was confident I could induce to bid against each other for me.

Slave auctions are one of the few entertainments available in places like Kiev, so the crowd was large and in good humor. Forest-, steppe-, and river-men thronged the empty spot in the middle of town that served as forum and marketplace. Spring was in the air. The sun was bright and a brisk wind thinned the flies and stench. The meanest of those for sale went first and, amid hoots and jeers and bawdy jokes, for a pittance. A half-dozen sad creatures who'd been badly used and, two of them, horribly mutilated, they were of the sort Heraclius, had he been in a benevolent mood, might have bought and had put out of their misery rather than let them endure one more cruel master. I might have, too, had I been Heraclius, but I wasn't and, though it does me no credit to say so, was too busy to spare them the pity they deserved.

The crowd was my audience and I played it adroitly, much as I had the crew when the rowmaster's son almost drowned. I juggled, danced, and swallowed a long dagger the captain had given me. I plucked trinkets from beards and ears and, from between the breasts of the only clean woman I saw, a hen's egg that, to great hilarity, I broke open and, with rolling eyes and exaggerated gusto, drank on the spot. And when the time was right, I approached Azak the Bulgar where he sat wrapped in a magnificent wolfskin, and handed him a small piece of parchment.

"What's this?" he asked, taken aback by my impudence.

"Words, Mighty Warrior," I responded simply.

He turned it up, down, and sideways, peered at it suspiciously and held it by one corner as if it might bite him. "An evil spell?" he asked.

"No, Prince," I said. "I'm not, like others, one to wish evil on so great a warrior and leader of men."

He looked in vain for someone who could read, saw no one, and thrust it toward me. "Read, then, Dwarf. What do the words say?"

I approached closely and, in private, pointed out each word as I spoke it. "Vengo the Slav owns a scribe, and boasts he's more civilized than Azak the Bulgar, whom he scorns.''

Azak grabbed me by the hair and turned my face to his. ''Who says these words, Dwarf?'' he demanded.

I didn't flinch. ''The whole world whispers them, Lord,'' I said. ''I only write what others dare not say to your face.''

His brow clouded. I'd seldom seen eyes so piercing, and though he frightened me and made me question if I wanted him to buy me, I didn't blink or back down. At last, he released me. ''Azak doesn't care what weaklings whisper about him behind his back. Get away before I buy you and give you to my women for supper.''

Sensing he was intrigued enough to bid on me, and at the same time more and more hoping he didn't, I bowed deferentially and melted into the crowd.

My second candidate was Kapsabelis, whose great bulk and colorful robes set him apart from everyone else there. I approached humbly and thrust the second parchment I'd prepared in the face of the great man himself, who I knew could read.

''Kapsabelis' greatest desire,'' the parchment read in Greek, ''is to satisfy his every smallest desire. He would do well to buy and be served by Musculus Herodes Formosus, who was Heraclius' dwarf, advisor, and friend, and who reads men's innermost thoughts.''

The Greek read and, his eyes betraying not one jot of emotion, gazed down at me. ''And what of Vadian Tertius?'' he asked to my surprise.

I'd known Vadian Tertius, had been aware of his machinations and scurrilous tricks, and had never trusted him. Had he taken bribes from Kapsabelis and then stabbed him in the back, as he had others? It was possible and, wagering he had, I answered without hesitation. ''Vadian Tertius will accept a bribe from a Greek merchant as quickly as a magpie will take a bright stone from a window ledge, and leave not so much as a small pile of wet shit in return.''

I saw I was right when the Greek allowed himself the luxury of a faint smile, so with the seed well planted, I bowed and once again disappeared into the crowd. Keeping myself hidden from the first two, I'd no sooner slipped up behind the third when I heard one of his men talking about me and saw, when he pointed, one of Azak the Bulgar's men approach the captain and whisper in his ear. Quickly, then, guessing I had no time to spare, I ducked behind a skirt, hurried to the block, and learned that Azak, seeking to buy me cheaply before the bidding started, had sent an offer. The contest already under way, we got me on the block immediately.

None of them was stupid, and each understood full well what the others were about. As, within minutes, did everyone else, and because the Bulgar, the Slav, and the Greek were proud men, each was reluctant to be the loser, especially in full view of a whole town.

What glares passed among them! Visions of unforeseen profit dancing in the captain's eyes, he proceeded slowly, and only when he judged the last ounce of drama had been wrung out of the contest let his closed fist fall. I'd gone for eight wolfskins, six clean female slaves (one reputedly a virgin), four pure white ermine skins, two blocks of beeswax, a large piece of red silk fabric, and, a final, irresistible item, a fragrant box of tea. Ecstatic, the captain wished me well, told me to keep the long dagger he'd given me, bade me good-bye, and pointed me in the direction of Kapsabelis the Greek.

The next morning, bathed, dressed in new clothes, and sitting a sturdy Mongol pony, I rode at my new master's side out of Kiev, and never in my life returned there.

# 6. *How I Fared in the Service of Kapsabelis the Greek.*

**K**apsabelis the Greek was as much like other men as a whale is like a minnow. In him were all aspects enlarged and exaggerated. I don't remember ever seeing a larger man who was able to get about in the world. His girth and weight were so great no horse could be found to carry him, so he rode in a two-wheeled cart he'd had especially constructed to fit his dimensions and carry him in comfort. His appetite was prodigious and, such was his wealth and shrewdness, never went unsatisfied whether for food, drink, or women. (He later told me he'd deflowered the reputed virgin, which he accounted a hilarious joke on the captain.) A lamb's haunch was an appetizer for him. He made short work of a roasted fish the length of my leg. He was partial to roasted sweet beets and onions—in his train were two asses whose sole function was to carry bags of these commodities—and, having in his cart a box in which was incorporated a ceramic pot that held coals from the previous night's fire, snacked on them hot as we traveled. Likewise, he sipped hot tea sweetened with honey all day, so we had to stop frequently and turn our heads while he micturated into a jug to spare himself the difficulty of climbing down and up again. His slaves erected a tent around him when he called a halt for the day and, after our evening meal, the woman he'd chosen for that night went in to him.

Kapsabelis was, in his own way, an emperor, a Heraclius of sorts. His fame preceded him and his arrival in the smallest settlement or encampment signaled the inhabitants to emerge from their miserable pit houses, haul out their accumulated beeswax, honey, furs, and amber, and mount a celebration. Like the ancient Greeks about whom so much has been written, he'd made himself a myth and, possibly, the only man who's ever made it an honor to be cheated by him. Everyone he'd ever met, and many he hadn't, had a tale to tell about him, and rare was the barbarian who wasn't awed by and didn't respect him.

He remembered everyone's name, they said, and the business they'd done together. He cheated them, yes, they said, but never very much. He made them laugh, they said, and released them for a day or two from the dangers and rigors that filled the tedium of their lives. He brought them stories, they said, tales of kings and heroes, of terrible engines of war and buildings as tall as trees but made of cut and shaped stones piled one atop another, and of a whole multitude of wonders found in the outside world, and eased for a while the loneliness that lay as thick and deep as the winter snows on their sparsely settled land. And, when he left, they invariably pressed surpluses of meat and other food on him, and accompanied him for a while along the trail before turning stoically back to their isolation where, for months, they fondly recalled his words, the splendor of his clothes, the size of his caravan (and himself), how they'd traded with him for this ax head or that knife, and how dearly they'd paid for it. Then, as often as not, they'd laugh and swear they'd gotten the better part of the bargain.

I genuinely liked Kapsabelis more than anyone I'd met in my travels, and thanked my lucky stars he'd bought me. I actually let down my guard in his company, partially because his was a harmonious empire and there was no need to nose out duplicity where there was none, partially because his talents in some regards exceeded mine because he knew his people so well, and partially because living and traveling with him was like being in a circus—or a court. I'd forgotten, until I experienced it again, how exhilarating life in a court could be, and enjoyed myself tremendously. I enjoyed the excitement, the fever pitch of arrival at a settlement, and the seemingly never-ending activity. I occasionally sported with a couple of the more affable female slaves. I delighted in and profited from riotous games of dice and draughts with the forty ferocious mercenaries Kapsabelis employed to protect him from bandits and raiders. They seemed to enjoy my company as much as I did theirs, and instructed me in the arts of the short sword and spear in return for the stories I told them about the mighty battles and feats of warfare I'd seen. I lazed through the quiet nights after the caravan had bedded down, and slept like a babe. I loved the gentle nicker of horses and the contented bleat of the goats, and a low laugh here and snore there were comforting sounds of human fellowship that made the vast and empty wilderness endurable. And, I enjoyed Kapsabelis. He'd read books (he was the only man I met north of the Caspian who had) and his questing mind roamed the universe. His sorrows were profound, his delights unlimited, and when he laughed, everyone in earshot turned to look at him and was soon laughing, too. He thought my intrigues in Kiev were a wonderful joke played on him, and was glad he'd won me even if I had cost, he said with a wink, ten times my worth. Often, as our caravan wended through the deep forest, he summoned me to ride at his side, there to describe life in court and its intrigues, or to dispute with him over philosophy. Sometimes, too, he called me to his tent and, unable to sleep, reminisced until dawn about the places he'd been and the things he'd seen and done.

Great men are possessed and driven by demons, I've come to believe after a long life. Heraclius was, I know, as was Azak the Bulgar, whom I'd meet again, and Einarr, also called Beowulf, toward whom my fate was steering me. These demons are powerful forces. I once saw Heraclius break three and dull six swords as he slew over fifty men in a single day's battle. I was there when Azak took a child from a woman who had incurred his wrath, broke its legs, cut it so it would bleed, and tied it out to bait a bear that had killed one of his men. And I guarded the door and listened to the cries of seven women Kapsabelis ravished in succession one night after a minor setback had uncharacteristically irritated him. I will say Kapsabelis' demons, though, if not exactly slept, at least dozed when he went into winter quarters.

Kapsabelis' excesses extended to his winter quarters, of which he had two that he used in alternating years. The first, where he'd stayed the winter before I met him, lay to the northwest of Kiev in the land of the Slavs. The second, where we went the winter after he bought me, lay to the northeast of Kiev in a valley that transversed the conjunction of forest and steppe near the river Volga. There, partially sheltered from the frequent and impenetrable white blizzards while he tallied the year's profits and planned the next summer's expedition, he attended to his wives and ruled as a benevolent tyrant over a minor kingdom that was cared for in his absence by one of his many sons.

The mercenaries had joked about how such a small man as I, and from a warmer land, would undoubtedly freeze to death in their winter. Constantinople was no stranger to winter, I told them, and we often had snow or ice, so I was little worried. They were very nearly right, however, because my ignorance of a northern winter was appalling. I had no idea it got so cold a man's breath froze in the air and dropped to the ground in front of him. I didn't believe whole rivers could be covered with ice thick enough to hold horses, sleds packed with goods, and, indeed, a whole village of houses built for fishing through the ice. I laughed when they told me how much snow fell—I was sure they were pulling my leg—and later stood gape-jawed in the middle of a large cave some of them dug in a drift deep enough to bury trees. Survive I did, though, but only because I was in good company who taught me well and rescued me—short legs and deep snow are a most unhealthy combination—more than once.

The demons that drive great men weary quickly of ease. When the ice-marble began to crack and groan on the river and a keen nose could smell a hint of spring in the air, our newly outfitted caravan left Kapsabelis' winter valley. His plan was to travel north to trade with the Bulgars, strike westward to the Dnieper, and float down to Kiev to trade some of his furs, slaves, and other commodities and parcel out the rest to be forwarded to a far-flung network of agents, some as far south as Constantinople, who sold or traded them for him. Then, sated with whatever entertainments Kiev had to offer and our necessities replenished, we'd trade our way toward his winter quarters in the west. His plan, the westward half of the great circular route he'd forged during thirty years of trading, would have succeeded admirably had we not, three days down the Dnieper, been stopped by a huge log jam.

Nobody knows where enough logs come from at one time or how a river knots them in a giant's brushpile. I thought Kapsabelis would be angry, but he'd spent his life overcoming obstacles and, knowing that stretch of the river well, put to shore, set camp, and sent out parties on foot to learn where the obstruction ended and which side of the river promised the easier path around it. We were in luck, we thought, when the parties returned to report that open water lay beyond a bend in the river not too far ahead, that the trees on the western bank offered the fewer obstacles to travel afoot, and that the bank at the far end on that side was gently sloped. Everyone set to work. Half the mercenaries deployed down the east side of the river to begin building new rafts out of some younger trees they found there, and the other half began clearing a road of sorts along the west bank. The rest of us warped the baggage rafts to shore and, with Kapsabelis shouting, waving directions, and generally making a nuisance and spectacle of himself, began the arduous task of transferring everything from one set of rafts to another.

Azak the Bulgar fell on us two days later at noon while our caravan was a shambles strung out a half mile through the forest. Our party was exhausted from wrestling with livestock, wagons, and a small mountain of goods. Our troop had laid down its weapons in order to work and, worse, was split by the river. I killed one of Azak's men with my dagger, but was quickly taken prisoner. The mercenaries on our side were overwhelmed and slaughtered before they could form a squad. Those on the other side tried to come to the rescue, but were easily picked off by bowmen as they clambered awkwardly across the jumbled logs. Within hardly more time than it takes to tell, every last mercenary was dead, dying, or captured, and Kapsabelis, I, and the rest of our caravan lay trussed like pigs ready for the pit.

If man may be called the laughing animal, he may be called the cruel animal as well. Wolves on land and sharks in the sea kill to feed themselves, but not for pleasure, as men do. Men everywhere I've been are cruel. I'd thought those of the desert, where food and water must be fought for daily, were the cruelest, but those of the steppe and forest, which are lands of bounty by comparison, vie with them for the honor: in one the soul crusts like bread kept too long in the oven, and in the other it hardens as solidly as a shallow lake frozen to the bottom. Azak was such a lake. His icily haughty demeanor in Kiev had warned me he was cold and ruthless, but I didn't dream of how cold and how ruthless until I saw him at his trade. If any emotion other than hatred and cruelty inhabited his breast, he guarded it as the great Sphinx its secrets.

Azak the Bulgar was young, no more than twenty years old, but already as dominant a leader of men as could be found. Squat, he was powerfully built but moved as gracefully as a swallow. His skin, the color of walnut juice, was smooth and stretched over a beardless face that was simultaneously round and full of sharp bones. Add the amoral, merciless eyes of a wolf and a complete wolfskin, from face to tail, that he wore like a mantle of state or, more ominously, a part of him, and he became the single most frightening man, including Heraclius in one of his rages, I've ever met.

Azak had no need to boast, but he was given to gloating. Strutting like a swallow wearing a peacock's tail, he ordered us dumped in front of Kapsabelis' tent, from which he emerged, once we were so unceremoniously assembled, with his wolf's head hat thrown back and a sea green flowing sash tied around his brow.

We knew, as he paraded around us like a boy emperor, that our minutes were numbered. Kapsabelis glowered but, having escaped more than one tight spot before, knew better than to say anything, even when Azak, in sardonic parody, stretched himself on the ground in front of him and, his head propped on one hand, showed his white teeth in a grim caricature of a smile. "You shame yourself, my fat Greek, by not welcoming guests into your camp. And you'd better not," he went on blandly, stopping Kapsabelis before he could spit, "unless you want to die more slowly than you can imagine, and be made into tallow for our lamps."

Kapsabelis nearly choked swallowing the sputum he'd nearly spat in Azak's face. "Welcome, Bulgar," he croaked, in a rage.

Azak clucked his tongue and shook his head sadly. "Welcome, Bulgar. Only welcome? No offer of food for slaughter-weary men? No offer of drink to quench the thirst brought on by the smell of blood? No offer to share your women with your visitors? You insult me, Greek, and you can see how angry you've made my men."

Tiring of his game, he sprang to his feet, looked momentarily as if he were going to walk away, then suddenly turned and squatted in front of me. "So, then, Dwarf, we meet again. Perhaps the Greek's more generous than I thought, to buy you for such a steep price and then give you to me, eh?"

I thought it best to guard my tongue, so only nodded.

"And yet you cost me." A knife appeared in his hand and under my left eye. "Do you think I didn't see you kill my man? What's a fair price for a man, Dwarf? One eye?"

I didn't blink. "He wasn't much of a man, Warrior, to let himself be killed by a dwarf."

Amazingly, Azak laughed, and withdrew the knife without using it. "Do you hear that, you lowborn gelded sons of one-balled goats?" he asked his men, who laughed appreciatively. "The dwarf's more of a man than he looks. Keep your eye, then, Dwarf, and live a little longer," he said, rising. "But don't be surprised when I give you to

them later. Because I lied.'' He winked conspiratorially and
jerked his head in his men's direction. ''They're not eun-
uchs, and when they're finished with the women, they'll
love the tight fit of a man.''

Needless to say, visions too horrible to contemplate
flashed through my mind and my fears flooded back instantly. Azak wasn't a man to flatter or influence with reason, and this wasn't a predicament I could juggle or dance
my way out of. He might, hope teased me, change his mind
on a whim or to suit his fancy, but logic dictated he'd not
lightly break the promise he'd made in front of his men.

Words can't adequately portray the orgy of violence that
filled the next two days and nights. Azak and his men had
a genius for inflicting pain on both the dying and the living,
and lucky were those who went first and were spared the
agony of having to watch, listen, smell, and speculate ever
more vividly on their own ends.

When asked how cruel men can be, I answer with the
certainty of having seen the distance cruelty can be carried
by depraved minds lacking a vestige of morality. They began with the captured mercenaries. Two they flayed alive
for their skins, which Azak ordered stretched, scraped, and
salted to cure. Two unfortunate souls were made the gam-
ing pieces in a gruesome contest between a pair of Azak's
lieutenants to see which one could get the most arrows in
his man without killing him. The last two met the fate Portia had planned for me, which, in addition to being the most
degrading prelude to death I can imagine, nearly drove me
insane with sick anticipation.

The drovers, carters, and male slaves were dull, witless
men, which, for the first and last time in their lives, was an
advantage because they were dispatched relatively quickly.
Their overseers, one a gentle and drolly humorous old man
I liked, were led to uglier deaths, the most ingenious one
being to hang a man from a tree, exsanguinate him slowly
with the blood dripping in Kapsabelis' face, and then disembowel him.

The women, with the exception of four Azak chose for
himself, were of course raped repeatedly. Seven older
women and two girls who hadn't yet got their menses bled

to death from their private parts, and one more, her jaw broken, was choked most hideously. Of Azak's four, three were Kapsabelis' companions and the last was a slave named Ilgen.

Our lives follow devious and unpredictable paths. One day, we walk east, only to come upon a sunset. Another, we are headed south for the winter and find ourselves hemmed in by ice. Improbable characters, like signposts, point our way, and we're obliged to swerve onto new courses. Heraclius, Elisaurus, Portia. The captain, the rowmaster. Kapsabelis, at whose side I traveled for eleven happy months, Azak, who tore me from my portly friend's company, and Ilgen, with whom I next took the road that has only one end.

My original excuse for this delay on the way to Einarr was Kapsabelis, who, as an old man maundering, I've taken great joy in recalling in his finery and preposterous excesses. But an even better excuse, I think, is Ilgen, who was as much Kapsabelis' opposite as Amin was mine. And if I recall Kapsabelis with fond chuckles and wry shakes of the head for his antics and love of life, I recall Ilgen gratefully for her sobriety—and the gift of her life.

Ilgen was a remarkable woman. Not beautiful, she was possessed of a naturally regal aura that made men who'd rather have a sheep that could cook than a woman listen humbly when she spoke, and address her by name. The man who sold her to us said she was a chieftain's daughter, but we knew not one whit more about her because she refused to speak of her past. She had a child she protected fiercely. Her son's father, of whom she likewise maintained a determined silence, was of some distant race, because the boy's eyes were blue and his hair a reddish blond, characteristics so rare in those parts that he was stared at as much or more than I was.

Azak's announced intent was to enjoy his women one by one on successive nights. When Ilgen was brought to him on the third night, she refused to surrender her child, spat in his face, and tried to stab him with a knife she'd hidden in her clothes. Azak was furious that a woman should spit in his face in front of his men, none of whom laughed or even smiled though they would have found it hilarious if she'd done as much to any of them. He was also so impressed by her he put her off to the fourth night, by which time he vowed to punish and humble her.

I mentioned some time earlier a child staked out to bait a bear. That was the night it happened. I was tied hand and foot across the clearing when Azak ordered the boy torn from Ilgen's arms, his legs broken and his face and arms sliced open so the bear could find him more easily, and carried out of camp. The scene was less gruesome in some respects than many I had seen in the preceding days, but has stuck in my mind like a persistent cancer. The child cried out when his legs were cracked and the knife bit him, and the hunched wolf shape with a man's face watched impassively as if nothing out of the ordinary were taking place. Kapsabelis knew he was going to die and accepted that vicissitude with equanimity, as he would any other that fate visited on himself or another grown man. He was, however, partial to children, and groaned as he revealed that he, too, could share in anguish.

The child's screams diminished as he was carried out of sight of his mother and into the forest, and faded into silence. I've never forgotten the look on Ilgen's face, her posture, and the utter loathing in her eyes as, in the terrible long silence that ensued, she returned Azak's stare. Not one muscle between them moved. Ilgen's shoulders were straight and her head was cocked slightly to one side, as if she were listening. Her lips, which I at first glance thought were turned up in a smile, on closer inspection were frozen in the mocking sneer of contempt nobles reserve for commoners: no matter what Azak did to her or her child, he could neither sully nor harm them.

Azak was a philosopher of pain and studied it as an astrologer studies the planets. Pain fascinated and obsessed him. All things seemed to come to him through pain. He inflicted pain for his enjoyment, true, but I also believe lovingly, because, as perverse as it sounds, pain may well have been the only love he ever knew. It was a grim love I saw displayed that night. Azak sat in quarter profile to me so I couldn't see his eyes, but I knew from his posture he was staring as intently at Ilgen as she was at him. He showed no indication he was troubled by her low opinion of him. Cross-legged, leaning slightly forward in order to more closely observe her, he sat as still and patiently as a statue.

I don't know how long we waited, but the silence, underlaid by the crackle of the fire and the intermittent, mad barking laugh of an owl, seemed interminable. It ended with the great coughing roar of a bear and a horribly thin screech. I momentarily deluded myself that the sound was the terror-cry of a rabbit, but knew in the pit of my stomach was in reality the cry of a child looking into the face of a bear, the cry of innocent humanity about to be devoured by the unknown dread made manifest. The shouts and roars of Azak's men and the bear doing battle followed a moment later, but no one around our fire cared very much. The boy was dead, we all knew.

Kapsabelis cried out, and in that cry the spell that held us suspended snapped. As if straining to hear a faint beat of wings inaudible to the rest of us, Ilgen lifted her head and, for a moment, left us. When she returned, her eyes, like falling stars that blaze most brightly just before they die, burned with a hatred so pure and palpable that Azak shuddered and his hands jerked as if he'd hold them in front of his face to shield himself from the heat. There was no need. The metaphor completed before he was burned, the fire in Ilgen's eyes died and she slumped, insensible, in her bonds.

Azak shook himself, rose to his feet, and stretched like a man, or a wolf, waking. "Bring the one I had last night," he ordered, turning to enter Kapsabelis', now his, tent, "and watch the Greek and his people closely. We'll finish tomorrow, and leave."

One Bulgar was killed and several others mauled, the camp learned when, sometime later, they carried in the gutted and skinned carcass of the bear. (The child was left to lie and rot where he died.) I barely noted, and took no interest, because I was drained empty by then, and had sunk into a deep torpor. I may have slept, I may have dreamed of Portia. Whatever I did, I became aware, sometime during

the dark, still hours, that I was in an unnatural state. I can't
explain or define it, but I felt as if I'd expanded to an
enormous size or, conversely, the world had shrunk. My
head and body overtopped the trees. My feet were the size
of an elephant's. My hands tied behind my back were large
enough to hold our entire camp with room to spare for
another like it. And in this mountain I'd become, a cloud
gathered and coiled and, a black and whirling wind-worm,
consumed my fear.

Azak, the bastard issue of a whore's congress with a pig!
Azak the Cruel. Azak the Monster, the son of Cain, of
Satan himself. Azak, who'd humiliated, debased, and killed
so many of my friends, and played with the rest of us as a
cat plays with a mouse before, with morning, our turns
came.

Where I found the strength or cunning to do what followed is a mystery. Perhaps I was inhabited by some of
Heraclius' or Kapsabelis' (or Azak's?) demons. Perhaps
they were concocted by the wind-worm of anger. In either
case, neither strength nor cunning would have sufficed had
Azak's men taken their charge seriously, but they were
sated with rape, slaughter, and bear meat, and slept the
sleep of the unjust. My dwarf's tricks and short legs made
the first step possible. No later than the thought, I held
myself off the ground on my fists, awkwardly worked my
legs through my arms, and set to work gnawing the leather
thongs that bound my wrists. Quickly, then, for hesitancy
attracts attention and loses a venture before it's well begun,
I moved to free Ilgen.

She was bound to a bale of furs. The guard set to watch
her snored gently until I clamped a hand over his mouth
and slipped his own knife into his heart before dragging
him behind the bale and stripping him because I, being
naked, had more need of his clothes than he.

Ilgen stared at me with empty, uncomprehending eyes
when I waked her and freed her ankles and wrists. "Lie
still," I whispered. "Let your hands and feet wake up. Wait
for me."

Escape from those men of the forest would be difficult
enough without excess baggage to slow us or to drop and

mark our trail. Taking only a pair of knives and a dagger with a steel blade, two long lengths of thong I tied around my waist, a pouch of food the Bulgars carry to eat when foraging is poor, and a slab of cooked bear meat, I dropped, when I saw his eyes following me, into the shadow cast by Kapsabelis' great bulk.

I didn't know what to say, but Kapsabelis rose to the occasion. "It will be a great joke on him, Musculus," he said.

"I wish—"

"I'm too fat, which we both know."

"I'm glad it was you who bought me, Kapsabelis. You've been kind and generous, and I won't forget you."

"Would you repay me, then?" he asked, with a glance at the dagger I held.

I knew what he was thinking.

"It would be a great favor to me, and a greater joke on him, if you'd slip that through my ribs."

I stared at him with tears in my eyes. His request was reasonable and I'd have asked the same had our roles been reversed, but I hadn't the stomach, even knowing the alternative, for killing a man who had so befriended me. "I can't," I whispered, ashamed and embarrassed by my weakness.

He understood, and was, I think, touched.

"Only this," I said, slashing his bonds so he could lie comfortably for his last moments on earth. "And this," I added, fitting his hand around the hilt of the sharpest of my new knives, to do with as he would.

Kapsabelis, that incredible man, that great fountain of welling life, actually smiled. "Godspeed, Musculus Herodes Formosus. Quickly, now, before they awake."

Ilgen hadn't moved when I returned for her. "Quickly, now," I whispered to her from around the corner of the bale. "Follow me closely."

"No," she replied, to my surprise. "I won't leave without my son."

"Your son's dead, woman!"

"I won't leave without him."

My heart in my throat, because luck won't wait on a

man forever, I slipped into the open and crouched in front
of her. "Azak will kill you."

Beyond care, her voice slurred and her eyes closed. "Let
him."

"He killed your son, and you'd reward him with your
body and life? You can't do that! I won't let you!"

Her eyes opened again and I could see I'd rekindled
some life in her. Suddenly, silently, she was on her feet.
"His wolfskin," she said. "I want it."

The skin hung like a standard on a pole stuck in the
ground outside the flap of his tent, and it was madness to
attempt to steal it. "No," I told her. "Better we should
escape—"

"The wolfskin," she hissed, snatching my new knife
from my hand. "Or I die with this in his tent."

"—with our own skins," I'd been about to say, but even
escaping with my own would be impossible if she attempted to kill Azak. I had no choice but to accept.

Great thanks to the grace of God, who sometimes looks
kindly on fools! The skin, which Azak supposed no one
dared touch, slipped silently off its peg and, my task completed more easily than I believed possible, I scurried from
shadow to shadow back to the bale and showed her my
trophy. With a grunt of approval, Ilgen took it and, without
another word, led the way out of camp.

I've no interest in writing a complete account of our
flight, so limit myself to three observations. First, escape
from experienced forest men is difficult and frightening
enough without taunting their leader by smearing his wolfskin symbol of authority with excrement and leaving it
where he's sure to find it.

Second, the only conceivable reason I can find to float
down the Dnieper on a log at night is to escape death at
the hands of a man like Azak. Danger lurks everywhere in
that Stygian, tree-roofed tunnel. Snouted fish and tailed
monsters with gleaming eyes and tooth-filled jaws have
been known to rise from the depths and drag men under.
Huge cats, arboreal bears, and giant snakes, which the captain said abounded there, drop from the trees and consume
their prey in a gulp. Unannounced rapids, as malign as any

living beast, crash and roil and throw logs about like bones thrown by a necromancer. The cold water leaches strength from muscle and bone, and entices the weary with the promise of sleep.

Third, the river widened abruptly the next morning and broke into slow and marshlike channels that meandered we knew not where. Not knowing which to follow, and not wanting to find ourselves trapped, we returned to the mouth of a small tributary we'd passed a few moments earlier, abandoned our log to the current, and struck out on foot upstream toward the northeast, where, if we survived the coming winter, Ilgen hoped to find her tribe in the spring.

Would that Heraclius had lived another dozen years! Would that I had been less contemptuous of Portia! But for my many subjunctive wishes, two objective facts were clear: I was alive and, unless Azak recaptured us, which I didn't intend to let happen, my fundament, which I was tired of worrying or even thinking about, was once again and forever thereafter, I sincerely hoped, relegated to its more usual and unremarkable place in the scheme of things.

# 7. Of Winter, and How, with the Pagan Gods' Help, Ilgen and I Fared.

**I**'ve often been intrigued and amused by the plethora and variety of gods people have in the past and still do worship. Two of the most interesting are the Egyptian gods Ptah and Bes, both of whom were—or are, according to those misguided souls who believe in them—dwarfs!

Ptah was an ancient god worshiped for creating the universe (did he say, "Let there be light," I wonder?), and on a more practical level as the patron of artisans and metal workers. Bes, my favorite, was bearded (as I was for many years), and knock-kneed. His images are still believed by some ignorant people to protect them from crocodiles, snakes, scorpions, and other dangerous animals. He was also worshiped as a god of pleasure whose domain included sexual intercourse, childbirth, singing, and dancing—which, childbirth excluded, is as pleasurable a combination as could be desired. I imagine him as a smiling, merry, and bawdily lascivious god whom a dwarf, especially one such as I, would be inclined to embrace.

Christians, since they worship only one God, dismiss other so-called gods as idols, demonic drummings of the imagination, and abominations. In that wide and dangerous land, I soon learned there were as many as dozens of gods for each of the unnamed scattered tribes I encountered. I learned, too, I was no Christian martyr, because I worshiped each as soon as I was told its name and province. However many there were, I heard of none who was a dwarf.

The summer weather was benign, and Ilgen and I became better acquainted as we marched toward her goal. We neither looked, sounded, nor thought alike, but for our many differences made no stranger a pair than any other you might find in the deep forest. She was taller than I, more darkly complected, and considerably younger, although she had no idea of her age because her people recognized only young and old, of which she considered me the latter. Her tongue differed from the way most barbarians spoke. More guttural, to the ear at first predominantly $l$'s and $g$'s and $u$'s, and I stumbled about in it in contrast to her natural fluency except in those areas where they had no words, for example, regarding the crystal spheres in which the sun, stars, moon and planets revolve about the earth, or how a ship sails on a sea, or even what a sea is.

I was at ease in the forest by natal influence, but lacked knowledge of the animals and their habits, what plants were nourishing and where they were found (especially difficult later, during winter), and many of the necessary arts of survival. The natural order in which women are inferior was therefore reversed, and Ilgen was my teacher and protector. She chose in which direction and how long we marched, and walked in front. She decided where we camped and how much or little shelter we needed for however long she decided to remain there. And, when we camped, it was I who became the mistress of the house, gathering firewood, replenishing our tinder, grinding acorns to flour, laying down boughs for beds, and whatever else she ordered.

I stood and walked in awe of Ilgen. She was a veritable encyclopedia, knew what needed to be done, and how to do it with minimum effort. She was always occupied. She collected nuts and pinecones, and shelled them while we marched. If she saw a suitable tree, she stopped to strip some of its bark for clothing or utensils. If we camped in one spot for a few days, as was sometimes necessary, she spent the daylight hours setting snares for small creatures and spear traps or deadfalls for larger ones, and the nights shaping flints for knives, axes, and spearheads. Her student, my clumsy attempts to imitate her in these endeavors were serious business for me, but were for her a constant source of amusement that I endured both because I was clearly ignorant and inept and because I'd thought she'd never laugh again after Azak killed her son.

My winter with Kapsabelis was a balmy spring in comparison to the one that followed with Ilgen. We had no houses and no well-supplied and sheltered valley. The snow was deeper, the winds fiercer, and the cold unremitting and unforgiving. And, in addition, our souls were stiff with the icy memory of Azak and his men, which haunted us and dogged our trail like an unsleeping wolf. Cold, hungry, and alone, we persisted with the help of the gods.

There's so little help and hope in those wilds that people understandably grasp for and cling to that which is available. When the wind blew and we had no snow to dig into, we prayed to the God of Wind for it to stop and the God of Snow for it to begin. We'd earlier gathered nuts, berries, and roots that we carried in sacks Ilgen taught me how to weave out of vines and bark, but we needed meat, too, and when deep snows made hunting difficult, we prayed to the God of Snow for it to stop and the God of Wind for it to begin and blow away some snow.

We prayed to the God of Hunting for animals to eat, but not vice-versa. We prayed to the Ice God to thicken rivers when they were too thin to cross, or to thin them when they were too thick to break through to catch fish. We prayed to the Sun God, who daily grew more pale and wan, and to the Moon God who, when he was full, was as bright as the winter sun, and in whose light shadows had the hard, sharp edges of slate. We, and most certainly I, prayed to the powerful Sky Fire God (he of the *aurora borealis*) who hung the sky with blazing sheets of color that, a gauzy curtain as strong as steel, saved men from madness. My polytheistic prayers at first discomforted me because Constantinople was Christian and I'd been nurtured in Christ.

The forest, however, was no more Constantinople than I am the pope, and Christ neither having seen nor addressed himself to winter, as far as I knew, I thought it prudent to err on the side of those who presumably knew the territory. Heaven couldn't have been too annoyed because lightning didn't strike me, and we sooner or later almost always got what we asked for.

We talked sparingly at first, and for most of the summer, but as the nights lengthened and the weather became more inclement and forced us to remain for days inside whatever crude shelter we built, talk became a solace. Sullen and uncommunicative as a slave, Ilgen was, as a free woman, an accomplished storyteller with a flair for the dramatic. She described her people, a tribe she called Wolun. They were nomads who wintered in the forest and emerged every spring to roam the far north where the land was perpetually frozen, there were no trees (so the forest did come to an end before the northern edge of the world!), and, in the middle of the summer, the sun never set, which, though I found preposterous, she swore was true. She told me lengthy stories, some amusing, of the Sky Fire God, and interpreted his moods as we watched him drape the sky with glowing sheets of red and green and white. She talked about her father, who was a great warrior and hunter, but had been tricked by wandering Bulgars whose lives he'd saved by giving them food, and who sold her to the tribe that traded her to Kapsabelis. She related tales of the exhilarating hunts for the great white snow bears her tribe prized, and of exhausting two-day battles to land giant fish as long as four men lying head to foot. She depicted her panic-stricken tribe fleeing a fire that consumed a whole forest, described trees so huge that people made houses inside them without cutting them down, and instructed me in many other wonders I'd never seen, heard, nor read about. But of the man who'd given her a son, she remained silent.

Strange to say, in those short days and endless nights, many of them huddled together under the same furs for warmth, we never knew each other carnally. There were times when I desired her so much that my stones ached fiercely, but her demeanor indicated she wasn't well disposed toward and would take no pleasure from it, and I was still so burdened by the excesses and horrors perpetrated by Azak that I had no stomach for force. The truth is, too, which as an old man I'm free to confess though as a younger one I never would have, not only was I in her debt, but I also feared her. I couldn't forget the look in her eyes when she spat in Azak's face and sat in front of him. I knew she was as strong as I because I'd watched her lift logs and carry heavy loads. My greatest fear, though, was that she'd simply slip away one night while I slept, and leave me alone to die.

One more reason still warms my memory: Ilgen didn't ridicule me for being a dwarf, but treated me as she would have any other human being, and I was glad for once in my life to find a woman who neither despised nor made mock of me. If her desire was to be my companion, I was delighted to be hers, and to this day am glad I was. Few companions in ninety years have given me so much so freely.

So, comrades and allies against starvation, the depredations of wild beasts, and the freezing cold, Ilgen and I passed the winter. Spring came slowly and, with it, we began to encounter other people who, because we didn't trust them, we circled warily and avoided. Our spirits lightened as the days lengthened. Ilgen changed while I watched. As the weight of winter slipped off her shoulders, so too did the weight of the memory of her son. Her eyes brightened with every step closer to her tribe. Her walk became brisk, and she often hummed while she worked. At night, first tentatively and then with a torrent of emotion, she sang the songs of her people, the work and play songs, the songs of pain and pleasure, of mourning and love. She became playful, and teased me unmercifully about how long it took me to make a fire or dress a bird for roasting. She laughed like a child when I produced pebbles and bits of bone from thin air and made them disappear again. She begged me to teach her how to juggle, mastered that art astonishingly rapidly and, always trying to get and keep one more stick or stone in the air, double-juggled with me at ever increasing distances until I wished I'd never shown her I knew how.

I don't know how far we'd gone or how far we had to go. Neither did Ilgen, she admitted, but like a dove that unerringly returns to its loft, she moved unhesitatingly and without an instant's doubt, always to the north and east. But I'll never know if she was right, because her gods ultimately failed her, and her journey came to an abrupt end before we reached our destination.

# 8. *Of Altruism, and Its Sometimes Terrible Cost.*

Spring was fraught with its own dangers. The cold itself ameliorated, but the dampness brought on by the melting snow in conjunction with the brisk wind seeped through our makeshift garments and chilled us as badly as the deep freezes on those clear nights when the wind was calm and the trees cracked and groaned. Accidents were potentially deadly, and one day I slipped when leaping from one rock to another while crossing a fast, spring-swollen stream. Beaten about by other rocks, I was carried some distance downstream before I could grab a limb and pull myself out.

I was soaked to the skin, had lost a valuable fur, a bag of food, and a knife, was bruised from head to foot, and chilled to the bone. We stopped immediately, of course. Ilgen had me out of my wet clothes and threw her fur around me, built a fire in front of a thick log that sheltered me from the wind, and there we stayed the night.

I'd supposed we'd continue the next day, but I was so stiff, sore, and racked with fever when dawn broke that I could barely move, much less walk. Ilgen made no complaint, instead heated water in which she boiled some dry leaves she said would reduce my fever, made sure I was warm and comfortable, and spent the rest of the day setting traps for game and catching a large fish, whose light flesh restored to some degree my spirit if not my strength.

I was as useless as a child. I quaked with fever and my teeth chattered until I feared they'd fall out. My lungs rasped and sharp pains tore my chest. My stomach tolerated nothing but water for two days, and that with an effort. Nevertheless, Ilgen made me drink cup after bark cupful in order to quench the fire of the lung disease, which was common among her people and with which, she explained, an evil stream spirit had infected me while I was helpless against it in the water.

Except for my illness, we were safe. We'd seen no people for days. Our shelter was dry and we had food in spite of the bagful I'd lost: meat, nuts, and an abundance of roasting tubers and crisp spring-green herbs that grew along the bank of the stream. We'd have lost two of the six or seven days we spent there in any case because of a violent storm, from which we were saved by prayers and the sacrifice of a spearhead embedded in a fine, long fish to Perun, who was a barbarian god of thunder and lightning. Two more days would have been largely wasted because the mud left in the storm's wake would have slowed us to an exhausted crawl.

The rest, however necessary for me, wasn't in our best interest, though, for a week is long enough to eat or drive away the small animals that are easy to catch and, in turn, attract larger ones whose hunting grounds you've invaded and who seek out men the way crows will hawks or owls. By the time I recovered sufficiently to understand where I was and what was happening, the local pack of wolves prowled the perimeter of our camp and, two nights before our departure, we heard the roar of a bear.

Ilgen was as at home in a wild populated with predators as I'd been in Heraclius' court, which was populated by predators as hungry for power and position as wolves and bears are for meat. Understanding their ways, she kept up the fire and, knowing she'd hear or sense if one came too close for comfort, slept soundly. She was right, as usual in those matters, for though the wolves came close enough for me to see their yellow eyes reflecting the firelight, they never intruded farther. Neither did the bear, which must have been hungry after his winter's sleep, approach any closer than an arrow-flight, which was the distance from us Ilgen found his tracks the next morning.

I've mentioned my fascination with the unpredictable turnings in our lives' paths, and I've especially wondered what path mine might have taken had we stayed another day. I was still weak when Ilgen said she was ready to leave, to which I answered that I'd rather stay. It was, remarkably, the first time I'd asserted myself, and she didn't appreciate it. She snarled at me, paced the camp like an animal in a cage, and, just when I was smugly beginning to believe I'd prevailed, told me I was strong enough to walk, and had better if I didn't want to be left behind. Restless to be on her way, she broke camp without my help and, weighing me down with only a spear and a small sack of tubers, led the way.

Why did Ilgen's sense of danger, which was tuned more finely than a poet's lyre, fail her? Because she was so anxious to put one foot in front of the other again? Because she was dull from an enforced and safe rest? Because no matter how well trained, no one can win the laurel wreath every time? Because, to be fair, the bear was simply more canny than she? Whatever the correct answer, there was no time for the question just then, for suddenly, with no warning whatsoever, I heard a sound behind me and, when I turned, beheld the end of my path in the shape of a brown mountain with teeth bearing down on me with the mind-numbing speed and intent of one of Hannibal's war elephants charging a Roman legion.

Ilgen could have saved herself. The bear would have struck me and, preoccupied with an easy meal, allowed her to escape. That she didn't is obvious, and in that remarkably selfless, astonishingly altruistic act, her path ended and mine, once again, was diverted in a new direction.

I can't recount what happened next with any veracity because the episode has become like the blurred cloud of a battle in which one sees bits and pieces of action amid a cloud of dust, but never the whole fray. I recall being knocked aside. I recall the bear rising, towering over Ilgen, then lunging to embrace her. I recall a mighty roar, and an answering primeval scream. (I was to hear, in vastly different circumstances, another such scream not too many half-years in the future.) I recall motion too fast for the eye to follow: the sweep of paws, the glint of sunlight on steel, a massive head swinging, dipping, spraying blood. And then I recall silence. Utter silence, no song of bird, no slap of feet on earth, no wind in tree.

I emerged from what must have been a trance to find myself looking down at the bear. Half my broken spear shaft lay at my feet. The other half, the head having entered the bear's mouth and pierced his brain, I suppose, protruded from his mouth and held his head propped off the ground like a trophy. Of Ilgen, there was no sign until, half fainting, I stumbled to one side and saw, protruding from beneath the shaggy fur, a hand and forearm painted red with blood.

The bear was so huge I almost despaired of removing it from her. She'd shed her pack as she knocked me aside, though, and in it was a length of rope she'd woven out of leather thongs patiently cut and chewed into pliability during our long winter nights together. With the rope, limbs from a tree shattered by lightning, rocks I rolled under the beast as I lifted it piece by piece, and most of the rest of the day working and resting, working and resting—nothing's as heavy or unmanageable as a dead animal—I finally pulled her out from under him and, exhausted and grief stricken, sat next to her and held her hand.

Oh, what a price Ilgen had paid for my life! The bear had chewed her face to a bloody pulp. Her breasts hung in tatters, shredded by claws as long as a man's thumb. Her back from her buttocks to her shoulders was ripped open with deep gashes that alone would have taken her life. So tired I hardly knew what I was doing, only that I must, I built a fire. In the dusk, with the wolves that still lurked nearby beginning to howl, I carried water from the same stream that a week earlier had tried to kill me, and washed her corpse. And then, with the fire in front of us and my back against the bear's belly, I held her through the night and, wrapped in the mystery of her sacrifice, eventually slept.

The milestones of my life, clear when I was a young man, are murkily obscured by a cloud of time in my old age. Some, like how I came to live in Heraclius' court, I accept without examination or question. Others grow more unfathomable with each passing year. Oh, I find, concoct, and rearrange answers and reasons, but in truth am assailed by doubts, hemmed in by inconsistencies, confused by complexities that pile one on the other, and am left peering into a well that sinks deeper every time I look into it until, at the bottom, I can see no light whatsoever, only an impenetrable, Stygian darkness.

I sometimes think, when I read the ancients, that I must be the only man to be thus plagued, but daily conversation tells me otherwise. And, while all men seem to be similarly afflicted to one degree or another, the finding of a cure is a matter for each as best he may. One friend, whose name I won't mention (he's a priest), to my certain knowledge has harked back to and secretly professes the heretical teachings of the Donatists, and thus embraces mystery rather than struggle against it. Another has less cynically become a cynic. For my part, I lower candle after candle into the well but, whenever I think I glimpse a spark or glimmer of meaning, the candle gutters and fails and I'm in the same darkness as I was before, which puzzles me because why, I wonder, should so many deeds, which on the surface are simply explained, become such great mysteries when one delves below that surface?

There was no mystery the next day when I buried Ilgen. She was of a warrior tribe that feared nothing, and I didn't believe she'd attacked the bear with any more trepidation or thought of her own safety than when she spat in Azak's face or smeared shit on his wolfskin robe. Those weren't wise decisions, I thought, but she'd have scorned that opinion and branded me a coward. Perhaps she would have been right: I'm not the one to judge. I am, though, the one who's still alive, and writing.

I buried her according to her tribe's customs, to the extent I knew them. I entwined green vines in her hair, placed a knife in her right hand and the bear's genitalia in her left. I hung a pouch of ground nuts and berries mixed with meat and fat around her neck, wrapped her in her ripped furs, and curled her on her side in a shallow grave I covered with rocks. Finally, I recited those Christian rites I remembered and, whether it was appropriate for a woman or not, charged Valos, her tribe's God of the Dead, to look upon her with favor and carry her with him on the hunt and into battle where she might savor eternal triumph. That completed, I removed and made a necklace of the bear's fangs and the rest of his claws, took his tongue and as much meat from one haunch as I could carry with the rest of my burden, and left his remains for the wolves, who, I hoped, would occupy themselves with gorging on him until I was far away.

What exactly far away was or meant, though, bordered on the meaningless since I was already as far away from any place I'd ever known as I could get. Any direction I took, therefore, must be toward somewhere. I considered the problem as I lay alone that night. Forest surrounded me for uncounted miles, and I had no idea where I was. The Wolun, Ilgen's tribe, lay somewhere to the northeast, and though I might be able to find them, I doubted I wanted to without her along to vouch for me. The steppe, I knew, lay to the south, and I had no desire to find myself in that featureless sea of grass. Azak and his men could have been anywhere by then, but they were to the southwest when we left them, so it was manifestly prudent to avoid that direction. I'd been told desert mountains lay to the southeast and, since I've never liked deserts, discarded that notion. Due north, Ilgen had said, led to vast marshes and treeless plains where the ground was frozen the year round, which wasn't to my liking. That left the northwest, where Kapsabelis had said a reddish-blond–haired race of warriors— might one of them have been Ilgen's son's father?—lived. No better idea presenting itself, I fell asleep and prophetically dreamed that a wild boar appeared and walked at my side. Content with his companionship, for he frightened off wolves and bears, I continued with him in the direction I'd decided on before I slept. When I woke the next morning, I took my bearing from the sunrise, and with stiffened resolve struck out toward the northwest.

I can't measure my journey in distance, and know only that I traveled many, many miles. I can't measure it in difficulties or dangers, for there were times when the difficulties seemed insurmountable and others when I might have been in Eden, and the dangers were occasionally so great I at first feared I wouldn't survive, but later learned to view them with equanimity. My sole measurement was the seasons, of which I used eight, for two years of my life. When I did find civilization again, I was more an animal than a man and, paradoxically, more a man than I'd ever been.

# 9. *Of Solitude, and How It May Change and Shape a Man.*

**I**'ve been a student of loneliness and the ways solitude affects men for a good share of my life. Some men wear solitude as naturally as a bird wears feathers, others no more than a wild horse does a man on his back, which is to say some of the latter may be trained to tolerate it, but others never will.

Few suspect the tyranny of solitude, the price it exacts from those who'd live under its rule. One man finds bliss when he takes the vows of an anchorite, departs from his fellows, and disappears into his hermitage: for him, Christ is sufficient company. Another discovers the calling he thought was founded as firmly as Peter's rock is set on a mire of sand: he must either abandon himself to lunacy or return in self-imposed shame to cloisters and the comfort of his brothers' company. No one can predict correctly every time which of these paths a new anchorite will follow, but I have a reputation for predicting correctly most of the time. In addition, when I've erred or come upon the scene too late and found a man hovering on the brink, I'm often able to help him with some gentle and useful advice other than "Pray, Brother!"—which isn't enough when prayer's been his sole occupation for what to him seems like forever. Now, I say this not to boast or flaunt my knowledge, but to explain why, other than for my ability to read men's motives, Mother Church ordained me (but I've never offered Mass) and has put up with me for nearly four decades, and, more important to this account, how fate, coupled with an ability to withstand and live with solitude, led me to Einarr, or Beowulf, whose story this is.

There are two kinds of solitude, the purely physical and that of the soul. Each is quite different, but they're often connected or mutually reinforce one another. One can be surrounded by people and yet quite alone: in this solitude, one can easily sink into a pit of despair, and the more people the deeper the pit, because one feels surrounded by riches that, like King Tantalus, he's denied. This solitude of the soul was my nearly constant companion when I was a child. People talked and listened to me, but they also treated me like a creature out of a bestiary and joked to my face. Even Heraclius, before he took note of me, treated me more like a toy than a person, and Amin, my one real friend, died an untimely death—though I now question if death is ever untimely. Eventually, beginning when Amin and I became friends, I graduated from my school of solitude and took my place in the world as a real person, but I was well trained in solitude by then, which later became a blessing and an asset when I faced purely physical solitude.

Two years is too long to live alone for one who's lived in the midst of turmoil and bustle for so long. Heraclius' court was a termitarium of activity with people always rushing about and underfoot. Solitude, after our return from Persia and in my new status, became a luxury rarely found except in sleep, which was often interrupted. Later, solitude was unheard of aboard the riverboat, as it was with Kapsabelis and the bawling, shouting, laughing, cursing crowd he surrounded himself with. Lastly, with Ilgen I was never alone for more than long enough for me to gather firewood or for her to set snares.

Man isn't meant to live alone (even anchorites receive

occasional visitors in their hermitages), and by nature bands together in settlements, towns, and cities. So ingrained is this tendency and so necessary this fellowship, that the man who's totally isolated is too soon more a dreaming animal than a man. I discovered how true that is during my two years in the wilderness.

If Ilgen had paid a high price for my life, so, by her loss, had I. I couldn't have been more numbed, initially, had a horse kicked me. I'd thought Ilgen and I would be together for a long time, and I couldn't believe she was dead. I spoke to her, and grew irritable when she failed to respond. Waiting for her to choose a campsite, I trod on well into dusk and sometimes until after dark before it dawned on me to stop. I forgot one fish was enough and caught two, and often prepared enough food for both of us. I excoriated her for not carrying her share of the load, and so on. All things considered, I was lucky the bear had been hungry after instead of fattening himself before his winter sleep, because I was in such a state I doubt I'd have survived severe weather.

I was subject to debilitating and lugubrious bouts of self-pity. The most ill-starred man in the world, I was sure, I questioned what I'd done to deserve such treatment. Witches, barbarians, and bears attacked me. God had betrayed me by giving me the body of a dwarf and making me the object of ridicule and scorn. Like Adam from Eden, I'd been expelled from the garden of mankind, and I was alone. Everyone I'd grown fond of, from Amin and Heraclius to Kapsabelis and Ilgen, had deserted and abandoned me.

The whole world, in fact, conspired and contrived against me. A log broke as I crossed a stream on it. Fish rejected the grubs I affixed to bone hooks. A ptarmigan I dropped with a stone flew away when I approached to pick it up. Rain leaked through the shelters I made of boughs, and tree limbs fell across my path. By the end of the first summer, I myself joined the throng and turned against me. It was as if I was toying with, or perhaps practicing for, the day when I fell into a depth from which no escape was possible. Once, I absent-mindedly used my hand instead of a pair of sticks to pick a rock out of the fire to heat some water. Another time, with a curious air of detachment, I watched my ankle trip a snare set across the path by a hunter who'd passed that way, saw the spear coming at me, and felt it graze my neck. Late that night, I lay curled in a hole in the bottom of an oak tree and contemplated the irony of God damning me with unnaturally short legs and, then, as if to mock me further, saving my life with them, because the spear would have pierced my breast if I'd been the height of a normal man.

Luckily, even in that haunted land populated, it often seemed, by nothing more than ghosts and spirits, I occasionally stumbled across other humans. Then, if I'd sunk deep enough to fear the effects of solitude more than possibly harsh treatment at the hands of strangers, I convinced myself I needed company and threw in my lot with them. Living in their low-walled pit houses, eating their execrable food, subjected to their inevitable squalor, the press of their vermin-infested bodies, their low intelligence and virtually complete ignorance of the world, always quickly cured my loneliness, and I moved on. I might have stayed longer if I'd been Kapsabelis and had his retinue to insulate me from their communal boredom, but I was only a dwarf, a strange and suspicious creature who wasn't quite human and was looked upon, I always thought uneasily, as something good to eat, a delicacy.

Thus, in one manner or other, I dragged myself through summer into autumn and, innocently, for I'd begun to shake my lethargy, prepared myself for winter. For once, luck seemed to be on my side. One morning I awoke to snow flurries, and the same afternoon stumbled on a cave that looked as if time and water had hollowed it out with my arrival in mind. My new home lay far enough up a cliff to remain dry if the small river at my front door flooded. Four or five times my height deep and wide, it was tall enough in the middle for the ceiling to be lost in the gloom, as dry as a bone left to weather in the summer sun, and empty. Everything I needed was close at hand. Fat trout swam in a deep spot where the river pooled fifty paces downstream. Another hundred paces away was a field of the tubers Ilgen had showed me how to dig and cook. Chestnut, hickory, walnut, and other nut trees were abundant, as were pine. By the time two weeks had passed, I'd gathered woven-bark baskets full of nuts and sun-dried berries and, before the ground froze solid, what I hoped was a winter's supply of tubers. At the top of the cliff, I stacked wood to tumble down to my front door. The day before the first severe storm shut me in, I finished smoking the trout I planned to save for emergencies and closed off the mouth of the cave.

A man has little time for introspection when he has a purpose and keeps busy. My labors lulled me into a false sense of peace, and I was as content as a worm in a fresh apple. Hauling and stacking, gathering and fishing, weaving baskets to hold food and lashing racks to keep my smoked fish off the ground, I quite forgot I was alone. As Ilgen had healed as she shed the weight of her lost son, so, though I'd by no means forgotten her, had I healed as I shed hers. How little did I know.

My ordeal began on a night I'll never forget if I live to be as old as Methuselah. Winter was young, the weather almost balmy. Pleased with myself, I sat soaking up the sun where it warmed the rocks outside the mouth of my cave. Around midday, though, clouds gathered and, more quickly than I imagined possible, a thunderstorm struck. The rain fell in sheets, the wind uprooted trees that, from the safety of my cave, I could hear crashing to the ground. The lightning was fierce and so close I could smell it, and the thunder would have deafened Perun himself, who'd produced it. Later, on the heels of the storm, the wind shifted abruptly and blew cold out of the north. As if what little light there'd been was frozen, the sky grew almost black, and snow began to fall.

I remained, throughout, as smugly complacent as a fat priest. What Kapsabelis' mercenaries hadn't taught me, Ilgen had. My cave was warm, and the branches I'd woven to cover its mouth, complete with a small door made of deer hide, kept the wind from sucking out the heat. I had food to eat and furs to keep me warm. I'd survived Heraclius' death, exile, Azak's depredations, Ilgen's death, and my own foolhardy urges to destroy myself. I was, in short, as safe as a flea in the armpit of a sleeping bear. Little did I know I was soon to descend into a hell that would test my powers of endurance as nothing has before or since.

When I look back, inasmuch as I ever could, or can, on the months that followed, I'm amazed I didn't take my life. How does one recall a gaping hole as black and formless as the cave I lived in? I ate, I know, because I didn't starve. I slept, too, sometimes for what seemed like days, except "day" had little meaning. I must have trudged uphill for wood—I didn't freeze—and downhill to chop ice for water and make holes to fish through. I recited as much as I could recall of the Gospels and the Psalter, both in Latin and Greek, and translated them into the barbarian's tongue. I recreated the multitudinous intrigues of courtiers, the soft and lascivious touch of beautiful women, the thrill of the hunt and battle, and wept that I was not once again in Heraclius' court. I tried to recall and imagine the many people I'd known, but they'd become ephemeral and their faces, even Ilgen's, which frightened me, were blurred and indistinct. For hours, I stared into the fire, but I don't remember what, if anything, I saw there.

And oh, the darkness! The unremitting, interminable darkness! The sun was a pale and mocking reminder of itself, seldom seen and, then, so low on the horizon it barely rose above the trees. The clouds were so persistent that the moon once went from new to full between my brief glimpses of it. Night. Nearly perpetual night, with the only sound the crackle of my fire, the moaning wind, and the rustle of ghosts assailing my stronghold, my very self.

And oh, too, my self! My soul was a stranger with whom I was forced to share uncounted hours. Such an unsavory, selfish, slippery soul! A veritable yapping dog or contentious crow of a soul. The soul of a petulant, argumentative child, a lust-ridden, deceitful lout. A soul that plagued me with obscene whispers and, when I closed my ears against them, insistently drummed inside my head.

As they might a bird sitting in a nest built at the end of a supple limb, the storms in my mind whipped me up and down, from side to side, and in dizzying circles. How I dreaded the approach of those soul-squalls! Unable to stop them, the grim interior of my cave blurred, shifted, formed patterns and designs, and, in spite of myself—oh, how I shouted myself hoarse and beat my thighs with slowing fists—I felt a chill steal over me, my eyes glaze, my mouth drop open and spittle run down my chin as I plummeted deeper and deeper into the infinite, hard emptiness of my existence and stood face-to-face with myself.

When the storms abated, I sat numbed, confused, frightened, exhausted, and as empty as a drum. I can't remember which of the two, the storms or the deadly calm between them, I dreaded more. Perhaps both equally, or, perhaps, as seems likely at this far remove, I was beyond dread. What I do recall, as ludicrous as it sounds, is how grateful I was for nuts.

I'm convinced I'd have slipped over the edge into raving lunacy without nuts. Fish, either raw, cooked, or smoked, I ate with ease and took care only to spit out the bones lest one catch in my throat. Tubers were simply baked in coals, split out of their skins, and eaten. Berries, taking care to make them last, were but a matter of munching a mouthful. But nuts required study, concentration, and hard work. I know that God in His infinite wisdom had a reason when He made nuts hard to crack (a reason as far beyond me as why He made squirrels, unless it was to eat nuts), and angrily assumed, when I first attempted to crack them, that it was to mash my fingers.

I sound as if I'm complaining, but I'm not, because those first attempts bore intellectual fruit that sustained me through the winter. Quite aware of what I was doing, I made nuts not only my sustenance but my vocation, my avocation, and my recreation. As a novice, I either bounced rocks off nuts and, like as not, smashed a finger or thumb, or shattered them into a myriad of pieces after which, like an ape rummaging through its mate's hair to pick off and eat fleas, I patiently, even obsessively, gleaned and savored the tiniest pieces of meat. I searched for the longest, flattest, fattest, and skinniest nut. I looked for faces in nuts. I found Heraclius and I found Portia. I found a merry Kapsabelis, a staunch Ilgen, and an evil Azak. I found one I imagined to be Ptah, and another Bes, and went on to invent a pantheon of nut heroes and nut gods and, in its dark corners, nut devils, demons, and rogues. I juggled nuts, and arranged them in geometric patterns. I made piles of nut primes— three, five, seven, nine, all the way to one hundred seventy- three, at which point I tripped, fell, and scattered them, which was so much for primes. I studied nuts the way an architect studies stone and wood, an astrologer the planets, a physician the humors, a theologian the nature of God, or Azak the many forms and aspects of violence and pain. I fell asleep to nuts and I awoke to nuts, and my efforts were rewarded. By winter's end, I was as knowledgeable about nuts as any man who's ever lived. By their heft and sound, I could tell the difference between those in which the meat was plump, juicy, and sweet, and those in which it was shriveled, dry, and bitter. With a glance, I knew where and how hard to strike one so, with two or three precise blows, the shell split and the meat fell out in perfectly twinned and convoluted hemispheres. Most especially, I was alive, sane, and in good health. Once again, I'd been put to the test, and had prevailed.

Spring's renewal came slowly. The sun crept ever higher into the sky. The snow receded flake by flake and the ice on the stream below my cave softened, broke apart, and was carried away by the rising water that, when it foamed and eddied an arm's length below my porch ledge, finally evicted me and sent me, however reluctantly at first, on my way.

I was of differing minds about resuming my journey. On one hand, my feet, legs, and back ached with the labor of carrying my pack, and the weather was devilishly change- able, with one day sun, the next rain or snow, and the forest floor accordingly frozen, sloppy, or slick. On the other, I was free of the constricting walls and the continual gloom of a cave, spring was in the air, which was comforting, and I was moving, which gave me a sense of purpose even if I had no particular destination.

How rapidly, and how slowly, that spring and summer passed! I can still taste, as clearly as the leeks in tonight's soup, the sense of wonder with which I greeted each day, and the inexhaustible joys of the solitude I'd learned to live with. I wandered in the soft greenness of a reawakening forest in which the only sounds were those of nature: no laughter, no cries, no wheel rattling on stone, no door closing, clatter of sandals or clank of spoon. No voice raised in raucous song, no housewife haggling with a fruit vendor or screeching at her mate or children. No neigh of horse, clop of hoof, or jingle of harness. No pipes, lyres, bells, cymbals, or drums. No voice, sound, smell, or sight generated by another of my kind. Not one.

I carried on my back all my possessions, nay, more, the total discernible evidence I saw of civilization, of an intellect that exceeded claw and tooth. No chair to sit on or bed to lie in, no cup from which I might savor wine, and no wine. No bread, either dark or white, neither salt to sprinkle nor sauce to pour. No manners to mend or fashions to keep, and no silver buckle, gold coin, or precious jewel to guard.

That didn't last forever, of course, for God dictates that everything (save His constant love) change and alter with time, which suits men who, like anxious war horses arrayed for battle, grow bored of and chomp on the bit of constancy. Thus I was pleased enough when my path crossed that of the occasional band of nomadic hunters or passed through a simple family holding. As before, I never stayed long in such company except once when I fell in with a trader much like Kapsabelis, and though it was pleasant to hear laughter and song again, and sit up half the night talking, I went my own way when they turned from their westerly course and headed south.

Luckily, I finally met one improbable soul to spend the next winter with. I'd stopped to rest, one day, and when I stood to resume my way, rose directly into the path of a raven as it fled a smaller bird that was chasing it. Both of us taken equally by surprise, I dropped to the ground and the raven swerved in his flight, flew directly into a tree trunk, and fluttered to the ground with a broken wing.

Needless to say, I was intrigued. Heraclius' court had been well supplied with falcons, parrots, peacocks, and even a crow that spoke a few garbled words of a language no one understood, but birds had never appealed to me and I'd kept my distance from them. This fellow, though,

wounded as he was, won my sympathy so, after he'd
wounded me with his beak a few times and I'd hooded and
tethered him, I set and bandaged his wing as best I could,
and kept him.

I was glad I had him when winter drove me indoors
again. My cave that year was too shallow to keep much
above freezing, even with the wattle-and-daub wall I built
to restrict the opening. The closest water was over two hundred paces downhill, which meant the climb back was
longer. The few fish I could catch were full of bones, and
I found tubers only a week before the ground froze solid,
which meant I was in short supply. I don't know where
ravens spend the winter, but Amin—I named him after my
giant Nubian friend—spent that winter with me. His wing
had healed and he could have flown away had he wished,
but I suppose he'd grown as accustomed to me and as glad
of my company as I was of him and his.

And good company we were. Like men who wallow in
laziness when others provide for them, he accepted the food
I gave him rather than search for his own. In recompense,
he amused me. Like an old man's wife in front of a fire,
he sat with his head cocked to one side while I prattled
until his eyes closed and he fell asleep. He took, with
croaks and shrieks, to reciting my Psalter in unison with
me. He learned to sit on my shoulder and pluck a seed from
my ear, or find one I'd hidden in my beard. Best of all,
when the nights grew unbearably long and cold and I felt
myself begin to slip into insanity, he sang and danced with
me around the fire.

What a sight that must have made! A bearded and flat-
faced, misshapen dwarf with bowed and bandy legs and
overly long arms leaping madly about, and a black bird
nearly half the man's height, its head bobbing and turning,
rising briefly into the air on outstretched wings. Our grotesquely enlarged shadows repeated and exaggerated our
every movement on the walls. Our voices, now hollow,
now booming—wild, indecipherable songs of madness, ecstasy, and glory—echoed as we moved like demons or lost
spirits contending against the unknowable emptiness. Had
anyone seen us, he would have guessed me a madman and

Amin a devil, and fled as fast as legs could carry him. But to what avail that flight? Where flee to avoid madmen or devils? Flee one, find another, I've found, and of the many of both I've encountered in this life, a man dancing with a bird is among the least to be feared.

# 10. *How, Upon Meeting the Geats, Amin and I Joined Them.*

**I** didn't believe my eyes when I found the ship in the middle of the forest. Winter and spring had passed. The summer day was hot and humid in the deep woods where little wind penetrates. Amin and I had been moving steadily, heading generally northwest. My naked feet made no sound on the soft forest floor, and Amin, too, was silent as he glided from tree to tree overhead. I'd just stepped around the bole of an ancient, towering conifer when, as if by magic, a boat, its keel hidden behind the crest of a slight rise in the ground, appeared no more than two-score paces in front of me. Dumbfounded, I stopped dead in my tracks and stared at what I thought must surely be an apparition, but it was still there after I closed my eyes and shook my head.

The boat—a most peculiar one at that—lay unmoving, as if docked in placid waters. Bow and stern rose in graceful quarter-moon curves to identical iron-ringed peaks that were indistinguishable except for an oddly carved spiral ornament at what I assumed was the bow. Neither mast, sail, nor oars were visible: instead, a row of seven round shields, each overlapping its neighbor from bow to stern, hid the top rail and gave to the whole a fierce, martial appearance. Frightened, for I had no idea how such a large ship had been transported into the middle of a forest, and was reasonably certain I didn't want to meet the men who'd done so, I was about to retreat—undiscovered, I hoped— when I heard a strange rumbling sound I took to be snoring coming from the craft. My curiosity piqued, I waved my arm in a circle over my head and pointed to the boat. Immediately, Amin dropped off the branch he was perched on, flapped his wings twice, and glided silently over the boat before circling back and landing on my shoulder.

More intelligent than I'd guessed a bird could be, Amin had an unerring nose, so to speak, for danger, and I'd learned to trust him without reservation, which more than once had saved me a great deal of effort and trouble and made up for the food I'd fed him all winter. "Well?" I whispered when, unperturbed, he began to preen his breast feathers. "Is there danger?" (I know it's ludicrous to talk to a bird, much less expect an answer, but I'd taken to doing so frequently during our winter of isolation together, and no longer gave it a second thought.)

His signal we were safe, he rubbed his beak as a man hones a razor across the top of my head and hair.

"You're certain?" I asked, still dubious.

Again, he honed his beak on my hair and, by way of emphasis, added a low croak.

Breathing shallowly to make as little noise as possible, although I don't know how anyone could have heard me over that wild snoring, I advanced slowly, this time close enough to see the whole craft from the keel up. Berthed in a sort of cradle resting on smooth log rollers, it was, on closer inspection, even more peculiar than I'd thought. The strakes were riveted longitudinally like any others, but with the long edges overlapping each other, which, it seemed to me, would have let water pour through between them. There was no keel to speak of, so a sail, if there was an unseen mast, would have been nearly useless because the slightest crosswind would have pushed the ship sideways through the water. The shields were nicked, dented, and

gouged, and, my heart leaped, a boar's head glared out at
me from fully half of them.

"The boar!" I whispered, awestruck, and crossed myself. "Like the one I saw in my dream!"

Suddenly, someone shouted in a language I didn't understand. Startled, I jumped back. Frightened in turn, Amin
let out a loud squawk and flapped into the air to take refuge
in a tree. I'd no sooner turned to run, though, than a man's
voice roared at me and, understanding the meaning if not
the words, I stopped as commanded, rooted like a tree to
the spot. Sure I was a dead man, I heard feet hit the ground
behind me and, a moment later, though I didn't know it,
saw my fate in the form of a giant reddish-blond bearded
man standing in front of me.

He was, as was immediately apparent from Kapsabelis'
description, a Northman, one of the kind who fathered Ilgen's child. And like his boat, I'd never seen a man like
him. Long golden hair that shone with a red cast in the
dappled sunlight hung in loose, flowing waves past his
shoulders. His beard, redder than his hair, was long and
bushy, and completely concealed his face from the nose
down. His eyes were surprisingly blue, and his skin, though
pinkened by the sun, was eerily pale. Twice my height, he
towered above me. His torso was naked, but he wore
coarsely woven, tight-fitting trousers and a pair of soft
leather boots laced from his ankles to halfway up his calves.
His chest was wide, finely sculpted, and as hairless as
Amin's beak, and his arms, the most remarkable feature in
a body that was wholly remarkable, were the most massive
I'd ever seen. His biceps were as stout as if they'd been
hewn from masts. His forearms were as thick as most men's
thighs, and his hands looked as if they could crush rock,
which, as it turned out, they very nearly could. Together,
they made the great broadsword he held pointed at my
breast look like a reed, and no more necessary than a knife
for a lion at feed, especially when, within a breath, he was
joined by fourteen other blond giants—though none so
large as he—who completely surrounded me.

I was frightened, I admit, but they, too, from the looks
on their faces, were taken aback. And why shouldn't they

have been? Dwarfs, in their scheme of things, I later learned, were dark and dangerous, often malicious and malevolent creatures, and I certainly looked the part. My squat bare legs ended in horny callused feet with thick misshapen nails. I wore only a short bark skirt to cover my lower torso and genitals, and my oversized and overdeveloped chest, shoulders, and arms were hung about with knives and pouches, a bear's tooth-and-claw necklace, and an overly large pack that held, with the exception of an iron-tipped spear I'd gotten from the trader, the rest of my possessions. Add a graying beard that, rather than disguise, accentuated the caved-in look of my face, and a head covered with a wild Medusa's nest of hair, and I suppose I must have looked more like a wild animal than a man, and for them as imposing a figure as they made for me.

But the Northmen never feared anyone for long. Recovering quickly, their leader, the one with the arms and sword, asked me something in his strange tongue. I answered with my name and, because they looked so unlike the barbarians, first in Latin and then Greek, something about being a traveler alone, which they unaccountably found amusing, for they doubled over in laughter. Their leader squatted so our heads were level, puffed out his chest, and made some further remark that elicited more gales of laughter. At which point, angered and not caring if they cut me to pieces, I pointed around the circle at them and declared myself ready to fight anyone who cared to.

I might have had to, were it not for Amin, who, having interpreted my pointing as a signal to come, obediently dropped out of his tree and, croaking in loud defiance of my attackers, landed on my shoulder.

The results were startling, to say the least. Like the elephant that fears the mouse, the Northmen collectively backed away from me in alarm, and one or two even went to their knees. Why Amin so frightened them I had no idea, but I did retain enough wit to take advantage of their fear, and boldly asserted myself while the iron was hot.

"I am Musculus the Dwarf," I thundered—even if "thunder" has never exactly described my voice—in the barbarian's language. "And who, I demand to know, are you to threaten me thus?"

We had at last found a common language, for the cowed Northmen looked to one of their number who, stepping forward but keeping his distance and a wary eye on Amin, answered, "We're Geats, sir, traders and adventurers from Vastergottland. We're moving our sea-steed from a river we explored to the east of here to the Vistula in order to return to our homes and hearths before winter sets in, for we've been roving for four half-years, and long to see our homeland and families. We mean you no harm, and earnestly beg your pardons for our jest."

My gaze was stern as I digested the implications of that plural and their reaction to Amin. I'd met in my travels men who revered a wide assortment of animals and objects, from wolves to round stones with holes in them, so it was entirely possible the Geats revered ravens, and no real surprise. My question to myself, then, was how to exploit that reverence, and my answer, I immediately decided, was to tread softly, because objects of reverence are apt to be reviled when things go wrong and, since something always went wrong sooner or later, I didn't want to put all my eggs in one raven's basket. Accordingly, I made a small sign for Amin to bend and inspect my ear for a treat, pretended to listen intently when he did, and forthwith nodded vigorously and broke out in a friendly smile.

"The Geats, the brave men of Vastergottland, would be welcome in my land," I said, bidding those who'd knelt to rise. "There, jests are prized, and he who makes others laugh is esteemed. This man, for example," and I approached the hairiest one of them, "would be such a man. Do you know why?" I asked, stealthily pulling from my belt a small bone comb I used to clean my beard.

Befuddled, caught off guard and still leery of Amin, they shook their heads in unison as the translator asked my question.

"Because," I said, startling the poor man by seizing his wrist and lifting his arm, which made Amin squawk and, distracting the Northmen, fly into the air, "he carries his comb in a most unlikely place."

Their mouths agape, the circled lot stared at their companion's armpit, where, as plain as day, a comb hung in his hairs. They were silent, at first, struck dumb by the ludicrous sight of their friend, who stood with his arm raised, head bent down and eyes rolled to stare at the comb that inexplicably appeared in his armpit. And, when he uttered what was obviously an oath, grabbed the comb and half tore out a patch of hair, which caused him to yelp with pain, first one, then another, and soon all of his companions were virtually rolling on the ground, laughing, holding their bellies, beating on each other, and wiping the tears from their eyes. As for me, I signaled for Amin to return to my shoulder and, when the Geats had collected themselves, approached my victim and asked the translator to tell him I apologized for making him the butt of my joke, and meant him no offense or disrespect. Fuming, his fists and teeth clenched, I thought for a moment he'd attack me, but their leader interceded, told him, according to the translator, that it was only a joke, and bade him greet me like a friend. And though he smiled and did, I didn't have to be too wise in the ways of men to know I'd made an enemy, and had better remember to watch my back when he was behind me.

My benefactors, Mother Church in general and Brother Benjamin in particular, have been generous. I've written as small as my eyes will allow and covered every available inch, but still have used more skins than are given to most men in a lifetime. And all, so far, for what amounts to an introduction, because it was with the discovery of the ship and the Geats that, though it be written on skins, we reach the meat of my account. And if my account be meat (though I shy from fattening the metaphor), here are the bones (some of them: the rest will follow in due course) that structure it.

To begin with, Einarr (or Beowulf, which name he did not assume for some months), also called Einarr the Clutcher, or simply Clutcher, whose song is quite properly sung by *scops* because he was a hero.

Hervarth, barely into his manhood and an apprentice of

sorts, untrustworthy, and their king's son. He treated me courteously during the rest of our journey, but later, as I'd predicted, attempted to avenge my joke turned insult.

Valgard Halfbeard, the old man of the crew, about my own age. Valgard had been shaved, in a fight, very nearly to the bone on the left side of his face. He killed his adversary, but was left with a monstrous flat scar that was as bald and shiny as my pate is today.

Askil, Asbrand, Olvir Iron-glove, Hugleik, and Hrothgeirr, of course, but what use a list of this nature? Let me come to them as my account unfolds. In any case, I can't for my life remember all their names. How could I after so many years? Some come to me as I write, but I have trouble connecting names and faces. Thorkel is an example. There's the name, but was he the one who was given up for lost after he fell overboard one night but was later found alive and well after swimming a mile to shore in a frigid and storm-tossed sea, or he who died in bed of a fever, an unfortunate death for a Geat or, indeed, any Northman?

The Northmen's names were as colorful as any I've found in my travels. Many were compounded with Thor, one of their principal gods; thus Thorkel, Thorhund, Thorolf, and so on. Some were connected with natural objects, as in so-and-so the Mast or Oak or, Sigurd comes to me, Sigurd the Crag. Teeth, eyes, and other body parts played their roles: Erik Gray-eye, Bluetooth, and Lief the Bald (a man without a single body hair). Exploits in the martial arts were frequently used too, as in Rorik Double-ax, Beo Gothsplitter, and Gnupa Storm-shield. I should add that some of the above are examples only, and play no role in this account.

If I don't remember all their names and faces, I do recall their strength and how hard they worked—even Einarr, with his aloof and cocksure attitude that so irritated me— which solved the mystery of how a sea-steed, their colorful term, got to the middle of a forest. After four half-years of trading with and harrying, or raiding, among the barbarian tribes, they were taking it, as the translator explained to me, from a river they'd traveled up as far as they could, overland to the Vistula, and in this manner: the ship was hauled out of the water and into a cradle built of light timbers they carried with them; they then cut, stripped, and fashioned a dozen or so log rollers and, with a great deal of pushing, pulling, smoothing the way, and cursing, made their way from one waterway to the other.

Short legs or no, my arms and shoulders were as strong as most other men's and, since they said they could use the help (and didn't say, but I believe it was true that I was an intriguing diversion), I was respectfully invited to join their band. In truth, after a winter with only a raven to talk to, I was pleased to accept.

The Geats weren't in the least like so many of the barbarians I'd met. They were a merry lot, with songs, jokes, and ribald comments about everything under the sun. They could be contentious, true, but seldom in the evilly sullen manner of the deep forest barbarians: there was no sneaking around and stabbing in the back (among the crew, at least: they were elsewhere as capable of deceit and betrayal as any other race) if one took offense at something another said or did. Rather, they argued the matter out—although argue is a pale euphemism for the fights that often continued until both were too exhausted to stand or launch a blow—and that night or the next morning acted as if their bruises, split lips, and cracked knuckles were badges of honor, and were once again the best of friends.

I took to my new life as if born a Geat. By day, I wielded an ax to help clear the way, foraged for food, pushed, hauled, carried rollers from stern to prow, and whatever else was required. I welcomed the labor because it gave me a sense of purpose and made me feel useful but, as I had with Kapsabelis, I enjoyed the nights the most.

What boasters the Geats were! Their boasts were of two categories. The first were blood-oaths, and served as a goad or inducement to a man to do what he knew he must or be excoriated or ridiculed. The second, story-boasts, were a combination of self-aggrandizement and pure entertainment. Now, I was accustomed to hearing proud men declare their prowess in no uncertain terms, but the Geats had turned that sort of declaration into an art of exaggeration that knew few bounds. They were very nearly incapable of uttering a simple unvarnished statement of fact once their bellies were full and they'd arranged themselves around a roaring fire. "I killed a wolf," a perfectly permissible statement by day, became transformed at night into an interminable tale in which the wolf was a fang-dog as large as a bear that had raided the teller's homestead and slaughtered his stock, whose blood-cries frightened normal men into panic-stricken flight, whose skull-cups were as big around as a man's fist and glowed like ghost-fire, whose snout-daggers (jowls, eyes, fangs: the Northmen delighted in these colorful constructions, and called the practice of using and inventing them *kenning*) could disembowel a horse in one slash, and whom the teller, with bare hands, slew after a meticulously described night-long battle.

The only rule was of proportion, so to speak. Thus, for example, Einarr, because he was their most formidable warrior and acknowledged leader, could concoct a tale of not merely carrying, which any normal man would have found challenge enough, but swimming a half a hundred miles of open sea in the middle of a winter storm while wearing full armor and laden with the swords, breastplates, helmets, and other assorted plunder from a vanquished enemy, and his men would applaud appreciatively as if that task were perfectly feasible. Let, however, Egil the Unfortunate (see how the names come to me!), he who'd once tripped, fallen, and knocked himself unconscious at the beginning of a battle and in this shameful manner lived to fight another day, step beyond a bloated account of how he killed a wolf or, perhaps, an amusing description of an escapade with a one-legged whore, and he'd be hooted derisively and driven offstage.

Such hyperbole was a nightly staple around our fire and played no small part in my mastery of their language. Norse was simple compared to Greek and close enough to the barbarian tongues to come easily to me. After stumbling about in it during the day, I listened at night and, by the end of my first month, with the translator's help, was ready to try an exaggerated tale of my own. In other areas, I needed no help. I couldn't compete in normal wrestling because the Geats had the advantage of long legs and youth, but I could hold my own in arm wrestling, which was as much a game of mind as of brawn, and even occasionally win, although never against Einarr, whom no one else had ever beaten, either. And in their version of evens and odds, in which they held from one to four pebbles in various combinations in one or both fists resting on their knees, I won so handily and monotonously that I soon had to allow my opponents to win frequently enough to keep them interested.

More an animal than a man, more a man than I'd ever been. Which statement prompts another digression, for which I hope my reader will indulge and forgive me.

I'm sitting, an old man with no duties or obligations, on the porch of a pleasant, cool cottage on the grounds of an ancient, opulent villa turned monastery. Novices bring my meals, and a small cup of wine when they check to make sure I'm still breathing and tuck me in for the night. It's a pleasant enough life, but somewhat somnambulant, too, which is an invitation for the mind to wander, to float about, to drift lazily like an old carp basking in a sun-warmed pool.

But something about me must abhor the vacuum of lazy peace because I've found, as I've proceeded with this account, that my mental powers, rather than being stultified, are stimulated. My mind bubbles like fermenting beer in a jug left in the sun. I'm rejuvenated. My muscles itch. I eat every crumb they serve me and ask for more. I disdain the proferred helping hand when I rise or sit, and put on my own slippers. And this stems, I believe, from an obsession with that earlier me, those earlier me's, I unearth as I proceed.

It strikes me that as difficult as it is to look at oneself with any degree of honesty in one's present, it's very nearly impossible to see, or even imagine, that self as a younger man. What strangers we become to ourselves! I find myself amused, sometimes astonished, often embarrassed, and totally fascinated by those earlier me's. I chuckle, I raise my eyebrows, brood, and, like the dwarfs of the Northmen's myths, dig and delve deeper into the mountain of my past.

And if that results in digressions, it also helps me understand the Musculus who was so strongly influenced by Einarr, who in turn played no small role in the Musculus I've become. Which is to say, in a circuitous manner, that Portia, in those days, saw me more clearly than I saw myself. She was, in short, right.

What a spectacular ninny I was! I was a vain, pompous, overconfident, preening, strutting, arch, pampered ass whose sense of honor was indeed as deformed as my body. I'd been feared and deferred to so long I'd become a miniature monster, and indeed belonged in a bestiary. I was as crafty and given to intrigue as the courtiers I so sanctimoniously despised. Flat on my moral back, I'd serviced Heraclius with my wit and ability to read men's minds (while remaining spectacularly illiterate when it came to my own) with the same meretricious devotion a whore lavishes on her customers. By metaphorically stripping me and casting me naked into and against the world, Portia's vengeance was perfectly conceived. And hating and fearing her as others hated and feared me, I dreamed of her.

But if that was one Musculus the Dwarf—as pitifully wrapped in comfort and the appurtenances of power as he was in the rags and ordure of a prison cell—another emerged in exile.

A mud wasp has made one nest and has started a second one a few feet to my left on the wall of the cottage where I now dwell. Just as when I was a boy, I've discovered that altering the landscape around the creature's nest (Musculus the malicious Wasp God!) reduces the poor beast to a confused and buzzing meander across the face of the wall. Is the analogy strained? I don't think so. Remove the landmarks by which a man retains his equilibrium, and observe how lost and confused he becomes. Which is to say I now recognize I in large part misrepresented myself in my account of the journeys after my exile from Constantinople. Not intentionally, really, because the events I related were essentially true, but as I tunnel ever deeper into this vein of honesty, I find a Musculus who was as unknowingly lost and confused as the wasp, and I'm amazed he survived. Survive he did, though, and by substituting Kapsabelis for

Heraclius and thus restoring his smug vanity, pranced blithely on his way to rendezvous with a barbarian version of Portia, Azak.

I haven't given Ilgen enough credit. Why she put up with that deplorable me who, it's true, had saved her life, but was also a bandy-legged incompetent without whom she probably would have lived to find her tribe, is beyond me. That she did, and furthermore died for me, was one of those incomprehensible demonstrations of altruism that not only saved, but ultimately changed, my life. Without her as my example, teacher, and guide, I never would have survived the winter of my excoriating emptiness that completed the job begun by Portia and left me, at last, stripped of pretensions. And after nearly two years with little human contact and my sole companion a raven, I'd become as close to a wild animal as you'll find but, at peace with myself and harmoniously one with the world in which I lived, more a man than I'd ever been.

Whatever I was, recalling how difficult it is to view our earlier selves objectively, I was tremendously excited by my good luck in finding the Northmen. Working, sweating, brawling, gambling, boasting, and occasionally trading when we chanced upon a river family or settlement, we made our way down the Vistula to the first village of any size I'd seen since Kiev four years earlier. Our arrival was blown into a monumental occasion. That morning, the Northmen prepared themselves with the care of maidens going to a dance. They bathed, trimmed their beards, shined and donned their war gear, tidied up their ship, and, when they were finished, presented a most impressive front. Then, with me stationed like a living figurehead on the bowplank, where the watch stood in inclement weather, and Amin on my shoulder, we were ready to make our entrance. Oars flashing and shields and helmets glinting in the sun, we dashed down the river, executed a full circle at speed— no mean trick with fourteen oars and a stiff current—and, to cheers of approval for our performance, bumped softly against the wharf.

In a land where theatrical gestures are valued (is there a land where they aren't?), our audience loved our perfor-

mance. Many of the transient Northmen there recognized
Einarr's ship and happily welcomed the hero returned.
Horns and drums blaring and beating the news, a crowd
quickly gathered and we were surrounded by well-wishers
and curious gawkers the moment we stepped ashore.

Truso was a rough-hewn trading center not unlike Kiev.
Low, thatched timber and plank shops, stores, and dwell-
ings were scattered in a planless maze on a high spot along
the river near where it split into a puzzle of islands before
it spilled into the Baltic Sea. The streets, if one wishes to
grace those narrow and twisting lanes with such a noble
appellation, were superior to those in Kiev by virtue of
occasional walkways of split logs that kept one's feet above
the mud and ordure bogs, but were so slick when wet that
the wise drunk—not that one was often encountered—
avoided them: better to slog along ankle deep than find
oneself flat on the back, or face, in that filth.

The population, too, with the exception of a number of
Northmen of various kingdoms, who stood a blond head
above most of the black-haired barbarians, was similar.
Traders, nomadic warriors, craftsmen, slaves, whores, and
a few honest wives rubbed shoulders indiscriminately,
gawked and traded jibes with each other and us as our band
made its way to a beer hall frequented by Northmen.

If Azak had strutted like a swallow with a peacock's tail,
how much more glorious was Einarr! His flowing blond
hair and great bushy red beard glowed in the sun and his
bulging arms and sculpted torso gleamed with a coat of
seal oil. Impressively resplendent, and yet vaguely ludicrous in his pompous vainglory, he strode through Truso
as if he were a god come to bestow his blessing on it. At
his side as I so often was with Heraclius, and with my
smashed-in face, patchy graying beard, burly torso, and
short legs, wearing on my shoulder a fierce black raven,
Odin's bird, whose piercing, expressionless black eyes and
thick beak stood well above my head and whose tail feathers brushed my waist, I waddled along like a grim reminder
that every god has his dark and dangerous side. We were,
I'm sure, the most imposing, impressive trio Truso had seen
in many a year, if not ever.

The main objective of our stay in Truso, it appeared, was for the Geats to get alternately roaring drunk and serviced by the many slave-whores. As for me, I indulged myself a half-dozen or so times—it had been, after all, over two years—but found the majority of them as repellent as those in Kiev, and decided I could understand why some men preferred sheep or other four-legged animals. Of course, when I said as much and added that I'd rather gamble and fill my purse with silver than my stones with pus, the Geats dissolved in laughter. They cared not in the least whom they bedded, floored, tabled, benched, or stood against the wall, whichever was handiest at the moment.

We arrived in Truso in the middle of summer and I thought we'd stay a while, but we weren't there more than eight or ten days when, one morning, I was booted off my sleeping bench and told we were leaving. I'd spent most of the night gambling, at which labor I'd profited richly during the past five days, and was so bleary-eyed I could hardly see. Imagine my amazement, then, when I stepped outside and there, as red of eye and half of them still too drunk to talk intelligibly, our band was assembled. My astonishment was even greater when, a disgruntled Amin croaking his displeasure with the early hour, we arrived at our ship and I discovered it resplendently refurbished and replenished for a long voyage.

Where in the midst of all the bacchanalian orgies they'd found time or energy for such a prodigious amount of work was incomprehensible to me. No less was why Einarr was so insistent that I accompany them, or, for that matter, why I complied so readily and without question. The answers can only be that my fate drove me in that direction, and to my further adventures with the Geats, so many other Northmen, and especially the man who would become my close friend, Einarr the Clutcher, who would also, so many years later, be sung of as Beowulf.

# 11. Of My Further Acquaintance with the Geats, and Our Journey to Their Homeland.

To think of the Geats bereft of ships and the sea is to think of a bishop without a crosier or miter. I didn't like the water after my sorry experiences on it. I'd been sick on it with Heraclius on our way to and from Persia, shackled and sick on it during the first stage of my exile, a slave on it up the Dnieper to Kiev, and betrayed by it on our raft trip down the Dnieper. Even a stream had tried to kill me. There I was, though, of my own volition marching down the street to take to the water again, this time with a band of mail-shirted, boar-crest helmeted, armed-to-the-teeth—oh, they put on a grand show!—half-crazed, three-quarters drunk, and wholly carefree adventurers in whose hands I was placing my life on a two to three month long voyage during which—not that they cared—I could very well drown.

"You're too drunk and sick to walk, much less man a ship," I said.

"We'll be sober and well tomorrow," they said.

"I can't swim," I said.

"So?" they asked. "Neither could you on the river."

"This is the open sea! I'll drown if I fall overboard."

"Don't fall overboard," they said and, being out of sight of Truso, began to rid themselves of their battle finery.

"I'm going to be sick," I said as smooth river turned into the choppy waves of the open water and our ship heaved and bucked like a horse drunk on rotten apples.

"Stick your head over the side if you do," they said, their voices heavy with scorn, "as any other woman would."

Needless to say, I needed no more incentive to clutch my gut with every ounce of willpower I could summon. I never did vomit, but there were times during those first few days when I'd have paid a raven to do so.

As for Amin, he loved the sea. We were rarely out of sight of land, so he had the best of both worlds. His normal perch, in which the Geats took enormous delight, was on the top of the spiraled insignia at the prow, where, to their eyes, he looked like Odin's blessing incarnate. He didn't like getting wet, which happened the first time we plowed into a sizeable wave, but he did enjoy the open water winds. Rising, letting them lift him as he spread his wings, he circled high as a falcon and then, with jubilant croaks, plummeted in arcing dives that ended with him skimming across the tops of the waves. However much he enjoyed these aeronautic exhibitions, though, the first thing he did every night when we put in to shore was light in a tree and look around as if to reassure himself he was once again home.

The Geats were not unlike Amin, in many respects. They viewed the sea with a stern and practical eye, as mariners must, but also loved it deeply. With reason were they called Sea- or Weather-Geats, because they became a new species once they were on salt water, and different from land-or riverbound men. They stood taller, breathed deeper, and looked prouder. They loved the sea as a mistress, as men have since time immemorial, but they also loved her, with heartfelt reverence, as a goddess.

Nothing in, on, or above the water was taken for granted: everything had a meaning. The color of the sky, the shape of the clouds, the velocity and smell of the wind, the way birds flew or fish swam, appeared like words to one who could read. Coded in the sound of waves slapping against the hull were secrets unknown to lesser men. The water's temperature, its swell and surge and chop, the taste of its spray, its subtle hues, were riddles they delighted in solving. The entirety combined to make a book they magically knew by heart even though it changed with every reading.

"She's nervous today," they said, and variously substituted angry, sweet, peeved, lonely, happy, or any other human emotion they assumed their goddess shared. They jocularly called her an ugly old hag, tenderly addressed her as a sweet bitch, earnestly begged her pardon when they were forced to relieve themselves in the water, and told tales and sang songs about and to her. The sea was their road, often their provider, sometimes their burial ground, and, in much the same way as earth and forest had been mine, their mother and father.

I was contemplating exactly that one evening when I received further proof of the matter. We'd landed on an island and I'd wandered off for a moment of solitude (how quickly we miss that of which we recently had a surfeit!) after we'd eaten and Einarr and his band had settled around the fire for a modest boast or two. Our ship, Spume-Spear, was beached in the lee of a short spit. Cautious, I picked my way across the jumble of rocks and stood on a more or less flat-topped boulder. It was nearly like being at sea. The dying west wind, delightfully cool after a day of hard rowing, teased my beard and hair. Twenty feet below, as if they, too, were tired after a long day, the unending march of waves halfheartedly slapped the ancient impregnable land wall and disintegrated in phosphorescent foam. Behind me, the forest's millions of eyes kept watch. Ahead, a myriad more eyes winked whitely opened and closed, the sea watching me as I watched it. The sky in the west was tinged faintly red and, in the east, a full moon was rising.

"Her hair's down tonight."

The voice startled me and I might have fallen had not a hand grabbed my arm and steadied me. Embarrassed, I looked up to see Valgard Halfbeard at my side. "I didn't hear you," I explained sheepishly.

He shrugged. "We say, 'Learn to have eyes and ears in your ass, or it won't be yours for long.' "

"I thought I did, but that was in the forest." I indicated the waves below us. "They're all I can hear."

He cocked his head to listen. "I didn't think of that. The sound's there and we hear it, but we don't." His brow knotted as he chewed on a thought. "It's the same as the silence in the forest," he finally said. "It's a speaking silence."

He'd carried the idea as far as he wanted and, returning to his original thought, gestured to the moon-road on the water. "She's lonely, and has let down her hair."

"The sea or the moon?" I asked.

"The sea who, when she wishes, borrows the moon's light and spins golden hair from it to beckon a lover." He spat, and rubbed the sputum with his foot. "A man will die tonight."

"One of ours?" I asked, taken aback.

His arm and hand swept the northern horizon from east to west. "No. One out there, whom she'll take to her bed and bosom, to sleep with her forever."

A hushed awe enveloped us as I digested this superstition and considered the man I stood with. When one meets new people, the inclination, nearly unavoidable even in the seasoned traveler, is to see them as alike as pebbles on a beach. Thus the Persians were vain, for example, the barbarians heartless, the river men sly, untrustworthy, and superstitious to a fault. Time invariably shatters those generalizations, though, and, with time, I was relearning the lesson: though from his looks you'd have thought him to be the most ferocious of the Geats I'd met—and there's no doubt he was ferocious, as he later demonstrated—Valbard Halfbeard had a streak of the poet in him.

Yet again made aware of that human truth—how often I have had to relearn the simplest lessons—I considered my companions anew. Einarr was absolutely confident of his strength and, with his cocky and quiet determination and unswaying perseverance, the natural leader. Hervarth, the youngest and under the others' tutelage, as it were, meant well but was better fitted for life in a court than the rough-

and-tumble of adventuring, and was possessed of a sly
streak that made the others slightly leery of him. Askil, their
navigator, was held in high regard for his weather luck, and
Thorfinn for his ability to build a fire in moments in whatever the weather. One, whose name I forget, was sometimes
mocked for a fear of drowning, but gently because he had
remarkable battle-luck. Another was said to have feared
drowning too, but challenged and conquered his fear by
becoming their champion oar-walker. Asbrand, a man I especially admired and liked, had a reputation for mending
anything that broke, and the band would have disowned his
opposite, Toki, for breaking half of what he touched if it
weren't for his phenomenal marksmanship with bow and
arrow. In addition, each played multiple other roles. Some
were always ready with a helping hand and others got by
with as little as possible, some were nearly always cheerful
and others more often glum. One could drink more than
the rest and still walk, another was renowned for his staying
power with women. Two men loved their wives and were
actually faithful to them and, as in every group I've ever
seen, from priests to prisoners, one, the clumsy Toki, was
an inveterate trickster. And, always to be remembered because I later (and still, now that I think of it) owed him my
life, my friend the warrior-poet Valgard Halfbeard was the
only Geat I ever met whose only boasts were blood-oaths.

One and all, next to the sea and in addition to a good
fight, drunk, or whore, they loved Spume-Spear. Their lives
and fortunes depended on her, and they spoke of her with
nearly the same reverence and called her many of the same
names as they did the sea, but with subtle differences because a ship could be replaced—as Spume-Spear later
was—and the sea remained eternal.

The Geats used Spume-Spear hard and expected great
things of her, and in return lavished extraordinary care on
her. Spume-Spear looked new from a distance, but her age,
five years, was evidenced by the thousands of minor repairs
and alterations made by those, some of them dead, who'd
sailed in her. Each man's work was as distinguishable as
his name or face to those who were knowledgeable, and
the longer I was with them, the more knowledgeable I be-

came. Every lashing, splice, and whip was distinctive. Oars were shaped to fit each man's hand and feel for the water, and each man had his own oar plus another in various stages of completion in case his old one broke. Oarlocks and seats took on the personality of the men who used them, this one grooved a little deeper inboard or outboard, that one broader or higher, and set farther fore or aft. Any fool could tell the difference between Asbrand's patches, which were as neat and precisely crafted as a king's armband, and Toki's, which a slave might have hacked out with a dull ax. All caulking had to be watertight, but no one ever stuffed a seam better than Ingald the Obstinate, Asbrand told me one day when I confessed they all looked alike to me.

"Alike?" he snorted, shaking his head in wonder. Grunting with effort, he worked loose the end of a three-foot-long pitch-filled cedar bark rope that had been packed in the crack between two staves, and held it up for me to inspect. "Ingald the Obstinate stuffed this eight half-years ago. Eight! Was ever a bitch so well stuffed?" He patted Spume-Spear's side as he might have a woman's flank. "She loved him for it, too! Not another caulk in her is half that old. Remind me, and we'll drink to the lucky bastard when we get home."

"Lucky?" I asked. "What happened to him?"

"In Valhalla. He single-handedly slaughtered six young men in their prime and had just taken off the seventh's sword arm when the eighth drove an ax through his skull. Is there a better way to leave one's companions? What a man he was! I myself carved the rune-stone that stands where he fell, and where we built his pyre." Whereupon, with a shake of his head, he pulled a new rope out of the pitch bucket, and began to teach me how to ram it home.

Men, even Sea-Geats, can row for only so many hours a day and so many days in a row, and then they must rest. This is more true if there are brisk headwinds and the waves are high and choppy, which was often the case in the Baltic Sea. Accordingly, our progress was agonizingly slow, and due to the lack of a keel, an improvement of which, to my astonishment, they'd never heard! That the Northmen had achieved such a mastery of the sea without the stabilizing influence of a keel was a marvel, because their sails were useless with any other than moderate winds from abaft. The Geats had used their sails extensively along the northern coast of Europe to the Vistula because the prevailing winds in the spring when they left their home were from the west, but the advantage in that direction became a disadvantage on the way home. Being an obstinate race, however, they refused even to consider the possibility of adding a keel. Their minds were set. In the first place, they'd built ships that way as long as anyone could remember and they worked well enough. In the second, since I knew so little about the sea and sailing, what could I possibly know about building a ship? Only one of them showed a modicum of interest, and he, to my surprise, was Einarr. But only through the intercession of a storm, and a story.

The storm came first. Summer, like the moon, was waning, and autumn storms, pushed ahead of the cold weather blowing in from the northwest, were a certainty. We'd had a rare tailing wind for three days and, though auspicious, it put the men on edge. "It will turn," Askil, he of the weather-luck, predicted. "When, is the question. If only before we take the whale-road!"

On the mainland some nights and islands others—never far from shore in case the weather deteriorated or we needed food or water—the prospects of the whale-road (a *kenning* I particularly liked) aroused in the crew a combination of anticipation and apprehension I failed to understand. Askil explained that night with a map drawn in the sand. From their present location, they had two choices. They could continue west through a maze of lowland islands, stick to the continental coastline, and finally turn back to the northeast, or they could work their way up to the northernmost point of the low-lying islands, which they called the Spit, and from there, by crossing open water, draw the short leg of a long, acute triangle and make a landfall on the southeast coast of the Danish Isles. The first way was safe, and the second saved a month of hard rowing. The problem was that the crossing required a night on the open water.

That made me nervous, I admitted, but I didn't understand, having had a belly full of boasts about the sailing prowess of the Sea-Geats, why it should frighten them. The answer was a complex formula whose factors were time, coastal conditions, the nature of the weather, and the perils of the open sea. If the storm hit the next night, as some of them thought, they could count on a protracted calm once it blew itself out, and they'd thank Niord, their God of the Sea Winds, and take to the whale-road. However, the signs were by no means clear. The storm could strike the next day or hold off for a week or more. If it struck the next day, leaving our present location was ill advised because the beaches between where we were and the Spit were uniformly dangerous. If they did reach the Spit and the storm held off, they wouldn't be able to stay too long because food and fresh water there were scarce. Neither dared they take the whale-road before the storm because, as perilous as the open water was under good conditions, they who found themselves on it at night in a storm were doomed. And while none of them feared death, they'd rather die in battle than drown. They'd cope one way or the other, but waiting took its toll of their nerves.

Who can say? Perhaps their prayers to Niord were answered. The decision reached to attempt the faster way, we arrived at the Spit in the middle of the next afternoon and, with the storm obviously imminent, the tension was relieved and the men cheerful. Hastily, we set to work improvising a long ramp and, a horrendous task, dragging Spume-Spear far up the rocky beach to the forest line. There, we snaked her between a pair of trees and, with forked stakes to hold up the now-landward bulwark rail, turned her over far enough for the tallest to walk in without bashing his head. By dark, lashed, propped, piled about with boughs, and the sail stretched from her top rail to nearby trees, we had as ingeniously devised and snug a house as, I imagine, could be found for miles in any direction. Happily, then, not only did the storm hold off until nearly the next morning, but one of the men brought in a fat wild boar. That night, with the boar stripped to bones and the marrow sucked out of them, we slept dry, content, and with full bellies.

The storm, when it hit, made mock of those I'd seen on the steppe. The wind howled, the rain fell in driving sheets, and the sea was whipped into an awesome fury. The river men would have been driven to a frenzy of fear, prayers, and extravagant sacrifices if they'd encountered such a storm, but the Geats paid it no more heed than a woman her menses: storms occurred with a certain frequency, and there was nothing to be done but wait them out.

It was during the wait that I discovered there was more to Einarr than met the eye and first heard the story of the Grundbur.

Everyone kept busy—one braiding a sealskin rope, another hurriedly putting the finishing touches on a new oar to replace the one he'd broken while hauling Spume-Spear up the beach to its haven, and so on—but there was time for talk, too. Old battles were refought. Sea stories, monumental drunks, women of various sizes, states, shapes, and dexterity, were woven in and out of conversations by way of warming up for their nightly boasting sessions. And I busied myself with my attempt to interest them in a keel. Boredom rampant on the second afternoon, I'd gathered a half-dozen around me and was busily drawing diagrams and designs with charcoal on a piece of bark when I realized Einarr was looking over my shoulder and listening.

I hadn't had much to do with Einarr. He'd virtually ignored me other than to parade me through the streets of Truso and summon me to accompany them on their voyage home, and our conversations had been limited to noncommittal grunts in passing. That had been fine with me. I'd learned early on to be suspicious of extraordinarily handsome and endowed men and, with Heraclius my mentor, believed extraordinary achievement, while meriting pride, should likewise be accompanied by a certain quiet modesty. Einarr lacking any vestige of modesty, I'd returned the favor of his inattention with that of my own.

There was no mistaking his curiosity, though, as I explained how a sail worked to drive a boat across the wind.

I felt his interest as he listened to his companions' questions and disbelief, as intently evaluated my responses, and, suddenly, grasped the concept in its entirety. Later, as the dim day darkened, I missed his presence, went looking for him, and found him standing alone on the beach. A great furred hulk with wind-whipped hair, looking much as Niord might, I imagined, he stood with his legs spread and mighty arms bared, looking over the sea. While I watched, he slowly raised his hand and, the fingers together and pointing up like a sail, turned it from side to side to feel the way the wind caught it. And in that moment, a chill passed through me. Because first, my case was as well as won, and second, because I'd misread the man so badly. That utter and cocky confidence cloaked an unannounced sense of privacy, and that endless boasting camouflaged an intellect capable of discarding tradition when something better came along. In addition, no mean trick, he'd purposefully concealed those aspects of himself from my discerning eye. There was, it suddenly became apparent, much, much more to Einarr than he let the others see.

At which point, to the story. (If man is the laughing, cruel animal, so, too, is he the storytelling animal.) Valgard Halfbeard was the *skald*, the Northmen's equivalent of a *scop*, and the Geats listened spellbound.

A better night for a tale of monsters and terror could have been devised by neither *scop* nor *skald*. A ferocious northwesterly wind howled and moaned like the ghosts of a thousand damned souls through the trees and around Spume-Spear and her lashings. A cloud of smoke and wind-driven rain and sea-spray assaulted eyes and noses with an unholy incense. The darkness outside the light cast by our campfire was so complete I'd have welcomed a circling ring of wolves' eyes, for any fellow creature, no matter how predatory, was preferable to the empty, eternal darkness of the universe in which we appeared to be the sole inhabitants. Grotesquely distorted shadows peopled the roof of our ship-cave, swayed on the undulating sail-roof, and stretched to join and become one with the darkness of the forest. Fur-clad creatures with incongruous men's faces and hands huddled shoulder-to-shoulder and thigh-to-thigh in a tight, protective circle as the story unfolded in Valgard's rising and falling, now hushed, now ringing, voice.

Not too far away, just across the whale-road and a week's journey north of our proposed landfall, an evil monster terrorized the land of the Scyldings, or Danes. So powerless were the Bright-Danes that their king and ring-giver, Hrothgeirr, son of Halfdan and Einarr's kinsman, had sunk into despair. His fabled folk-hall, a shining tower that stood on a high hill overlooking a placid bay and a fertile valley, was reduced to a shadow of its former glory, for within its environs the Grundbur stalked, slew, and devoured on the spot or carried away to his cave the ring-giver's best men, those experienced and widely acclaimed in battle. No man could describe the Grundbur, for he came by night and committed his grisly crimes in darkness. Only this was known: he was huge, fast, voracious, and powerful beyond imagination. He was invulnerable, so fell were his powers. Many were the boar-crested heroes—Starketh the Devastator, terrible in battle, Rorik Double-ax, who laughed at shields, to name two—who had pronounced their boasts widely, only to die and leave behind not a single body-beam. Many were the famous gold-wound, rune-adorned swords, some it was said forged by the same Sindri who forged Thor's hammer, whose steel was turned and dulled by the monster's thick skin. No spear could pierce the Grundbur's body-cave, no sword sunder his body-locks, no mere man tear him from earth's lap.

He went on, Valgard Halfbeard, warrior, *skald,* and poet, but I needn't recount his tale because you'll hear much more about the Grundbur before I come to the end of this account. Enough, for now, to know the wide-eyed Geats absorbed every exaggeration like gospel, and I, in my foolishness, believed the story no more than a tale told by a mother to frighten into obedience a child who failed to turn a roast on a spit. I did, though, view with more than passing interest the gleam in Einarr's eye and the set of his jaw as his gaze turned to the north, where the Grundbur lived. And, unless I'd lost my touch completely, I knew I was as good as warned to tighten my belt and gird my loins, because sooner or later, that was where I would find myself.

## 12. Of Grend and the Sea-Geat's Folk- and Mead-hall, and of Hugleik, Their King.

Was Askil's weather-luck unnecessary, or uncommonly effective? Can one ever answer that kind of question? Whatever the answer, the storm blew itself out, the sea calmed, and, other than being reduced to quivering hulks of exhausted, aching muscles and bones, we spent our night out of sight of land and crossed the whale-road uneventfully. Even Amin paid his way. After a haphazard landing on an oar, he decided he liked the rhythmic up and down, back and forth, and took to riding until the rower tired of the extra weight, cursed him soundly, and shook him off, whereupon he croaked in loud indignation, flapped into the air, and settled on another. Watching his antics and betting on whose oar he'd land on next took our minds off our aching muscles and helped the hours pass.

Ah, youth! I tell myself I remember its glories but, especially when I look into the faces of the novices who serve me, realize I don't. Even at the time, nearing or around my fortieth year, I felt ancient in comparison to the Geats, who, with the exception of Asbrand, Askil, and Valgard, were for the most part little more than half my age. No sooner had we landed than, like plow horses that appear ready to drop from exhaustion as they plod around a field and five minutes after being turned to pasture frisk about like colts, they were cavorting and gamboling, shedding their clothes for a swim in the freezing water, and in general acting as if they'd just woken from a nap. And then—how could such innocent-looking youth wreak such unholy havoc in battle?—polished off a dolphin someone had speared that morning and a keg of beer and, boastless for once, were asleep before the fire had died to embers. I'd slept earlier while they'd played, so wasn't as tired. Awake, then, idly musing on who knows what, I heard one of the crew mumble in his sleep. The distraction was irritating, but I ignored it until he stood. And then, the strangest thing. Facing north, and me, over the fire, he slowly raised his arms from his sides. As he did, his fur fell to the ground, and there was no mistaking that torso and those titan's arms profiled against the sky. Einarr the Clutcher, his fists clenched, raised a threat and a promise, a bold boast in fierce determination, to find the Grundbur, whose name I at last recognized from his sleep-choked mumbling, and which he repeated not only with his voice but with every nuance of his posture and the wild, barely restrained energy that emanated from him.

"Grundbur," he swore. "Grundbur!" he promised. "Who are you? What man of what unknown clan or race? Why do you linger to harry the Danes? Wait for me, you Grundbur, whoever you are. Save for me your vaunted power, your fell skills, your terror-roar, and your blood-luck. Save them for me, for you're my fate as I am yours, and I will come. On my blood-oath, my mighty boast, Grundbur, I'll come to you!"

Did I breathe during that lengthy speech? I don't remember. Only, as he sank to the ground and wrapped himself in his fur and sleep, I found myself gulping air, and was faint. And with that scene, that fierce aspect, itself reeking of fell skills and blood-lust, my own musings faded to insignificance and I, too, wrapped myself in fur, rolled onto my side by the dying fire, and slept, and dreamed of ring-choked and spiral-adorned ships that left foaming wakes across the whale-road, of grim-visaged slaughterers wreaking havoc on dark, moonless nights, and of hot blood spilling and etching symbols and memorials long read in the glass of time.

I'm not a Tacitus, who wrote, I discovered some twenty years ago, about the Northmen. Were it my intention to write a history of the Northmen and their ways, I'd have done so fifty years ago (and more accurately, having been there) when they were still fresh in my mind. At this late date, as with their names, I've forgotten too many details of their daily lives, and often confuse them with the other races I've known. And if not completely forgotten, I'd have to dig and delve much deeper than I care to in order to dredge them up. Suffice to say that for their many differences they support the veracity of scripture, because they were also similar enough to men of other races to have descended from our common ancestor, Adam. Vagaries aside, men everywhere eat, breed, fight, and die in amazingly similar ways despite the multitudinous laws and customs that order their societies. Men, in short, will be men whatever their color, wherever they be found, and whoever their gods.

That said, the Geats at home were a breath of fresh air after the forest barbarians. My first impression of their homeland is indelibly etched on my mind. The days were growing shorter and winter was bearing down rapidly when, two weeks after our landfall on the Danish Isles, we rowed up the final stretch of coastland toward a bank of clouds that concealed Knar's Fiord, the waterway from the sea to their homeland. With what anticipation, then, we shipped oars long enough for the men to don their battle finery and raise jubilant pennants, then bent again to the task and, with Askil at the rudder, headed for a dimly discerned gap in the cliffs.

They'd told me what to expect, but mere words hadn't, and couldn't have, prepared me for the sight that met my eyes. No more than two or three score strokes after we entered the mist—the result of cold mountain air encountering the relatively warmer air over the open water—the sea calmed and the chopping sound of waves diminished into a silence broken only by the sound of our oars. Scant moments later, we rowed out of the mist into clear, cool air, and a scene of such magnificence that it took away my breath.

One is to ten as ten is to a hundred, and the Hagia Sophia was to the lake on the Dnieper as the lake was to Knar's Fiord. I've traveled farther and seen more than most men, and know no place to equal Knar's Fiord in majesty and splendor. Sheer rock walls towered hundreds of feet above us on either side. Strangely, I don't remember the sky, but I do recall water as black and smooth as polished obsidian. At first, I heard only silence, but it was a silence that grew to a whisper and then a roar as the splash of oar was added to the creak of line and wood, as the clatter of tumbling rocks was added to the stuttering hiss of falling water, as all, enclosed within the looming walls of rock, echoed back and forth on themselves and were magnified to a roar that culminated in one blast after another on the ram's horn.

I saw, later, similar ships make their way up that fiord, and can picture the sight we made as we rowed out of the deep cleft through the sea-bordering mountains; the walls shrank, and the land opened into a deep, wide, and dark green valley painted with spots of yellow and orange where trees had changed into their fall raiment. Spume-Spear, so large when I was in it, appeared at first as a toy. The last rays of sun angled steeply from behind us to pick out the white foam streaking from our bow, the glistening oars rising and falling in unison, the diamond points of light reflected from gleaming helmets and breastplates. Ever closer, the eager, gliding, foam-flecked, ring-choked and spiral-ornamented ship, and, standing tall and wide in the bow, an indomitable sea-king with arms to contend with the sea itself, the gold encrusted ram's horn he blew winding challenge, greeting, and safe return, the mighty Einarr, a ring-giver in his own right, as natural a king as God has ordained.

Einarr and our crew, one would have guessed, were Alexander and his merry band returned from conquering the world. (How wrong he was: how much more of the world

there is than he thought!) Mellow-toned *lurs,* long and doubly curved ceremonial horns, answered our horn's call. A
din of spears rattling against shields floated across the water. Wooden drums beat to the rhythm of our oars. All
combined in a great, throbbing, echoing roar, through
which we proceeded directly to a wharf filled with cheering
men, women, and children, each of whom had that much
more reason to rejoice, for every man who sailed away in
Spume-Spear nearly two years earlier returned that day.

Do I wax poetic? Hyperbolic? Old men are prone to
those sins, so perhaps I do. And perhaps, too, I'll be given
license to invest those thrilling echoes of the past with a
rosy glow of exaggeration. But however thrilling the scene
and happy the arrival, there were proprieties to be observed
which excluded, to my surprise, word or embrace, because
the crowd fell curiously silent as we touched the wharf,
shipped oars, and tied down.

I was in the dark, for as much as they had told me about
our return, no one had instructed me on what exactly would
happen or what I should do. Protocol is protocol, though,
as I'd spent a good share of my life learning, and I recognized a procession in the making, so wasn't overly worried about making a fool of myself as long as I kept my
eyes and ears open and maintained an air of modesty. Silently, purposefully, the men prepared to disembark. I had
neither armor to adjust, sword to buckle on, nor shield to
carry, but followed their example with my best dagger, my
iron-tipped spear, and Amin, whom, as excited and nervous
as he was, I persuaded to sit quietly on my shoulder. When
we were ready, Valgard Halfbeard whispered we were going to see Hugleik, who was their king and, as they called
him, ring-giver, and that I should accompany him, follow
his lead, and speak only when spoken to.

Einarr, as befitted a leader and the king's nephew,
walked alone and led the way. Valgard Halfbeard, as a
token of respect freely bestowed by the rest of the crew
(each of whom considered himself his fellow's equal), followed with me (an honored guest) at his side. The rest,
Hervarth included in spite of his birthright (if he wanted
honors, he had to earn them), followed in a file of pairs,

and the welcoming crowd tagged along in the rear.

Our destination, it soon became apparent, was the largest building in sight, which I knew would be Hugleik's folk-hall and mead-building. Our march passed through Grend, which settlement was approximately the size of Truso but at least four times as clean, then through a wide meadow and along a broad path that wound upward through a grove of widely spaced and ancient oak trees among which stood scores of shaped boulders and stone tablets on which were carved scenes of battles and inscriptions in runes, a method of writing I'd yet to learn, and have long since forgotten. Presently, we emerged from the grove and clattered along a broad stone path laid across a modest but pretty meadow that commanded a view of the fiord.

Hugleik's folk-hall couldn't be described as monumental when compared to other palaces I've been in. It was, however, the largest building I'd seen since my departure from Constantinople, and I was duly impressed by its comparative splendor and the inarguable magnificence of its siting. No less impressive were the ceremonies following our arrival. The hall doors—taller than a man on a horse and wide enough for eight men to march through abreast—were guarded by a pair of fully armed and armored warriors sitting on matched bay war horses of, I guessed, sturdy Mongolian stock. His pace unbroken, Einarr marched up the three broad steps and stopped a hand's breadth from the tips of the ornate spears the guards lowered to his breast.

"Halt, Traveler," the first guard ordered. "Speak your name and purpose, that we may tell our king, Hugleik, son of Hreithar and ring-giver of the Sea-Geats, whom all men know as a mighty warrior and, for those who have earned his love and loyalty, a generous bestower of treasures, both ring and sword."

"I know well the mighty Hugleik," Einarr responded formally. "He is my king and kinsman. It was he who gave me this sword I wear for deeds of warfare in his service, and who calls me his table-companion and hearth-mate. Tell him, then, in all modesty, that Einarr, son of Eggther, and his travel-companions, each of them seasoned warriors hardened by battle, have returned from their travels and greatly desire to be welcomed home by our noble lord, and to pay him due respects and honors.''

"Well spoken, Einarr, son of Eggther. I'll tell Hugleik what you've said, and I don't think you or your travel-companions will have long to wait before he bids you enter his folk-hall.'' Whereupon, he dismounted and, opening a small door set in one of the larger ones, disappeared inside.

Are men anywhere gathered in a state without having invented ceremonies to puff themselves up and increase their importance? The crew, more ready to swing swords or fists, chafed at the delay, for wives, families, friends, and slave girls waited, and their agenda included more than fancy words. One shifted, another shuffled, a third coughed impatiently. Who, after all, wanted to stand around like a rune-stone? Which Hugleik knew full well, for suddenly we heard a clanking of iron, the outer guard led his companion's horse to one side, and the great doors swung open.

"Enter, Einarr, and you men, too," the guard who had carried Einarr's message boomed. "Keep your swords, your spears, and your battle gear, for the ring-giver, Hugleik, your king, knows you well and is anxious to greet and welcome you.''

There was more, of course. Kings being kings, no matter how small the kingdom, there generally is, but the formalities finally came to an end. When they did, the Geats reverted to form and the riot was on. Not only on, but went on for the rest of the day and night, the next day, and well into that night, too.

And where was Musculus the Dwarf during the festivities? How was he met and entertained, how did he explain his presence there, and his remarkable bird that so awed his guests? The answer, sad to say, is I don't have the foggiest recollection, which gap may be laid at the sticky feet of that magic potion, mead.

Mead is unknown in Italy and Constantinople because it's brewed only in the far north in places like Denmark and Vastergottland. This is how the first mead was made, and how men came to have it.

Kvasir was the first poet and *skald*. Wise beyond belief and loved for his healing songs and the joy and comfort he brought men, he was slain by two avaricious dwarfs, Fialar and Galar, who envied his wisdom and his power over men's hearts. (O, how we're calumniated! Almost all dwarfs are, in the Northmen's stories.) As clever as they were avaricious, Fialar and Galar mixed Kvasir's blood with honey and made the first mead, which was so potent and magical that anyone who drank it was taken with Kvasir's wisdom and spirit, and became poetic. Fialar and Galar, though, either drank none or were beyond its effect, because they continued in their evil ways by murdering a pair of giants. Found out and nearly drowned by the giants' son, they bought their lives with the mead, which the new owner carried to a cave guarded by his daughter. Father Odin (also called Wotan, and he corresponds most closely to Zeus), however, had been told all this by his ravens, Thought and Memory, and, wanting the mead for himself and the rest of the gods, tricked the poor girl out of it. (The story fails to say what happened to the unfortunate giantess when her father learned she'd let his magical potion be stolen.) Later, Odin in his munificence showed men how to make mead, and to this day the Northmen speak of drinking Kvasir's blood.

Mead's principal ingredient is fermented honey. The Northmen also call it honey beer, but it more closely resembles, to my palate, a frothy wine. It's almost nauseatingly sweet for the uninitiated, insidiously and dangerously potent, and induces monumental and debilitating hangovers. Whether because the mind is burned clean by mead or the hammers beating in one's skull the next morning drown out whatever vestiges of memory may remain, I can't say, but the heron of forgetfulness that's said to hover over mead bouts is as real as crows in a barley field. Which, considering the outrageous excesses in which I evidently indulged myself on that first night, is probably just as well.

It wasn't what I'd call an appropriate introduction to a royal court, but the Geats thought it was. They later told me I had a marvelous time and, in light of my disquieting display of abstinence in Truso, were suitably impressed by and made jokes about my prowess with the drinking horn and the slave girls. My only serious blunder had been propositioning Thyri, Hugleik's wife and queen, an act that would have brought instant death to anyone else, but was forgiven in a stranger who was ignorant in the first place, was vouched for in the second by such stalwarts as Einarr and Valgard Halfbeard, and in the third was protected by Amin, whom the Geats didn't dare offend lest they bring Odin's wrath down on them. My cause was apparently helped, too, when, appropriately regretful, I swallowed a sword in apology. I was lucky I didn't slice out my gizzard. Lucky, too, I'd had a good time, because I was so violently ill for the next three or four days I'd have hated to have had a bad time as well.

Hugleik was no Heraclius (anyone who propositioned Martina would have died before he finished the question, with ignorance no excuse), but he didn't have to be. Heraclius' empire was far-flung and its daily administration was the responsibility of layered corps of functionaries, the vast majority of whom had never been seen by or laid eyes on the emperor himself. Hugleik knew and was known by every one (slaves excluded) of his subjects, and ran his kingdom with an intensely personal hand. Under those conditions—lucky dwarf I was—he could afford to make allowances, and often did.

Hugleik was over fifty years old and had ruled for more than twenty years when I met him. A bold and daring battle-leader, he'd led the Geats on raiding and harrying parties far and wide and had brought home silver, goods in abundance, and slaves. He'd overpowered many princes and chieftains, who sent emissaries and tributes to him from as far away as sixty days' travel. The Geats had prospered under his illustrious stewardship, and he was unstinting with gifts, both ring and sword.

Considering the score or so of kings (including popes, who are kings of a sort) I've known and served, Hugleik was by no means the worst of the breed. His courage was unquestioned and he bore battle scars, some caused by wounds that would have killed many a lesser man, to prove it. Physically, he was one of the shorter and leaner Northmen I saw, but he'd been renowned in his youth for his cunning, surprising speed, strength, and especially stamina.

No man in memory, it was said, could sustain a battle-rage for as long as he, even when wounded, and his name still evoked fear and respect. Of equal if not greater importance was his strength of character and conviction, without which no man leads others. He faced men squarely, feared neither contradiction nor dissension as long as it was fairly and soundly based, and occasionally went so far—a rarity in kings—as to admit an error or miscalculation. And on top of everything else, he was uncompromisingly fair in mediating disputes, and generous in the extreme. His loyalty to his men was absolute, and repaid in kind.

Reading the above, I sound like a Geat warming up for a boasting party, but I'm not. In the first place, I hadn't traveled so far and undergone so many rigors to become a court dwarf again, and didn't appreciate him making me one by asking me to perform tricks and tell stories, which he scoffed at as impossible, of the southern lands. In the second, no one is more aware of a king's weak spots than I, and Hugleik had two, his son and his wife. Each was as apparent and as unsightly as a chancre on a courtesan's lip to an experienced and observant dwarf.

His son, Hervarth (he had three daughters, who were married and away from court, but only the one son), first.

Hugleik's father, Hreithar, had been king before him, and visions of a line of succession danced in Hugleik's head. Unfortunately for Hugleik, few kings climb to a throne by birth alone, and this is nowhere more true than in the northern lands. There, as elsewhere, a king's son has an advantage, but still must prove his worth or be set aside for a better man. There, too, as elsewhere, the royal father more often than not wants his son to succeed him, and frequently bends heaven and earth to that end. Not, however, always wisely.

How often is it true that an overly solicitous father cripples a son! Hugleik might have sent Hervarth away from court to toughen him on a farm in his youth, as Hreithar had him, but he didn't. He might have exposed Hervarth to the grueling discipline of the sea by apprenticing him for a time to an unsympathetic trader, as his father had him, but he didn't. He might have forced Hervarth to learn his battle skills in a neighboring court, take his cuts and bruises and broken bones with a smile, and nurture his determination to do better the next time, as his father had him, but he didn't. True, he'd sent Hervarth adventuring with Einarr, but that was too little too late. The damage had been done. Sadly, and the more so because it was his own fault, the line was very likely to end with him.

Did Hugleik know this? Yes, I think. Did he admit it, even to himself? No, I think. Few kings do. Rather, they suspect the more able of their subjects, and silently scheme to discredit them while advancing their sons' chances. Which brings me in a roundabout way to Thyri, his wife and second weakness.

And to Einarr, the most able of his subjects.

# 13. Of a King's Jealousy, a Queen's Demeanor, and a Hero's Decision to Build a Ship.

Is there anything new under the sun? If so, I can't imagine what it is. I thought, once, the Grundbur and his female, but reflection leads me to reconsider. Because no thing and no being exists as an isolate. For a being to exist, with the exception of Almighty God, there must have been a predecessor, a progenitor. There must have been, therefore, earlier Grundburs and Grundburs' sires and dams, as there undoubtedly are later ones today and will be more tomorrow. They lurk here and there on the face of the earth, engendering both in seclusion and under our noses more of their foul progeny who in turn will surely reveal themselves to future generations of mankind. Plagues and scourges incarnate, we'll have them until Christ returns in his glory to rid us of them.

If this sounds unduly pessimistic, given the light shed by our Lord and Redeemer, forgive me, but a visitor last night brought the news that an old friend, one Aurelius, has been found slaughtered and mutilated in his hermitage. And for what? His only possessions were an undyed wool robe, a cracked wooden bowl, and a cross made of sticks. And for what? A Grundbur stalks.

Interestingly, that younger me I spoke of earlier shrugged off slaughters of this nature. That men killed men was neither a surprise nor particularly troublesome. And why should it have been? I'd been figuratively weaned on the slaughter of thousands. Heads, arms, legs, and entrails were nothing new to me. Granted there have been times when the enormity of violent death (Ilgen's and her son's, for example) has struck like a blow between the eyes, but for the most part, outside of anger and a brief period of mourning in the case of a friend, it's occasioned less pain and anguish than a stubbed toe. Everyone dies, anyway. I have never heard of a two-hundred-year-old man in these modern times.

So the Geats' and other Northmen's propensity for slaughter seemed unremarkable. Their history, as I pieced together a bit here and there, was as fraught as anyone else's with brawls, feuds, raids, internecine skirmishes, and pitched battles incited and provoked by the usual combinations of petty greeds, slights, and jealousies. They were proud of their pugnacity, nourished a combative spirit, and fiercely maintained their desire to die in as bloody a manner as possible. I probably would have, too, if I'd believed in Valhalla.

It was just as well I took slaughter so offhandedly, because my new companions were so single-mindedly devoted to it. The Geats relished battle and made it one of their highest virtues. Battle was high drama, and their purest form of play. Battle was better than mead, and they swilled it thirstily, and got drunk on it. And when the battle was ended, if any of their foe were alive, one of their great delights was to make a blood-eagle by splitting open a man's back on both sides and pulling out his lungs. Then, their victim running and screaming, they roared with laughter at the sight of his lungs filling and deflating, and flapping in the wind. I never saw this done, and am just as glad.

Hugleik bragged he could assemble a thousand men under arms, if need be, and with them conquer the world, though it was just as well he never tried (to my knowledge), because he was even more badly misinformed than Alexander. Also, I'd wager my sinecure that a third of those thousand weren't as much as half as good as Valgard Halfbeard, say, or Einarr, of course. Constans II, as hard-pressed as I later learned he was then, would have wiped them off the face of the earth with a sigh and a roll of his eyes if, indeed, his generals even bothered to tell him about them. Whatever their numbers or abilities, two—Einarr and Hervarth—of Spume-Spear's crew remained in Grend all winter. The vast majority owned farms and had families and, since travel was difficult and often hazardous during the deep winter months, seldom visited. Perhaps three or four hundred people, however, were permanent residents of Grend and the complex of buildings surrounding the royal hall, and they were enough to keep the pot boiling.

Winter in Vastergottland and elsewhere in the far north is as boring as bread. The ineffable excitement of snow, ice, and freezing temperatures quickly fades, and claustrophobia reigns. I spent a week snowed in at Asbrand's freeholding. His house was a palace compared to the pit houses of the barbarians, but by the time they'd packed four cows, three horses, seven sheep, four goats, a pair of swine, and a mixed flock of chickens and ducks in the east end, and two sons, a daughter, a wife and her sister, a sharp-tongued mother-in-law, a crippled uncle, a senile grandfather, two slave girls, Asbrand, me, two cats and a dog in the west, they were left with quarters that were as cramped and stuffy and smelled about the same as the inside of a half-cooked sausage. The bawling, neighing, baaing, grunting, clucking, quacking, barking, hissing, crying, belching, farting, snoring, blithering, bitching, arguing, shouting, and general unceasing babble became a din to drive the devil to heaven. Asbrand claimed to thrive on it, and he did seem to enjoy the pandemonium, but he'd also developed a tic in his left cheek and a furtive, hunted look in his eyes that I hadn't seen during our voyage on Spume-Spear.

I offer the following conversation that took place some days after my arrival, and that I've remembered for its sheer inanity.

| | |
|---|---|
| ASBRAND: | "This soup is cold." |
| WIFE: | "Be happy you have soup." |
| OLDER SON (*age seven*): | "Mine's too hot." |
| WIFE: | "Don't contradict your father." |
| GRANDFATHER: | "We didn't have cold soup in my day." |
| UNCLE: | "My back hurts. We're going to have snow." |
| MOTHER-IN-LAW: | "What day's today?" |
| ASBRAND: | "Wednesday." *(in unison with)* |
| WIFE'S SISTER: | "Tuesday." *(in unison with)* |
| UNCLE: | "Thursday." |
| GRANDFATHER: | "It doesn't snow on Wednesdays." |
| WIFE: | "We already have snow." |

Is it any wonder Asbrand returned to Grend with me?

A host of factors made Grend and its environs more tolerable than the hinterland. Grend was the most important village in Hugleik's widespread but sparsely populated kingdom. It boasted a gold and silver smith, a harness maker, a wheelwright, a barrel smith, a wire maker, a tinsmith, two blacksmiths, fletchers, armorers, and sword makers, four master boat-builders, five beer halls (two of them with slave-whores), and a half-score other establishments, any one of which served as a place to while away an afternoon.

The royal grounds offered their own divertissements. The folk-hall was the center of activity. A dormitory for fifteen or twenty regulars and any number of visitors, the tables and sleeping benches were stacked against the wall during the day to make room for wrestling matches, mock (occasionally real) sword fights, and practice and contests in spear throwing or archery. Hugleik and Thyri received visitors in their quarters, a sumptuously appointed house larger than Asbrand's and minus the livestock. In addition, there were kitchens, granaries, a brewing house, stables, an armory, and so on, whose occupants, as bored as everyone else, were always eager to show off their skills or spend an hour gossiping with an inquisitive traveler. I, in other words, managed to occupy and amuse myself. The Geats, however, spending their winters doing the same thing over and over again, were prone to what they called white, or black, fever. After my winters alone, I was sympathetic.

You saw it first in their eyes when they stepped outside. Always, there was snow and ice in every direction as far as the eye could see and, except for a short daily respite during which a pallid sun hung low over the hills, it was dark. You heard it in the strained quality of their voices. They had trouble going to sleep unless they were drunk, and slept troubled when they were drunk. Like Asbrand, many developed tics, and eventually everyone, with the exception of one poor fellow named Gnar, who'd been shot by an arrow in the middle of his forehead and right through his skull, and unluckily lived, and who became agitated only when a fit seized him, was edgy, contentious, and spoiled for trouble. That they survived the winter with their sanity intact I ascribe to—no, not nuts or dancing with a raven—mead, and an almost total lack of inhibition.

The old Romans are known far and wide for their licentious debauchery during their banquets. I don't doubt for a minute that the stories I've read are true, but at the same time question if they could have held their own with the Geats. I don't know who collected the honey to make their mead but, even with the enormous number of kegs imported from the barbarians, there couldn't have been a skep or wild swarm of bees spared the collector's smoke in that part of the world. My introductory party was only a taste of what was to come with mind-numbing regularity.

The Geats drank as much as they boasted, and their drinking bouts had to be experienced to be believed. The mead-hall was sixty of my paces long and twenty wide. A fireplace set into one of the long walls was big enough to roast a young bullock, and required the constant attention of a slave turning the great spit and carrying wood in and ashes out. The preparations for a full-fledged knock-down tooth-rattling debauch took two days. On the first, unless a blizzard was raging, in which case they relied on domestic meat, the men split into parties of four, five, or six, and went hunting. Boar, deer, elk, and even bear, when someone stumbled across a lair, were fair game. Rabbits, squirrels, ptarmigan, grouse, or any other of the smaller animals were taken too, destined for stew pots that were periodically replenished with onions, turnips, barley, oats, millet, and other starchy foods that would ameliorate the effects of mead and beer, and settle the stomach.

The vast majority of the visitors arrived the second day. All were greeted with flagons of warm, spiced beer. The women went inside to gossip, I assume, and the men amused themselves outside with races and wrestling matches, and wood-splitting and throwing contests. Einarr never won a foot race that I know of, a quick and clever man could occasionally pin him wrestling, and he often failed to find the weak spot in a log, but what he lacked in speed and agility he made up in raw power. Give him a rock to lift, a young bullock to carry, a stick to break, a piece of iron to bend, or a log to throw, and he was as invincible as he was at arm wrestling. Not once, ever, did I see him lose one of these contests.

Inside, the slaves were busy. The first dressed and seasoned carcass (others were started in outside kitchens and brought in as needed) was put on to roast, and stew pots were filled and hung to simmer. Blankets and furs were taken outside and hung to air. The floor was swept and clean rushes laid. A half-dozen scoured wooden tubs for people to puke and urinate in were strategically placed. The tables and benches were scrubbed, and the raised platform for the royal table installed at the end opposite the great doors. New torches were fitted in the wall sconces, and fat beeswax candles were put in three circular chandeliers that hung from the ceiling and were let down with ropes. Finally, they brought back the blankets and furs, and set the tables with plates, cups, and drinking horns. When they were finished, the hall fairly sparkled, and it was difficult to believe so many people had worked so long and hard in order, by the next morning, for the place to be turned into a shambles.

I've read, in one account, that the Northmen were slovenly and practiced disgusting habits like, for example, spitting in the water they used to wash their faces. That may be true in some places, but the Geats, whatever else their faults, were more fastidious. Yes, male and female alike used the tubs in full view of everyone, but they could hardly be blamed in light of the winds and temperatures outside that would freeze a nose, not to speak of whatever else might be exposed, in seconds.

(They had a male and female joke that illustrated how cold it got. In the male version, Oleg was drunk and had to micturate, but his urine froze on contact and he was soon pushed onto his back, and attached to his penis was a yellow icicle that arced four feet into the air and connected with the earth a dog's length beyond his feet. In the female version, Olga squatted and, again, the urine freezing as it touched, pissed herself a sword's length straight up in the air.)

Inhibition and temperance were concepts alien to the Northmen, and the words, that I ever learned, not easily translated into Norse. Like children, the Geats were given to extremes in virtually everything. Boisterously happy one moment, any one of them could in the next be sullen and down at the mouth. The unpredictable moods shifted more frequently and dramatically as winter wore on and the effects and severity of the white or black fever increased.

If a keg of fermenting beer is bunged lightly on top, the bung will be ejected when the pressure inside becomes too great, and the keg will be saved from destruction. So it is with men. The Geats innately understood this, I believe, and because passions and tempers were apt to exceed safe limits at any given time, they'd made their mead banquets the safety bung of their society.

The winter's gasses of discontent were vented during those banquets. They began in a dignified enough manner, but, after Thyri and the other wives excused themselves, got down to serious eating and drinking. The hall rang with jokes, laughter, and bawdy songs. People shed clothing as the temperature rose. They gorged on food and swilled beer and mead until they puked themselves sick, passed out, woke up, and began again. The slave girls were put to the test, and there was no shame when the crowd counted in unison a man's thrusts and cheered at his moment of release. (Amazingly, the women seemed to take as much pleasure in these public exhibitions as the men.) Fights broke out. Most of them were between two men, but sides for full-scale brawls were sometimes chosen, and bodies, benches, and other objects often flew through the air. Prudently, the use of edged and metal weapons was prohibited during these free-for-alls, and though they hung in full view on the wall behind the high table, where they were accessible in case of an attack, the ban was honored.

Eventually, the seething volcano of energy having been released and expended, one, then another, and finally all lay scattered about where they fell. Soon, the hall reverberated with snores. A while later, slaves entered and covered the sweating, cooling flesh with robes and furs, doused the candles and torches, banked the fire, and crept off to their own beds. Another week had passed.

It was in this setting that Einarr and I learned to respect each other, and become friends. I hadn't expected to, really. I've said before that we didn't have a great deal to do with each other, and mentioned his aloofness and cocksure vanity. I mentioned, too, that there was more of him than met the eye, and the longer I knew him, the more I saw beneath the reserve he so little understood but so carefully maintained. Einarr was different from other men, and knew it. Unlike Valgard, he was plain spoken (except when boasting) and simply didn't know how to engage in the quiet, lazy banter that was so characteristic of the Geats. He couldn't tell a joke to save his life, and became tongue-tied talking about his sexual exploits. He wasn't clever with his hands like Asbrand, couldn't have walked the oars if he'd tried, and wasn't a particularly accomplished hunter. Ironically, his unparalleled strength mitigated against him in his daily contacts with his fellows because he was so far head and shoulders above other men that he was a freak of sorts, which I of all people should have understood earlier. Knowing that, and as much as he wanted to be like everyone else, he remained aloof and essentially alone. I don't believe he had one close friend in the world other than Valgard and, later, me. He did, however, have admirers, and this is where the trouble I hinted about earlier began.

There have been exceptions, but most men who don't want to become kings succeed in their ambition. With exceptions, too, most kings' desire to rule is so fierce they assume everyone else wants to, and suspect the worst of those who qualify for the job. I know the look of men who want to rule. It's as plain as if written in large red letters across their faces. Cassius, it was said, had the look of a hungry wolf, and Caesar, who'd seen that look in his mirror, knew it. Einarr didn't. Einarr told me and others that he had no royal pretensions, and while I and most others believed him, Hugleik didn't. You couldn't really blame Hugleik, because no matter what Einarr said, he was still the heir apparent to the throne. First, because the Geats were no more likely to elevate Hervarth than they were me, and second, because they feared and respected Einarr's strength and battle-rage, heeded his advice and opinions when he had any, and admired him immensely. These twinned truths gnawed at Hugleik's guts and, though he pretended otherwise in public, I could see he hated Einarr with a sick passion.

At which juncture, I return to where I left off before, namely to Thyri, Hugleik's queen and second weakness.

It was easy to see why Hugleik had wanted Thyri. The daughter of a Heatho-Scylding noble, she'd come to him two years after his first wife died as part of a pact between him and that nation. She was tall, blonde, buxom, and, no mean consideration in Hugleik's fifty-year-old eyes, young—not, I imagine, a day over twenty. She was also smart, spoiled (having been brought up in a court), and, in that hotbed of virility run amok, a born troublemaker.

Hugleik had bargained for and won Thyri a few months after Einarr and his band left, so Einarr can't be blamed for being curious about her when he returned and found her sharing his uncle's bed and throne. No one thought anything strange about that—everyone had been curious when she arrived—but whispers soon started circulating. The fault was more Thyri's than Einarr's. Einarr was young, handsome, wondrously constructed, and exuded an aura of virility, so he could be expected to sniff around bedroom doors and paw the ground like a bull at stud. Thyri was his feminine match, true, but was also expected, especially in the close confines of court, to keep her regal distance. Instead, she flirted with and led him on, and in the process added the fuel of sexual jealousy to Hugleik's already burning distrust of Einarr. In short order, Hugleik was soon convinced that Einarr wanted not only his throne but his wife as well.

But what could he do? Thyri and Einarr were never alone together, that anyone knew, so he couldn't accuse her of infidelity or Einarr of making a cuckold of him. He couldn't admit he feared a younger man's attraction or virility for fear of raising questions about his own. He certainly couldn't admit—in public, because who knows what he said to Thyri in private, or how she responded—his queen was undermining him, because that would have raised questions about his ability to rule his woman and, by extension, his kingdom. And to make matters worse, Einarr was his nephew, his dead sister's son, whom years earlier he had virtually adopted. His only option was as subtly as possible to turn a cold shoulder to Einarr and, in small but pointed ways, distance himself from him.

The simmering conflict between Hugleik and Einarr was a welcome diversion in the small snow- and winter-locked court. Einarr's place at Thyri's left at the royal table was given to someone else on one pretext or other, and he was moved two seats to Hervarth's right, which was an insult. Hugleik found occasion to remark disparagingly on Einarr's well-known fear of the dark during his childhood, and subtly ridiculed his lack of agility, which left Einarr seething. When opinions were sought, the quest ended when Einarr was about to give his, or when what he said was dismissed with a peremptory grunt. And to add insult to injury, Hervarth, in his sly and smirking way, pushed Hugleik's verbal daggers deeper with every chance, which seemed to please Hugleik. Einarr showed what I thought was astonishing restraint, but any fool could tell trouble was brewing. The pot boiled over near what I'd guess was our Christmastime or New Year, to judge from the stars.

And it was precipitated by, of all things, the leg of a goose.

"That's a goose leg, isn't it?" Hugleik asked when he saw Einarr holding it.

Einarr was already deep in his cups. Dreamy-eyed, regarding the crisply bronzed skin oozing with fat, he either didn't hear or ignored the question, and was about to take a bite when Hervarth reached a long bone across the woman sitting between them and stayed him. "What do you think you're doing, bunghole?" Einarr growled, coming out of his trance.

Hervarth smirked. "Father asked you a question," he said.

"Oh? What's that?" Einarr asked.

Hugleik, the ring-giver, pointed with the joint of meat he held. "I said, that's a goose leg, isn't it?"

It was a stupid question. Einarr knew he was being baited, from the look in his eyes, but remained civil. "Yes, Lord. A goose leg."

"A plump and tender goose leg, is it not?" Hugleik asked.

Einarr glanced at it and back to Hugleik. "Taste will tell," he said with a shrug.

The men and women on the floor, unaware of the drama being played above them, went on eating, drinking, talking, and laughing. A hush soon spread down the royal table.

"Please be so kind, then, to pass the joint so I may taste and tell."

Walk warily when kings speak softly and politely is an adage and policy that's kept my head on my shoulders more than once. It's difficult, though, to walk warily while being backed into a corner, and Einarr, from the set of his shoulders, was beyond caring in any case. A dangerous edge crept for the first time into his voice as he glanced at the joint Hugleik held. "And what of the goose leg my lord is already gnawing on? One isn't enough?"

"The meat is dry and stringy," Hugleik said. He tossed the leg over his shoulder, whereupon a bitch snapped it up and hurried off with it. "The joint, Nephew."

A courtier in a more sophisticated court would have

looked at the bitch long enough to convey the message that a king wasn't the only one who could throw a bone to a dog, and then graciously handed it over to win the day. Hugleik's court was as far from sophisticated as London is from Baghdad, however, and Einarr's concept of subtlety was as developed as a chicken's of Pythagoras' theorem. So instead, having to have known he was courting the devil, he merely smiled, looked fondly at his juicy goose leg, smacked his lips, and prepared to bite into it.

Hervarth should have known better. He was young and counted a great deal on his royal birth, to be sure, but he was no fool. Perhaps he thought he'd be perceived as bold. Perhaps he thought Einarr would forbear. Perhaps, too, he simply didn't think when he reached for and grabbed Einarr's wrist.

The Geats on the floor, with their noses well trained to sniff out violence, had become aware of the approaching storm. The revelers quieted, and every eye turned to Einarr and Hervarth. As for Einarr, he glanced at Hervarth's hand on his wrist and then, as if it were no more than a fly or gnat, bent his arm and bit into the goose leg.

The woman sitting between them was sensible enough to get out of the way. Just in time, too, because no sooner was she gone than Einarr struck. Hervarth raised his left hand to ward off the blow, but he would have needed at least another pair of arms to make an appreciable difference. His right arm bending like a rag, the bone broke with a popping sound clearly heard through the hall, and the back of Einarr's fist, still holding the goose leg, smashed into his face and sent him flying backward off his seat.

No one moved, no one said a word. Stunned—unthinkable, to so challenge Hugleik—we watched Einarr deliberately stuff a dangling piece of skin into his mouth, chew, swallow, wipe his mouth with the back of his hand, and belch. "Tender, plump, and tasty," he said, to no one in particular. "A fine bird." Whereupon he stood and casually tossed the leg, minus a great ragged gouge torn out of the thigh, onto Hugleik's plate. "Your goose leg, Uncle. I took only one small bite," he added apologetically, and turned on his heel and stalked out.

What, then, was Hugleik to do? The contest of wills that he probably would have won had become a political dilemma with Hervarth's impolitic interference. On the first horn, leave though he had, Einarr won the day if Hugleik let it go at that. But as sharp as that horn was, the other was sharper, because his thanes would believe he'd come to his son's rescue if he persisted, and they'd never crown a man who needed his father's help in a fight. To Hugleik's credit, I think, he chose to bide his time and, the black look on his face a warning there'd be another day, he stood, told somebody to look after Hervarth, and, followed by a subdued Thyri, retired to his private quarters. As for everyone else, poor Hervarth moaned and bled, the thanes and their women began to eat, drink, and chatter, and I, for some reason, quietly slipped away from the table and went to look for Einarr.

"The bastard!"

"Your mother's brother a bastard?" I asked.

Einarr turned, saw who it was, and grunted. "What are you doing here?"

"I lost my appetite. Too much mead too early. I needed to clear my head. Move over."

Half irritated by the intrusion and half welcoming the company, Einarr grunted again. "You're asking for trouble, taking sides like this," he said, moving over.

I sat, huddled in the fur cape I'd brought with me. "I'll take my chances."

It was colder than a nun's crotch on a winter morning after the blazing, steamy heat inside. We sat on an ice-covered stone bench near the edge where the cliff dropped into Knar's Fiord. At our feet, ice and snow covered the ground. The ice-cascaded mountain wall across the fiord was black with trees and purple with shadows, and the mountain behind us and the mead-hall was silhouetted by a faint green diaphanous tapestry of *aurora borealis*. The sky overhead was clear and a setting half-moon dimmed the stars. A slow, wet, cold wind blew steadily inland from the sea and found the seams in my furs. From the hall, an occasional loud laugh or shout drifted our way.

"He should have known better, damn it!" Einarr said, breaking the unreal silence so suddenly that I jumped.

"Which he?" I asked.

"Both of them. Piss on their throne. I don't want it."

"So you've said. But what about his wife?"

Einarr frowned, and I saw I'd touched a sore spot. "Why's an old man want to marry a bitch like that anyway?" he asked. "I thought Hugleik had more sense."

I shrugged. "We had a saying where I come from. The older the man, the tighter the pussy."

Einarr snorted in disgust. "Hugleik's court is full of tight pussies. He can have one any time he wants."

That was true. The Sea-Geats had women to spare. Beautiful women and a wide variety, too, for they'd captured or bought as many of the best on the continent as they could find. Furthermore, though it was reprehensible for a man to lie with another free man's wife—the husband was entitled to the interloper's head, even a king's, if he could get it— wives are susceptible to kings (that power is the most potent aphrodisiac was as true in Vastergottland as it was in Constantinople), so he could have had his choice of them, too.

Einarr, however, needed something more practical than idle musings. "So can you," I pointed out. "And one tight pussy—even a queen's—is very much like another."

Einarr opened his mouth to say something and, possibly considering the number he'd sampled and knowing I was right, closed it again.

"Then by the Christ," I swore (I'd told him, though to no effect, who Christ was, which tells you something more about the *scop*, who made Einarr a Christian), "why offer the man your head on a platter? Because he'll take it. Mark my words, he'll take it."

"And die trying."

"No. This is no time for boasts. I don't give a shit how strong you are, he's the king, and outnumbers you." I paused to let that unpleasant truth seep in, and finally added, "I don't know if the throne's worth it or not. That's up to you. But she isn't, Clutcher. She simply isn't."

"I know," he said with a sigh. Silent, he tilted back his

head. Above, Cygnus flew on his southerly course through the diaphanous ghost-path we call the Milky Way. Behind him, the regal Cassiopeia, wrapped in diaphanous sheets of fire, fixed her eternal gaze on the Axis Star, around which the heavenly sphere revolves.

"Our eyes meet. In them, I read a saucy boldness, but then her breath quickens, her eyes widen and her lips part, as they will when you caress a woman in her soft and secret places. Then her eyes close, as if in sweet pain, and I know in her mind I am entering and riding her, that her legs are encircling me, her nails raking my back."

So much for the throne. As for Thyri, Cassiopeia hadn't, and I wasn't, moved. "What?" I asked. "Has Einarr, the boar-crested warrior, become love's *skald?*"

Heaven forgotten, his head dropped and his eyes closed. Across his face, which he'd so well trained to mask intent, emotion, or motive, the confusions, fears, and torments that plague the strongest men at one time or other paraded openly. And as that anguished procession passed, those enormous hands closed into boar-head fists and smashed onto his knees. "By Odin's one good eye, Dwarf, I swear she sets my balls afire, and makes them burn."

And there it was. She set his balls afire and made them burn. In the history of the world, what excursions and what wars, what daring, foolish, reckless, ill-advised, and hopeless ventures have been launched by the testicular fever that, unchecked, spreads quickly to heart and head and provokes the infinite multitude of follies in which men indulge themselves? Helen, it's said, by the force of her beauty, unleashed whole armies and navies in the war that saw tens of thousands of men slaughtered and Ilium reduced to rubble. On the contrary. Her exertions were limited, by Odin's one good eye or Zeus's lust, to setting four tiny balls on fire and making them burn. Paris and Menelaus did the rest. While Helen, no doubt, pouted and posed, and attended to her toilet.

I may sound like, but am not, a misogynist. Label me instead a cynic, for if women beguile and lead men into folly, men seek folly as certainly as water seeks the lowest level it can find. They'll also, if they find a suitable exercise, sometimes exert their efforts in a different direction. Which is where I got the idea, God forgive me, to save his neck by using him to further my own designs.

"She's bored, Einarr. Like everyone else, she has the black and white fever, and seeks excitement."

God bless the simplicity of brawn. "She does?" he asked, surprised.

"She plays you like a pipe, and your only victory is to win the fabled Battle of the Goose Leg."

His brows knit as he chewed on that. "You're right," he said at last. "The bitch!"

We were almost, but not quite, back where we'd started. "The fault isn't entirely hers, my friend. You were easily led. And once at table, reached for the joint."

That, too, was food for thought. Once digested, he nodded. "And right again," he agreed dolefully. "What am I to do, Musculus?"

My heart raced. He'd called me by my name for the first time, and I knew I had him. "Well, you've lost your seat at the royal table, I imagine, and will generally be about as welcome as mead gone bad. What about—" I paused, ostensibly to think, though I knew what I was going to say.

"What about what?" Einarr prompted.

"What about . . . Why don't you build a ship?"

He looked at me as if I'd lost my mind. "A ship? Why would I want to build a ship?"

I pointed to the sky, and Cygnus. "To follow the swan," I said, and added, as my finger dropped to the horizon, "south, where waits the Grundbur."

# 14. Of a New Ship and the Men Who Built It, and a Bold and Adventuresome Band Assembled.

W hy do men treat women worse than they treat their ships?"

I thought I'd forgotten that question. I'd certainly tried to. It lies at the end of a thought-path that began with ships, and branches into various inherent contradictions. One has either forgotten or not forgotten. If one thinks he's forgotten, then a memory lies embedded in the thought. Trying to forget is similarly impossible, because the attempt only strengthens memory. In any case, I awoke this morning thinking about ships, as is natural since I left off last night thinking about ships, and suddenly that plaintive question I heard so many years ago was reverberating in my head.

Two or three weeks had passed since I'd put the bug of a new ship in Einarr's ear. We'd kept busy and, by the nature of our industry, avoided Hugleik, Hervarth (who was laid up much of the time), and Thyri. I'd taken to sleeping in one of the outbuildings in order to find surcease from the constant noise and bustle in the hall, and that particular night, after dinner and enough mead to stir my juices, had

spirited a slave girl away from the general throng and retired with her for a night of pleasure.

Yrsa, her Norse name, was barely more than a child.
Sexually adept—what relatively intelligent fourteen-or fif-
teen-year-old wouldn't be after three or four months in the
sexual free-for-all of a mead-hall?—she was as bright-eyed
and cheerful as any of the girls there and, like the others,
flattered to be found desirable by Hugleik's heroes. Yrsa
had been bought from one of the northern barbarian tribes.
Her life expectancy as a folk-hall concubine was perhaps
six winters, with time off for a child or two. Her children,
boys or girls, would probably be taken from her unless, as
happened occasionally, a free man took her for his wife.
The odds were, if, indeed, she thought of odds, the thanes
would tire of her by the time she was nineteen or twenty,
after which she'd most likely be given to some *thrall* who
needed a woman—they wore them out and used them up
at an alarming rate—bear three or four children for him,
and then succumb from overwork at an early age. The prospects weren't pleasant, but they were better than had she
remained with the barbarians, who treated their women
worse than draft horses, which were counted as more valuable.

To return to the night in question. The weather was bit-
terly cold with a howling wind, but one wall of my quarters
was the rear wall of a fireplace, so we were warm enough.
We'd played the game of the beast with two backs a time
or two, and we were tired. Content and cooling from our
ardors, we lazed half under furs, sipped the last of the mead
I'd brought with me, and talked desultorily about nothing
much, as I recall. Lapsing into ever longer silences and
finally dozing, I felt Yrsa looking at me. When I opened
my eyes, she was propped on one elbow and, her dark hair
falling around her breasts, sadly gazing down at me.

I suppose I said something. I don't remember. But I do
remember the wistful look in her eyes, and her question:
"Why do men treat women worse than their ships?"

It seemed an odd question, and I told her to go to sleep.

"No, Musculus. I want to know. Why do men treat
women worse than they do their ships?"

Disgruntled and groggy, I pinched out the wick and plunged the room into darkness. "They don't," I said, pulling the fur over me and settling in to sleep. "They treat their ships like ships and their women like women. Now go to sleep."

She was gone when I woke the next day. Shortly thereafter, I heard she was pregnant, had been temporarily retired from the arena, and made one of Thyri's serving girls. Whose child it was and what happened to her after that, I have no idea, but her question, and my answer, linger.

My topic, however, was ships, or one ship in particular, and Einarr's passion.

My ploy worked more effectively than I'd hoped. No sooner did I mention the Grundbur than, as water diverted from one channel to another when a gate is turned, Einarr's mind turned to new matters. The furrows in his brow smoothed as tension faded. His fists opened and his hands, cupping, mimicked a shiplike form. He was silent for a long moment, and then, after a glance to the south, fixed me with a purposeful gaze. "Can you really," he asked, each word slow and ponderous, "build a ship that will sail across the wind?"

I'd been unceasingly and uncompromisingly positive in my earlier attempts to persuade, but, with the possibility that my advice might actually be followed, a note of caution seemed prudent. "Yes and no: I know the principles, not the craft. To build one, we'll need a man who knows ships, will listen, is bold and wise enough, and will add his own innovations and improvements. But you must remember, the first attempt at anything often falls short of the goal."

A particularly loud shout from behind us broke the silence that followed. With it, Einarr stood and, with clenched fists and an angry glare, faced the folk-hall. Conflicting emotions driving him toward Thyri and the Grundbur played across his face like swirls of fine snow driven over ice. "Then come," he said abruptly, and, not looking to see if I followed, strode off across the snow. "We must start now if we're to sail with the weather."

\*    \*    \*

Hugleik's immediate family rated private quarters. Einarr's room was one of four in a long, low building that jutted at right angles from the rear of the royal quarters, and while not sumptuous by our standards, it was by theirs. Einarr had a man and a woman servant, and his room was neat and well kept. A fire burned in the pit. Benches covered with furs lined the walls and on one, a rarity, lay a pillow. Various accouterments of war hung on pegs driven between logs near the top of the wall, and clothing was similarly hung on the wall facing it. The room was austere and, lacking any feminine touch, looked more martial than homelike, but I doubt Einarr cared since he spent so little time there.

There were, of course, no writing materials available. In their place, after ordering food and mead, Einarr cleared one bench, lay the smooth bottom boards between the stone fire-pit wall and another bench, and dumped onto the improvised table a few handfuls of sand he scooped from the bucketful kept there to quench the fire, if need be. Once smoothed, and with a piece of kindling he sharpened to a point, we were ready to begin.

I didn't have that much to show him, really. Most of what I said and drew was a reiteration of what he'd already heard and seen, and any real work would have to wait for discussions with a boat builder. Mostly, we talked about this and that and, after having known each other for six or seven months, got acquainted.

Einarr's father, Eggther, had died twenty years earlier during a raid on a Wendel clan on the continent. His mother had followed a few months later during the birth of Einarr's younger sister, who also perished. Alone in the world at three, he was taken in by Hugleik, who raised him as a son. His extraordinary strength had made him nearly as much of an oddity as I was as a child, and he couldn't remember not being strong. That strength was at the root of many a problem. Children his own age feared, taunted, and ran from him. Jealous adults mocked him for the slightest weakness, and teased him unmercifully for his fear of the dark, which was natural and went unremarked in many other children. He was simultaneously expected to perform at levels undemanded of any other child, and again mocked when he fell short of the mark. He remembered, vividly and painfully, for example, his mortification when, as a young man—still a boy, really—of twelve, he was reduced to tears when he failed to bend a piece of iron that, he discovered later, none of Hugleik's thanes could bend, either.

The results were predictable. As was I, Einarr was well versed in the pain of isolation, and had learned early on to conceal his thoughts and emotions and to keep his own counsel. He resolved never to be mocked again and, though it made him appear slow of thought, to think before he spoke or acted. And if he was expected to be stronger than other men, he became obsessed with fulfilling their expectations beyond doubt, and developing his strength to the fullest. As far as I could tell, he'd succeeded remarkably well in both endeavors. Succeeded, too, unfortunately, in creating a demon that drove him as inexorably as Heraclius' or Kapsabelis', because he knew as well as anyone that strength alone wasn't enough, and that there were men who questioned—not to his face—his ability. "He's strong," they said, "but as slow and bumbling as an ox. Starketh the Devastator or Ingald the Obstinate could have slaughtered him like a pig."

Was that true? Who, since both were dead, could say? It didn't matter. One demon laid to rest, another born, Einarr was driven to prove he was invincible, and to silence the damning innuendoes. How better than to defeat the Grundbur, whatever he was?

Einarr and I talked early into the morning. My last thought, when I wrapped myself in a fur and lay down to sleep across the fire from him, was that I'd added, that night, another name to my very short list of true friends. He forthwith joined Valgard at the top of that list, where, by virtue of being alive, they reigned alone.

I'd forgotten the delights of greeting a new week unencumbered by a hangover. It was a pleasant change, first, to actually wake up Monday morning, second, to be possessed of a mouth that didn't taste as if Askil had flushed the east end of his house through it, and third, to be able to think without a din of drums beating in my head.

There was also, for once, something to think about and to do. Our first task was to retain a ship builder. Einarr and I had considered the four men available and, with his knowledge of ships and mine of men, had decided to approach Egil, who was reputedly the best and most experienced in Vast- and Oostergottland. Early Monday morning, a day I remember as still and relatively warm, and with great half-bezant snowflakes floating down through the dim predawn light, we walked down to Grend and pushed into his shop.

Egil was known far and wide. He was said to be slow, hidebound, irascible, and stubbornly insistent on having his own way, but those were minor drawbacks given the impeccability of his craftsmanship and the utter reliability and seaworthiness of his ships. If a man were to set sail on a quest to find and slay the Migard serpent, the giant snake that with tail in mouth was said to encircle the earth, it would be the best part of wisdom to hire Egil to build his ship.

Egil's so-called minor drawbacks became more formidable, however, when considering the ship Einarr and I wanted, and when we wanted it. More than outweighing them, to my way of thinking, was his apprentice, Gurd. Sonless, and having given up hope for progeny, Egil had adopted, freed, and apprenticed Gurd at age ten, and the two, by the time I knew them, were partners. Of prime importance, though, was this single, salient fact: Gurd was in many ways Egil's exact opposite. If Egil was hidebound, Gurd was an innovator. If Egil was slow, Gurd, while not as meticulous, was fast. And if Egil was irascible and stubbornly insistent, Gurd was affable and willing to let a suggestion lead him where it would. Between them, each with his own particular strength, they made the perfect man to build our new ship.

Their initial reactions to my crude charcoal sketches were about what I expected. Egil's brow furrowed and his eyes narrowed as he shook his head from side to side and pronounced the very idea an impossibility. Gurd, on the other hand, proved I hadn't lost my touch. His brow furrowed, too, true enough, but his eyes lit and I could tell his mind was racing with possibilities.

"No. You're wrong, Father," he interrupted Egil. "Come."

Picking up a billet, he strode to the tank in which they boiled and softened wood, smashed the inch-thick layer of ice that had formed after the fire had died down over the night, and scooped the largest chunks onto the floor. "He's right," he said, picking up a short piece of planking and dropping it into the water. "This is a bottom board, agreed?"

Egil grunted assent.

"Pretend my finger's the wind," he went on, nudging one end of the plank and sending it the length of the tank. "All well and good as long as it's abaft." He retrieved the plank and shoved it from the side. "But on the beam," he said as the plank slid across the water and bumped into the side of the tank, "it's useless."

"So?" Egil asked, unimpressed. "That's why we have oars, and men have arms to pull them."

"Of course. But watch." His imagination fired, Gurd drilled a hole near one edge of the plank, tied a string with a weight attached to it to the plank, and returned it to the tank where it floated on edge. "The wind abaft again," he said, and again sent the plank the length of the tank. "But from the side," he said, retrieving it and giving it a sideways push, "nothing!"

True enough. The plank tilted a bit, but moved laterally only slightly. "You see how stable it is? We can do it, Father! A new ship that will keep its course, better than any we've ever made!"

"You'd still need oars anytime you wanted to go into or across the wind," Egil pointed out.

"That's true. But if you can use wind from seven points, is that not better than from three?"

Egil wasn't about to be convinced too rapidly. A skeptic for too many years to be rushed, he pushed the hurriedly built and clumsy model this way and that, frowned and grumbled. "Play with it if you will," he said at last, spitting to one side. "I'll give you a week. In the meantime, we can't all be dreamers, and I have Bjerne's ship to build."

What a week that followed! If anyone in court missed us, we were too busy to know or care. Gurd's wizardry with a knife and wood put to shame mine picking baubles out of the air. One after another, he produced three, then a fourth, and final, hull model. The details escape me after so many years, but there was much more involved than the hull. He had to devise a new way to cut, shape, and bend the keel so it would rise evenly at bow and stern, a new method of attaching the ribs, a new and stronger stepping post, rigging for a thicker and taller mast and a larger and heavier sail, and an improved rudder. Nothing, it seemed, was simple or easy, but by virtually moving into the shop and sleeping only when we could no longer keep our eyes open, we—more properly Gurd—were able to show Egil a finished model in, as I recall, a short eight days.

It was, I must say, a victory. Complete in most details, our tiny ship floated proudly in the tank. And when, with sail and rudder set properly, we huffed and puffed until our faces turned red and it sailed very nearly across the wind, the phlegmatic Egil was so impressed that he, too, caught fire. Before the day was out, he'd assigned a crew to finish Bjerne's ship, dismissed Einarr and me, and, closeting Gurd and himself with food and mead, set to work on a finished design and a detailed accurate model.

The following weeks—the breaking of the ice on Knar's Fiord looming with increasing immediacy—were hectic for everyone involved except me, who was hardly more than an observer and errand boy. Egil and Gurd drove themselves nearly to exhaustion. The strange new ship they were building became a cure for the black and white fever. They were plagued by the other ship builders, the king and his thanes, and the rest of the town. With imaginations fueled and fired, gawkers and scoffers besieged them. Problems they hadn't foreseen in the model-building stage cropped up and had to be solved. The weather was foul and, though they worked under a shed, they and their helpers were more often than not cold, wet, and miserable. Still, men's souls revealed by the work of their hands, the keel was laid and ribbed, strakes cut, steamed, and riveted in place, and the sleek lines of a ship, the likes of which hadn't been seen before, took shape before our eyes.

Einarr, in the meantime, was consumed by the task at hand. A torrent of questions, he haunted Egil's and Gurd's shed. With me as his scribe, he drew up a list of a hundred or so names of men to accompany us on our journey, then started winnowing through them. Some, of course, were easy. Valgard Halfbeard was an obvious choice. Askil was included for his weather-luck and navigational skills. Asbrand, who could repair anything, was enlisted early on to work with Egil and Gurd so he'd know the new ship from keel to ringed prow. Olvir Iron-glove, whom I hadn't met until then but remember vividly for the fate that befell him later (the *scop* was correct in that detail, as you shall see), was Einarr's distant kinsman, and deadly with the long ax, with which, at full force, he could split a wheat straw lengthwise on the first stroke. I, too, was included, not because I was liable to be much more than a diversion in a fight, but because Amin, who Einarr considered a powerful talisman, would have nothing to do with anyone else but me and because, rather grimly, I thought, he meant me to be aboard in case anything went wrong with the ship that had been my idea. All told, when gathered in early spring, our number was to be fifteen. And if the strength, skill, and luck of fourteen of us were any indication, I'd wager my remaining days without fear of losing so much as a sunrise that a more ferocious or daunting crew had never been assembled.

# 15. On Einarr's Crew, the Naming of a New Ship, and a Dwarf's Banishment and Blood-oath.

Einarr alone, as I've said, was worth a score of the best fighting men I've ever known. But as if that weren't enough, as if he weren't as confident of his prowess as a terrier pitted with a toothless rat, he also took seriously the stories told about the Grundbur, and set out most assiduously to improve himself.

No athlete was ever more disciplined. Mead slowed his speed, so (miracle of miracles) he drank in moderation. He ate voraciously, huge chunks of half-raw meat, bowl after steaming bowl of a thick fish, barley, and onion stew he instructed one of the cooks to prepare for him, and drank copious amounts of fresh water to cleanse his system. Twice each day, he ran, scrambled, and climbed a steep and perilous path down to and back up from the fiord. He ordered, from one of the blacksmiths, a pair of heavy iron ingots with handles. These, each as heavy as a dozen shields, he repeatedly lifted straight up from his sides to shoulder height or, with his upper arms tight against his sides and twisting his hands as he did so, lifted them over and over again by his fore-and upper arms. He likewise had a heavy log he lifted in various ways, but my favorite exercise was the one in which he squeezed raw onions until the juice and pulp oozed between his fingers. It was a feat I wouldn't have believed possible if I hadn't seen it with my own eyes.

(The hand is quicker than the eye. One Atticus, a strong man in Heraclius' court, was renowned for this same feat, but he used partially cooked onions. I know, because he wouldn't do the trick unless I was there to make the switch. And if one need beware of charlatans in as frivolous a matter as squeezing an onion, think of how important that advice may be when money is at stake or politics is involved!)

Never has there been, I think, a name more apt than Clutcher.

And so winter passed and spring crept northward. Night, on her dark horse, Hrimfaxi, who scattered dew and rime on the sleeping earth, daily tired earlier and awoke later, and Day, with his beautiful horse, Glad, whose glowing mane lit the sky, awoke earlier and tired later. Arvakur the Watchful and Alsvith the Rapid daily rose farther to the north and, escorted by Day and Glad, traveled their lengthening journey across the sky. Vernal undercurrents stirred winter's pattern. No more snow and ice fell and formed than melted and thawed. The north wind became confused and erratic in the face of an occasional reluctant breeze from the south.

A tense and expectant excitement gripped Grend and the folk-hall as the heroes, Einarr's chosen few, gathered. Rested and bored after months at home with their families, they were eager for action. Valgard, Askil, and Asbrand were old friends, and I've mentioned Olvir Iron-glove. As for the other nine (I made the fifteenth), I remember Ulfberth the Fair, he with the baby face, the morals of an inflated pig's bladder that goes in whichever direction it's kicked or the wind blows, and nearly as sick a love as Azak's for blood; Sigtrygg, an older, cautious man, Valgard's half-brother, and a consummate artist with the long ax; Thorfinn, the fire-builder, who was with us on Spume-

Spear; Olaf the Silent, a quiet, one-eyed man who was said to be, in battle, as coldly efficient and emotionless as a shark; and an amiable young bear of a man, yet another Egil (the third in this account, and I knew four or five more) Blackbeard, a boyhood friend of Einarr's who was said to be clumsy but lucky in battle, and with whom Einarr liked to wrestle because he was so unpredictable. As for the last four, I've lost their names and identities in the murky halls of time.

And oh, what a band of warrior-heroes they made! From the swaggering Einarr, pure muscle and brute strength, to Olaf the Silent, as lean and tough as a fire-hardened ash spear, they dominated the court and Grend. They were indefatigable. Combat was their business and their pleasure, and they worked and played at it with a combination of grim determination and merriment that left me, when I joined them, exhausted. One against one, two, three or four, sword against spear, spear against ax, they fought for hours on end. Each practiced his art alone, as well. I saw Olvir spend half a morning charging an imaginary foe, planting the butt of his spear in the ground, levering himself high into the air, and landing two spear lengths away with his long ax drawn. When they weren't fighting or practicing alone, they climbed up and down the cliff with Einarr or, for amusement, raced each other halfway up the mountain behind Grend. When they weren't doing that, they shaped oars and benches, studied and played with the model of the new ship, or, when the wind was blowing hard enough to make the task difficult, practiced setting and furling the new sail, which was several times larger and heavier (we soaked it to heighten the challenge) than the smaller sails they were used to. And when they weren't doing any of the preceding, they ate prodigiously, drank inordinate amounts of beer and mead, and sported lewdly, lasciviously, and at length with the slave girls. Needless to say, any hopes I had of maintaining their grueling pace were quashed early on, so I soon gave up any pretense of trying and settled into a less vigorous regimen that was more appropriate and better suited for an aching, somewhat antiquated, forty-year-old dwarf, namely, watching the watchers.

Hugleik was the most interesting, the one man who held his peace, who said not one word of approbation or disapproval, who voiced no opinion. The others paid him not one whit, but I had long ago learned to be wary when a king broods. Oh, I knew what was going through his mind, that he was caught again on the horns of a dilemma as he had been on the night of the Battle of the Goose Leg, only one that this time persisted over a period of months.

He was king, and theoretically had the power to break Einarr's dream with a word. But if Einarr challenged him, as was his ultimate right? Einarr was, after all, a free man and himself the son of a king, and the clash of those two wills could easily have led to mortal combat in which Hugleik's cunning and years of experience might not be expected to prevail over Einarr's youth and strength.

A king as well as a commoner may be haunted by questions that have no easy answers. A king may fear and a king may vacillate. A king may be indecisive—but not for too long a time if he wishes to remain a king. And so, as I kept a wary eye on Hugleik, I at last understood his thoughts. They were simple enough. He would not deny Einarr, for his court would know why he was doing so and he would thereby lose the game without a doubt. Rather, he would give Einarr, like any colt, his head, which could lead to one of only two conclusions. In the first, Einarr's death at the hands of the Grundbur, the succession was assured. And in the second, however unlikely Einarr was to prevail, Hugleik could only wait, hope, and load the dice. And though it was beyond my powers to ascertain exactly how he would do so, I was sure in my bones that he would.

As for the rest of the inhabitants of Grend and Hugleik's court, the reaction to the heroes' goings-on was divided between the white of virtually abject hero worship and the black of blind jealousy. Speculation on the nature of the Grundbur and the odds on Einarr slaying him ran rampant. For the women, the monster's powers were inflated beyond those of a mere human and Einarr was destined to return a hero. For the rejected thanes, the creature about whom they'd listened wide-eyed and shivering before Einarr's announcement suddenly became an implausible fabrication, probably nothing more than a powerful warrior who'd defeated and cowed Hrothgeirr's men.. As for whether or not Einarr would return, they supposed he would if he was lucky, but then any one of them probably would, too.

"Then why not go yourself?" Olaf the Silent asked one night after hearing a retort of that nature to one of his boasts. A circle of expectation spread around him and the smug young man who'd spoken so rashly, for a blood-boast challenged wasn't a matter to be taken lightly. "My brine-hog lies wintered across the fiord. It's yours, if you've the will and guts."

The poor fellow! Drunk, befuddled by the torrent of words from the usually monosyllabic Olaf, and skewered by the gleaming dagger of that one narrowed eye, he hesitated too long.

"Then keep your tongue from wagging," Olaf said, spitting his disdain, "if you don't want a man to cut it off like a dog's tail."

It was folly to attack, but folly was as natural for a Geat as crowing is for a rooster. The young man, however, was luckily more drunk than he thought, and Olaf was in a mellow, if not benevolent, frame of mind. Consequently, when the young man stood and struck with his heavy tankard, Olaf merely leaned back and, after the tankard whistled harmlessly past his nose and crashed into the table, grabbed the young man's wrist with his left hand and pulled. Off balance, the table acting like a fulcrum, the young man pitched forward to strike his forehead on the edge of, and bury his face in, a heavy bowl filled with cold, greasy stew. The fight was over almost before it began, and might have been the young man's last had not Olaf pulled him out by his hair and shaken him like a rag so he could breathe before casting him aside. His point made, Olaf yawned, rose and found his favorite slave girl, and took her off to a corner, where he used her and, sex the soporific, slept. Need I mention that no one cared—or dared—to disturb his slumber?

Altercations being as common in court as Our Fathers are in Rome, there were more fights, of course, but to catalog them one would merely recite a rapidly boring litany in which Einarr's men were invariably the victors. Of more interest was our new ship. The scoffers won over, for the most part, the majority of the settlement became caught up in the drive to be ready for a launch by the time the ice broke on the fiord. Egil laid on an extra half-dozen men to drill rivet holes and shave planks. The rope makers were put to the test to make the thicker, and yet still supple and easily handled, lines needed for the taller mast and heavier sail. Two iron smiths labored night and day to produce rivets, reinforcing rings, and sundry other necessities, including four sets of thick wrist and ankle manacles with accompanying chains in the hopeful event we captured the Grundbur alive. Slaves were sent out to gather and shred cedar bark, and a gang of older men cheerfully pitched in to help make the hundreds of feet of caulking to stuff between the strakes. My favorite, though, was Ethelred the Blind.

Ethelred was the oldest man in Grend: rare is the life as full as his had been, and rarer the awe and respect he commanded. Experienced and renowned in battle, he was blinded while rescuing Hugleik from a fire when the one-day-to-be king was a week old. He could have rested on his laurels and royal largesse, but that wasn't his way, and he became first a healer, then, as a storyteller, a repository of history and lore, a veritable Geatish Herodotus. And sometime in the past, he'd learned to carve to while away the time. Such became his art and, through the sight of his fingers, such was the sailing-luck his touch conferred that every ship launched in Grend in the previous twenty or so years was preceded by the spiral prow-ornaments decorated according to the way the ship felt to him when he sat in its unfinished hull. Indeed, those talismans had become a necessity for even the humblest craft, and it would have required a brave soul to put to sea without the old man's luck-charm at the bow of his ship.

The carving itself, which was never revealed until it was finished, was preceded by a solemn ritual that had evolved over a period of years. The proceedings, like many other things in the Geats' lands and lives, were new to me, and though I saw only this one example, I was told it was representative in every detail except two, which differed drastically from the normal and caused a great deal of consternation.

The day after the hull was finished and moved to the water's edge was eagerly awaited by everyone. That morning, Egil and Gurd, Einarr and his band, and what looked like at least a hundred others—the ceremony was more of an occasion than I'd understood—gathered around the hull in the dim light of dawn and stood, stamping feet and blowing on fingers, waiting for Ethelred.

Ethelred was a recluse, if not a hermit, and I'd seen him only once or twice without, having been acquainted with my share of so-called seers and holy men, being overly impressed. I must say, however, he won me over that morning when, accompanied by his great-grandson and striding along in utter confidence, he arrived and passed through the waiting throng of spectators. He looked like what I imagine the hard-edged, tough-minded ancient desert prophets of the Jews—a Geatish Jeremiah or Ezekiel—might have looked like. Huge and powerful in his youth, I was told, he'd wasted with age, but what was left was no mean measure of a man. As tall as Valgard Halfbeard, he was as thin and sinuously resilient as a walrus skin rope. His long, flowing hair and beard were as white as fresh snow. His arms were bare in the morning cold, tanned brown with age and smoke, and virtually fleshless. His most prominent features were his eyes, which, in spite of milky occlusions, gave the impression he was looking at, if not through, every one and thing in his path. Seldom in my life have I seen a man whose eyes simultaneously so attracted and repelled, so utterly fascinated, so elicited fear, respect, awe, and raw, commanding power.

Master shipbuilder Egil met Ethelred, escorted him to a stilelike ladder erected amidships over the freeboard, and led him to a special seat placed there earlier. When Egil retreated, an eerie, almost haunted hush fell over the crowd which stood and stared at the apparently empty hull. Black in the gray light, Amin circled overhead like an omen. Someone coughed. A dog barked in the distance and, closer by, two fighting pigs squealed their rage. Then, as if arranged by a master planner with a flair for the dramatic, and accompanied by a prolonged cracking sound similar to that made when a leaning tree sometimes splits lengthwise, the ice split and a wide, black crack opened from the shoreline to my left and extended out and seaward as far along the fiord as I could see. As if he had been waiting for that signal, Ethelred rose from his seat, stared with those blank, white eyes into the heart of the echoes and the mountains across the fiord, then raised his stick over his head and cried:

"I hear, Father Wotan, and name this ship Boar-Rover!"

The crowd was stunned! The privilege of naming a ship was reserved for the man who commissioned its construction, and for Ethelred to usurp that honor was unprecedented. Such was Ethelred's reputation as a seer, though, and such was his stature, that no one said a word as, upon being beckoned, Egil reentered the hull, assisted the old man back to firm ground, and, not knowing what else to say or do, returned him to his great-grandson's care. Imagine Egil's state, then, when instead of leaving, Ethelred pivoted and fixed him with those terrible eyes.

"Continue in all haste," he commanded in a voice that rang and echoed across the fiord and, indeed, through the following days. "Finish him quickly, for Boar-Rover will be a fast and able craft, a ship of renown, long sung of. I will bring his luck-charm to you soon."

And with that, he turned on his heel and stalked away in silent magnificence.

"Him!"

Oh, Einarr fumed!

"By Odin's overworked cock, but what kind of a ship is a *him?*"

No one else knew what to make of it, either. Ships were feminine: a ship was a she. Every reference to her—to him—would stick in the craw and choke the speaker. With what, for example, would they replace, "She handles like a whore on the rag in this quartering sea"? Or, again, echoing Valgard's earlier reference, "Was ever a bitch so sweetly stuffed?'' The very idea was ludicrous, and beyond the ability of the imagination to comprehend. There had never, in anyone's memory, been a masculine ship.

To make matters worse, Einarr had his mind set on naming his ship Grundbur-Stalker. I'd thought that name an unfortunate choice for a number of reasons. What would happen, for example, if the Grundbur turned out to be no more than a good story grown out of proportion? Einarr himself was prone, on occasion, to be skeptical in spite of all he'd heard over the past half-year and more. Would it not, since renaming a ship brought devastatingly bad luck, be burdened with a name that would rapidly become a joke among the Northmen of whatever kingdom? And who, Einarr included, wanted to sail in a joke? What would they do, then? Beach it and leave it to rot, after all we'd gone through to build it?

I might as well have addressed myself to a rune-stone. Grundbur-Stalker he wanted, it wasn't for me to question his choice or judgement, and my questions alone tinged the name with a shadow of bad luck. Upon hearing that, luck being a magic word for the Northmen, I'd shut my mouth. As, indeed, I did that afternoon while Einarr carried on.

''I don't give a shit if he's as old and wise as Mimer. He had no right to name my ship!'' he raved, in the next breath polishing off his second horn of mead.

I sipped on my cup, kept the fire between us, and a close eye on the door.

''A wandering pig! Paugh! The blind old fart-maker's lost his other senses as well!''

I recalled that boars, as symbols of virility and ferocity, adorned the Geats' helmets, nose-guards, shields, hilts, and virtually everything else, but said not one word.

''The sea will swamp me with storms for calling her a hog wallow,'' he said, filling his horn for the third time, ''but he didn't think about that, did he?''

I doubted the sea would take any more heed of Einarr than Neptune did when Caligula attacked his ocean in France, but saved my breath.

''It's said a good ship, like a woman, is a pleasure for a man to slip into and ride,'' he spat. ''By Odin's blue balls, but they'll laugh me off the face of the deep with that one!''

Woe to the man who laughed at Einarr to his face, no matter what the reason! Woe to me, for that matter. "Dwarf!" he slurred as the mead, to which he'd become unaccustomed, overtook him as a hare will a tortoise. Rising, his body quivering like a gigantic fist clenched, he lurched around the fire-pit toward me. "You've brought this on me, creature of the earth's bowels. Your magic, and your ill-omened black bird!''

Were I magic, I'd have put myself far away from my friend turned Grundbur. "Not true, Einarr," I protested lamely, half rising to meet him.

"I'll grind your body-struts! I'll . . ."

Whatever else he had in mind went unsaid because, stumbling, he simultaneously cracked his shin against a protruding fire-pit stone and his head on a low beam. Howling, then, his eyes wide, he stared at my hunch-backed, looming shadow that, like an evil spirit, danced menacingly on the wall behind me and the ceiling above me. Had he been a Christian, he'd have crossed himself.

"You see, Gods! He makes the beams and stones of my own house attack me!" Mead-frightened, most unlike a Geat, he backed away from me until, tripped by his sleeping bench, he sat heavily. "Should have killed you on the spot and left your life-bag to rot on the forest floor!" Groaning, he slumped to one side and pulled a fur over his head. "Get out, Dwarf. Take yourself back to the earth's bowels, or whatever pit you came from." Muffled by fur and mead, his voice faded. "Leave. Leave. Leave. . . ."

Needless to say, I did. My heart heavy, and not knowing where else to go, I crept out silently and took myself to the folk-hall, where, as I might have predicted, the same subject was on every tongue.

The hall was divided into two camps. The cheerful larger camp consisted of those to be left behind on Einarr's quest. Smirking and laughing, they were led by Hugleik, who said little aloud but was openly amused by Hervarth's sarcastic and caustic remarks about masculine ships and a floating boar struggling to keep its snout out of the water as it snorted and grunted its way along the whale-road.

The other camp, the thirteen chosen, were sullen and morose. Normally, they'd have annihilated their tormentors, but they were too disheartened by Ethelred's imposition of name and gender on the ship they'd been so proud of the day before, and merely grumbled in their cups.

"Behold, the runt of the litter!" some wit jeered when I was noticed, eliciting gales of laughter.

I should have known better than to enter that den of antagonism without Amin, but I hadn't seen him since that morning.

"The piglet who'd teach real men how to build a ship," Hervarth sneered. "And what a ship *he* is. As much a ship as this piglet is a man!"

"You are witty tonight, my lord Hervarth," I retorted. "I give you as much, but will take it back the day *he* sails circles around the best sea-sow you or anyone else can put in the water."

Riding the crest of a wave of popularity, Hervarth laughed off my challenge. "Brave words, spoken only because I didn't toss you overboard in the middle of the whale-road, as I should have. So hear me, Dwarf! If you've a wit left, or care for your life, be gone from here by the time the sun sets tomorrow, or I'll stuff you under a mountain where you belong. There, with others of your kind, you can *oink oink, oink oink oink.*"

I've never lightly suffered being threatened or mocked, even by a king's son, but what was I to do when the cry was joined and the hall resounded with a chorus of oinks, grunts, and squeals? Stick combs in their armpits? Helpless for the moment, I retreated to the far corner where Einarr's band skulked, and to an equally disappointing reception.

"So, Flat-face," one of them said. "You see what your knife-keeled boat has brought us to?"

"You were singing its praises yesterday," I reminded him.

"A dwarf's wiles and dark arts at work."

"And what do you say, Valgard Halfbeard?" I asked, looking to my friend for support.

Valgard, as bleak of face as the rest, frowned and shook his head. "The mead has soured, Musculus." He shot his eyes in the direction of the epidemic of porcine merriment convulsing the rabble. "Foolish is he who follows a luck-stricken man. Luckless, a man stands alone. Where, now, is your life-luck?"

Luck-stricken, luckless, and bereft of life-luck. Was that me? Evidently so, for he believed it, and so did the rest of them. Bravery, courage, talent, wisdom, all of men's finest traits bowed, in the Geats' and other Northmen's minds, to mere and senseless, unthinking luck.

I have never been a believer in luck, and yet, contradictorily, recognize its existence. How many times, for example, had I seen Heraclius ride through a storm of arrows and spears, and not lose one drop of blood? Had I not been contrarily blessed with Portia-luck? Kapsabelis-luck saved me from Azak once, and Ilgen-luck, yet again.

One sorts out luck, like love, only from a distance, and even then is left with little more than a bagful of trick questions, illogical suppositions, and unverifiable conclusions. Good or bad luck is unrecognizable when encountered. If I'm hungry and find meat, I'll say I'm lucky. If, however, the meat is tainted and I become ill, I'm unlucky.

Luck is a thread that runs through a life and ends only in death. Only after death, if one were alive, could one sort out one's good and bad luck, and even then it likely would be hard to say. One simply never knows. Was I lucky when I emerged a dwarf from my mother's womb? Was I lucky when I was given to Heraclius? What might I have been if I hadn't been that gift? Another (though not so large) Kapsabelis? Another Azak? A feeble-witted boy who fell into a river?

If luck is too difficult to sort out at this stage in my life, I can't imagine I tried to then. Enough, at that point, to fly in luck's face, meet it head-on, and deny the pessimistic Geatish consensus that threatened to drive me from them. Enough to throw luck in their faces, and make my own.

What choice, after all, did I have? Where should I have gone, had I obeyed Hervarth? Up the mountain behind Grend? Found a boat as narrow as a boot and sailed away down the narrow crack in the ice-covered fiord? What should I have eaten, what drunk?

I've always been slow to anger. Hervarth's jibes and the pig calls, for example, had little more than irritated me. Portia with her vituperation and Azak with his threats had, in the end, instructed me. But when a man I admired and considered a friend deserted me, that did rouse my anger.

"Wrong, Valgard Halfbeard," I said, openly displaying my contempt. "A luck-stricken man's no more than a product of his own weak imagination. You may gnash your teeth and bewail your ailing luck until Loki breaks his chains and escapes the dripping poison that burns his forehead, but I tell you, a real man makes his own starry luck. So chew on this, you crestfallen heroes. I, Musculus the Dwarf, will warm my hands and ass in front of this very same fire tomorrow night.

"And that," I swore, preparatory to turning on my heel and leaving them, "is a lesson for a handful of moping, groaning Geats—and a dwarf's blood-oath."

# 16. Of a Blind Seer's Sight, a Prow-spiral that Was No Spiral, and a Blood-oath Fulfilled.

To say I understood isolation isn't to say I enjoyed it. Certainly not on a cold night in a far northern land. I was hungry, weary, and confused by the sudden onslaught of events beyond my control. Amin was missing, and I feared he'd deserted me or, worse, been killed or stolen, which could have ominous ramifications. I'd been mocked, cursed, reviled, deserted, and banished. A dwarf in a land of giants, I slipped out of the folk-hall through the small door in one of the larger ones, and trudged across the trampled white meadow to the same bench on which Einarr and I sat a scant two months earlier.

Even the elements had arrayed themselves against me. Heavy clouds driven by a south wind spilled up Knar's Fiord and dumped wet snow on me. The night was as dark as my soul. Nothing stirred. My legs crossed, I sat in the center of an abyss of silence while the snow built around and entombed me so I must have looked more like a rune-stone than a human. Inside that stone, the banked fire of my anger, as much as the thick bearskin I'd wrapped around me, kept me warm.

Flat-face. A pitch-filled twig of memory flared and died away to coals.

A dwarf's wiles. A chunk of fat bubbled and burst into popping flames.

A luck-stricken man. The stench of burning hair filled my nostrils.

Creature of the earth's bowels. Incandescent, sulphurous fumes writhed like angry snakes.

The runt of the litter, the piglet, *oink oink, oink oink oink.* Oh, I burned, I burned!

Dwarf! O, God, is a dwarf any less a man than a Geat? Was I, by my flat face and the length of my bowed legs, any more a monster than men who made blood-eagles out of other men? Did rare and beautiful creatures spring from their loins alone? Did their stuporous drunken orgies confer on them some wisdom not privy to me? Were their features more pleasurable than mine in the eyes of the one God of us all, of whom they were, and chose to remain, ignorant?

Who were these men to so demean a dwarf? I took pride in my dwarfishness. I, a dwarf, swung out of my bonds and freed Ilgen, as none of them could have. I, a dwarf, had counseled an emperor of a far larger kingdom than they could imagine. I, a dwarf, had lain with not only their women, but sloe-eyed Mediterranean voluptuaries, with long-necked and lithe women as black and sleek as night, with a diminutive and mysteriously slant-eyed yellow woman whose silken black hair fell to her feet, and who could do tricks with a knotted silk cord that would very nearly pop a man's eyes out of his head. I, a dwarf, who admittedly couldn't read the book of the sea, had given them a keel and, with it, the key to the wind. And I, a dwarf, didn't care if a ship was a male or female (where, after all, the cock, and where the cunt?), and didn't fear a blind old man who named a ship.

I'm amused, at this far remove, by how, with ne'er a nut to crack or raven to dance with, I ranted and raved in my snow-covered bearskin cave. Amused, too, after having slept, by how I found myself looking at the morning through a small ice-encrusted hole made by my breath. The clouds had snowed themselves out or been blown away. I was, to my surprise, comfortably warm and rested, and my anger, like a demon scourged, had left me in peace. It was a strange moment in which I felt much as I do now, calm, detached, even serene. And in that moment of quietude, as I do now, I recognized the folly of wasting anger on men for being men. What else, not being gods, should they be? Men (myself included—I never claimed to be more than a man) are in the final analysis poor, weak, superstitious creatures, and to spend anger on them wishing them to be otherwise is a waste of time, emotion, and energy. As soon chew a rock in the hopes it will become a melon, or use a loaf of bread as an adze in the hopes it will cut wood. That in mind, and suddenly ravenously hungry, I broke free of my snowy cocoon and, after waggling my legs to wake them, trudged through the calf-deep virgin snow back to the shelter of the folk-hall.

The usual snores greeted me. Mouths agape, legs and arms flung every which way, the Geats were sleeping off the previous night's carouse. There being no need to wake sleeping children, I picked my way quietly through the scattered bodies to the fireplace where, in an empty bowl from one table and with a half loaf of dry bread from another, I made a breakfast of still warm stew dipped from a giant black cauldron. And there, warming my hands and ass in front of the embers of the previous night's fire, as I had vowed I would in front of the next night's, I filled my belly and, such as it was, laid a plan.

Such as it was, I say, and in the unfortunate singular, because the only plan I could think of was to visit Ethelred, and trust that something more concrete would come to mind. With no more than that—actually, my belly was full and my hands and ass were warm—I once again slipped outside and, leaving a bowl of scraps in the open where Amin could find them, made my way toward Grend.

Why do I remember that morning so well? Probably because wagering for high stakes tends to sharpen and clear the mind so the minutest details stand out. As so often occurs, the previous night's storm had preceded a calm. The morning sky was a clear and fragile pale blue. The winds coming up the fiord and down the valley from the mountains had laid aside their differences, and not so much as a puff stirred the air. The fresh snow crunched lightly underfoot, and I recall thinking it was a shame to mar its beauty as I started downhill and entered the sacred oak grove.

I'd been told, but had never fully understood why until then, that the Geats held the grove as the holiest in their domain. The underbrush had been cleared and the tended trees loomed silently like dark, brooding giants. High overhead, an antithesis to the thick, gnarled trunks covered with twisted bark specked with tiny piles of contrasting snow, a lacework of twigs filigreed the sky. Below, some short and squat like cairns or sleeping dwarfs, others taller, bare-flanked tablets in which epitaphs, encomiums, and admonitions had been carved, snow-capped rune-stones haphazardly lumped the grove floor. As did the Geats and other Northmen, I could well believe, during my hushed passage, that oak trees housed mighty spirits, some of whose powers imbued the trees with powers of their own.

(Indeed, maidens or favored children, who were thought to be especially vulnerable in the afterlife, were often buried in a box carved out of a hollowed oak trunk, if one could be found that had fallen of its own accord. By way of contrast, a warrior might be cremated, other adults accoutered lavishly or simply and laid out in a grave or barrow, and slaves thrown into a bog to appease the marsh monsters who were said to reside in those dank and dreary places.)

The view, when I emerged from the rune-stone grove, was spectacular. Knar's Fiord, the crack in the ice startlingly black in contrast to the previous night's snow, stretched seaward. Nearer at hand, the low-slung, heavily thatched and snow-peaked huts that made up the sleepily bucolic Grend clustered in a rough circle. Boys in an empty lot, their cries competing with the barking of dogs and crowing of roosters, waged a snowball war. Smoke from eave vents rose in narrow columns to a level somewhat above my position, where it mysteriously flattened into an ill-defined but vaguely circular milk-white sheet. Here and there, a figurine bustled along the spider-web network of paths etched in the snow between the houses. At the water's edge, close by the sleek-lined hull of the unfinished Boar-Rover, smoke from the blacksmith's forges and a thick cloud of steam from the wood-bending vats rose to thicken the flat cloud overhead, and the thud of mallets, the clank of metal, and the sharp ringing of adzes mingled in a sustained yet rhythmic note that fed on its own echoes. However Ethelred might have astounded or appalled the inhabitants the day before, life went on as usual.

Ethelred's hut stood apart from the rest of the village and under an ancient and renowned oak in whose crown was said to reside the spirit of the giantess Skadi, the Skee-Goddess. His was a hermitage of sorts and, indeed, mine were the first footprints to mar the new snow filling the narrow rut of a lane that led to his door.

I don't know what I expected. Not, of course, a cross and an alms bowl, but certainly neither, when I beat on his door, to be called by name and commanded to enter.

Hermits and holy men, seers and saints, are often endowed with powers not given to the rest of mankind. Whether they become hermits, etc. because they exercise these powers or enjoy the powers because they are holy, etc., I don't know, but I've learned to separate the wheat from the chaff. There was, and remains, no doubt in my mind that Ethelred was, though no Christian, wheat of the highest quality.

For my part, I chose not to answer—he knew what he knew, and would ask what he didn't—as I opened his door and entered.

"Sit on that bench, Dwarf," he said, pointing with a short-bladed knife, "and give me a moment."

There are times when a blind man enjoys an advantage, which truth strikes a seeing man when he walks out of a snow- and sun-bright morning and into a darkened room. I was, the moment the door closed behind me, blinder than Ethelred.

"Three short steps," the old man said and, as if reading my mind, added, "don't worry. The floor is smooth and there's nothing to trip over."

How many times, while ascending a stairway in a dark

house in the middle of the night and knowing from having counted that there are, say, eight steps, will a man reach the eighth and, like a fool, wave his foot around looking for a ninth? A blind man I knew some years later once told me he found this amusing, which I find plausible after, as an old man, I've watched young men blindly wave their pride and fear about like a foot groping for a ninth step. Be that as it may, and though he, too, may have been amused, Ethelred said nothing as I shuffled forward, ran into the bench, climbed onto it, and closed my eyes to hasten their adjustment to the dark. Evidently knowing what I was doing, and that men who can see think and talk better when their eyes are open (a blind friend once pointed out this phenomenon, and I believe he was correct), Ethelred, from the sound of a knife plied on wood, returned to his work, and waited. And furthermore, had the good grace to remain silent once—I felt he sensed when—I opened my eyes and looked around.

Ethelred's hut, as far as I could tell in the deep gloom, looked much like any other I'd been in. A dull fire of mixed peat and hardwood burned in the sand-filled, stone-walled pit in the center of the room. Barely visible around the periphery, the usual household implements hung from the ceiling and walls. At one end of the room, its eyes glowing like brushed gold, what looked like a stuffed eagle perched on a branch. On the opposite wall, a sword and a long ax crossed poignantly on an aged and battered shield, no doubt relics of Ethelred's youth.

The light cast by a hissing tongue of flame springing from the end of a log bathed Ethelred's wrinkled, shadow-lined face and turned his blank, unseeing eyes into eerily glowing amber marbles. He sat cross-legged, with bony knees sticking out from under a blanket draped over his lap. His arms and chest were bare under a heavy sheepskin vest, his long white hair was kept out of his work by a thick leather band tied around his forehead, and his equally white beard hung well down his chest. Altogether, he looked more like a benign, avuncular craftsman at his bench than a prophet or seer, and I was put at ease.

A chunk of wood hidden by shadows, the blanket, and

his calm, competent hands that seemed composed entirely of joints and fingers lay in his lap. "The prow-spiral?" I asked.

"You could say so."

"You don't let anyone see them until they're finished, they say."

"It is, very nearly."

I'd heard he often spent upwards of a week carving one of his charms, and was surprised. "You've worked rapidly," I said.

His mouth turned up slightly at the corners in what I took for a smile, and he shook his head no. "Nine half-years ago, an old woman brought me this piece of wood and told me I'd know when to use it and what to make out of it." His shrug, I thought, was almost apologetic. "The Gods created it many, many half-years before then. I have only to make it look like itself."

"But how do you know when it does look like itself?" I asked, mystified.

"It's evident," he answered shortly. "As you'll see for yourself in a while."

"And if a while's too long?" I asked, thinking of the coming night and Hervarth's warning.

"I know why you're here, Dwarf," Ethelred answered. "Be patient. You'll have time enough."

I'd gone to see him simply because I hadn't known where else to go or to whom else to turn, and in the hope that my blind, so to speak, cast of the die would suggest some other, more useful course of action. I was disappointed but, reminding myself there are times when a man must lay his fate in another's hands, resigned myself to the patience he advised. Who, after all (other than he), knew? If waiting to look at Boar-Rover's finished prow-ornament was the way out of my predicament, wait I would, and gladly.

Wait I did, too. The fire died down: Ethelred—could he feel light?—added kindling so I wouldn't have to sit in total darkness. The hut warmed: I shed my bearskin. My legs cramped, there being no back on the bench: I made my bearskin into a pallet and, the crossed forelegs my pillow,

lay down. Ethelred worked without pause: the steady slice
and rasp of steel on wood, the sharp, rapping taps of mallet
against chisel, the intermittent brush of steel on stone and
leather as he honed his blades, melded into a sound as lull-
ing as a soft breeze in spring leaves, and I lapsed into a
stupor in which my senses played tricks on me. Was the
pile of rags in the corner really a crouching hag? Did the
stuffed eagle preen itself? Did the sword, longing to be free,
strain against its scabbard, and did I smell the stale reek of
old blood?

"I need your eyes, Dwarf. Wake up."

Groggy and disoriented, I sat up and caught a leather bag
he tossed across the fire to me.

He threw a handful of shavings in the fire, which blazed
up. "Give them to me one by one, and tell me their color."

The bag contained amber pieces that ranged in size from
a thrush's egg to a child's fist, and in shape from rough
ovals to smoothly faceted polygons to jagged chunks. I
walked around the fire to his side, but not before he covered
the prow-spiral with a flap of the blanket.

"Milky white," I said, handing him the first, a sphere
the size of a human eyeball.

Ethelred smiled faintly as he, too, I thought, compared
it to his own useless eyes, and set it to one side. "Next."

They followed quickly. Most he returned to the bag, but
a half-dozen or so, when we finished, lay in a small pile
on the blanket. These, to my amazement, he held up one
by one and described each one's color to the word, as I
had.

"So they've blamed you for what I did, eh?" he said
after I returned to my bench.

"Yes," I said, letting it go at that.

He bent anew to his carving. "And have banished you,
I hear."

"My lord's hearing is acute."

He smiled. "Yes. It is."

"They're brave warriors," I said, "but superstitious to
a fault."

"Oh?" he asked. "Are men less superstitious where you
come from?"

I admitted they weren't, really.

Ethelred's smile was wan. "Do you ever wonder, Dwarf, why warriors who'll fight through a sea of blood will also be cowed by an old blind man?"

I shrugged. "There was a time not too long ago when men as fierce as these feared a dwarf."

He pondered that as he concentrated on a particularly delicate series of cuts. "Which is to say," he said at last, "there may come a time when these warriors will no longer fear me."

"I didn't mean that," I said quickly and, after a pause, added, "but it's possible."

Ethelred fumbled behind him and produced another bag, from which he extracted a coil of silver wire.

"Any name can be faulted, my lord, as I faulted Grund-bur-Stalker, and though Boar-Rover was not Einarr's choice, it's a good enough name and one they'll accept in time. But the idea of a masculine ship unnerves them. And without a dwarf, who may be short but is nonetheless tall enough to make a target, where next will the lightning strike?"

He frowned as he measured a short piece of silver and, by repeatedly bending it, broke it from the coil. "I understand their confusion," he said, "but I've weathered too many storms and am too old to worry about lightning." Shaking his head in puzzlement, he turned over the prow-ring and began what appeared to be a series of nearly identical operations on the opposite side. "Still, the God's never spoken to me like that before. It's a mystery."

"What god isn't? Every god I've known delights in ambiguity and riddles. You'd think a god, being a god, would say what he wanted and why, straight out."

"It's clear to me one did yesterday."

"It is?" I asked. "I wouldn't know. I don't read gods' minds."

"But you do men's, they say, and I think they're right." Ethelred's mallet slipped and he hit his finger instead of the chisel. It must have hurt, but he continued as if nothing out of the way had happened. "So tell me. Will they heed the God's command?"

I assumed they would, and said so.

"You're quick to answer. Do men where you come from always heed their gods' commands?"

"You read men's souls better than I their minds," I said with a laugh. "And the answer is no, they don't. Our God—we have only one—has made his wishes known, but each man is free to interpret those wishes as he pleases, and act accordingly."

"So then men sometimes choose the path that pleases them more than your one god?"

"Sometimes, my lord? Say, rather, often."

Ethelred nodded to indicate my answer was expected. "Then don't be surprised," he said, breaking off another piece of silver and beginning to tap it into place, "if the Sea-Geats, too, balk at following the God's advice."

I didn't care if they did or not. Of vastly greater importance was the completion of the prow-spiral, for time was running out. On edge, I imagined sand streaming through the neck of a glass and measuring my remaining moments. Finally, though, and none too soon, he was finished. His milk-white eyes glowing like gold amber in the dim firelight, he ran his hands over his work and, evidently pleased, smiled. "So, then! Perhaps this will convince them to obey the God's command after all, eh?"

I cared no more then than I had earlier, but restrained myself. "And if they don't?" I asked.

"That, we will see in due time."

"You're blind and I'm banished. We, my lord? See?"

Ethelred laughed aloud, and with that laugh his mystical aura cracked and fell from him, leaving the man exposed. "Ah, Dwarf! It's been too long since I've laughed so heartily. We could be friends, you and I, and I'll be sorry when you take the whale-road. But, yes," he said, leaning forward to throw a handful of pine twigs on the fire, "you'll see, if you'll be bold."

The fire blazed, filled the room with light, and evoked a rustle of wings and a familiar croak from my left.

"He's been visiting me," Ethelred said. The blanket fell from his lap as he stood. "Raven, go to your master!"

Dumbfounded, I too stood as Amin slipped from his

perch, flapped his wings once, and landed on my shoulder.

Ethelred's voice rang with authority as he held up the finished prow-spiral that was no spiral. "Go now to the folk-hall," he said. "Show them this, and say the following: . . ."

Night had fallen when Ethelred dismissed me. The days were still short, to be sure, but I'd been in his hut far longer than I'd thought. And if I felt a certain thrill of anticipation as his door closed behind me, it was leavened by more than a hint of apprehension. I was banished, after all, and if Ethelred was sanguine about my fate, I wasn't.

The sky was still clear, but the moon had not yet risen, so trees, rune-stones, and Amin and I were reduced to silhouettes against the snow. Had anyone seen us as I retraced the morning's steps, he could have been forgiven for believing a monster with three heads stalked the land. Up we climbed, up the rock-strewn slope, up through the sacred oak grove in which the trees, at night, whispered freely among themselves and spread the rumor of the boar-and bird-topped intruder. Out of the grove and across the meadow, its snow by then trampled in a fan of ruts spreading from my path to a half-dozen royal destinations. And three heads on one body, a dwarfish Grundbur stumped and waddled along the deepest rut, the path that led to the main doors of the folk-hall, inside which thanes caroused and, that night, more fates than mine would be sealed.

They had, of course, no idea I was coming, no notice of my arrival. On the porch, I transferred Amin to my arm, rested my burden against one of the great doors, and pushed my cowl off my head. The small door, as was the custom, was opened a crack to welcome travelers seeking food and shelter. Pushing aside the skin hung there to keep out the wind, I saw a hall divided. Smug thanes, though careful not to push their luck too far, reveled and caroused at the king's end. Boar-Rover's dispirited crew, Einarr included, I was pleased to note, drank silently and sullenly alone in a corner to my right. There being no time like the present, I crossed myself (yes, I still remembered how), took up my boar and bird, and slipped inside.

If the Northmen counted luck a virtue, I was a veritable saint. No one at Hugleik's table—they were all preoccupied by an arm wrestling match—not one of the smug thanes, not even Einarr and his men, noticed me. As if cloaked in invisibility (the slave tending the fire saw me, but I pointed at him and he fled silently), I wended my way through tables and benches, climbed onto a table in front of the fireplace, and waited.

Thyri saw me first. Her jaw dropping, she stared at me and with her silence drew Hugleik's attention. Half rising, then stopped, frozen like a statue carved in ice, his attention caught another's eye, and then another's.

The circle spread rapidly. Laughter and loud talk faded. Heads turned, eyes widened, and faces blanched with fear. Silence, too, at Einarr's table, where the men rose and edged forward the better to see me.

"You proud thanes!" I roared, my voice ringing with Ethelred's strength. "You approved my banishment last night, but tonight, as you see, I stand before you. What say you now to Musculus the Dwarf?"

Hervarth once had dared seize Einarr's arm. He would have waded unhesitatingly, as Ethelred said, through a sea of blood. The sight I presented terrified him, though, and he said nothing. Neither, superstitious louts that they were, was there a word, nor so much as a move, from any of the rest.

Imagine with me, as I hark back to that night.

A dwarf, a bandy-and bowlegged, ominously shaggy truncated lump of a man wrapped in a bearskin above which protruded a human head with a flat face, pug nose, and, lurking in a grizzled beard and graying hair, black eyes that glared (as fiercely as I could) at the assembly. Imagine, too, like a bloated scepter, its base supported on an upended bowl, its own head towering a foot above mine, a prow-spiral that was no spiral, a fiercely carved arch-necked, sharp-tusked, dragon-snouted boar's head with one sharp-edged and silver-ringed eye blazing red as blood, the other, as large and smooth as a hen's egg, a baleful amber fire. Imagine, too, perched on the fierce boar's head, towering even taller to complete the three-headed monster, a bird black of wing and beak, black as the inside of a cave, or an evil thought.

And imagine, too, in the strained hush, my voice reverberating as I repeated Ethelred's words:

"What say you, Sea-Geats? Will you be the Sons of the Boar and sail behind this insignia sent by the one-eyed Odin, Wotan himself, or will the Grundbur feast at will and laugh in his lair until sterner men be found?"

Einarr was slow and took time to think, but not Valgard Halfbeard. Without hesitation, he stepped forward and, a dangerous, fell glint in his eye, stepped onto the bench alongside the table I stood on, seized the boar's head insignia in one fist, and raised it high over his head.

"There are no sterner men," he said. "What say you, Sea-Geats, and especially you, Einarr, son of Eggther? Shall lesser men bathe their hands in the Grundbur's blood?"

All eyes turned to Einarr, who welcomed danger more than any other man. His mind made up, then, a terrible smile masked his face as he stepped resolutely forward and onto the bench.

"There are no sterner men," said Einarr, his voice ringing with authority, with command. He in turn raised the arch-necked and dragon-snouted boar's head. "I tell you the Grundbur's fear-slobber will drool down his chin when he sees the Sons of the Boar approach. And this, my blood-oath, I swear to you! That I, Einarr, son of Eggther, by my own beating heart, will bathe my hands in the Grundbur's blood, and cast his body into Niflheim's icy pit!"

There was more, of course. Each of the other twelve took his turn, raised the boar's head insignia capped by the black and croaking raven, and swore his blood-oath. As for me, I was content to watch and listen, and close this section of my account with two observations.

First, the *scop* wasn't there, so how could he have known the part played by the dwarf?

And second, though Hugleik frowned and Hervarth gnashed his teeth, neither said a word as, my own blood-oath fulfilled, I stood in front of the great fire, and warmed my hands and ass.

# 17. Of Boar-Rover's Success, My Last Days at Hugleik's Court, and a Friend Remembered.

No one apologized, because to apologize would have been to say they'd caused my fall from luck. Contrariwise, I wasn't congratulated because to congratulate would have been to say I was responsible for my reversed fortunes. Enough for them my luck had changed for the better. Enough for me, though Ethelred had played a major part in the proceedings, to leave well enough alone. My oath was fulfilled, Hervarth put in his place, and my coin once again valued. That's not to say I had any faith in it retaining its value. Outsiders are always precariously perched in a society they don't fully understand, and it can be up one day and down the next. Fortunately, spring was knocking on winter's door, and the Geats had more to do than worry about a dwarf in their midst.

Spring was a busy time of year for the Geats, as it is for every race. Their blood stirred and they were energized after being cooped up all winter. The ice had cracked and, though the open water had frozen over, would crack again soon. If they were to thrive and survive the next winter, they had to be ready to take advantage of every warm summer day given them. The list of preparations was long.

Their fleet of fishing and trading ships had to be re-floated, reoutfitted with mended or newly made gear, and made seaworthy.

Artisans and craftsmen prepared and packed crates with the trade goods they'd been busy producing for the past year: weapons and armor, jewelry, utensils, and so on. The royal complex and Grend were put in order for the horde of visitors that collected there each spring and turned it very nearly into another Truso.

In addition to this annual flurry, Boar-Rover had to be completed so it could be floated at the earliest opportunity and, while its crew learned how to sail it, put to the trial in the fiord and at sea.

The pace quickened as the spring wore on. Men arrived from their freeholdings and farms with trade goods their families had made during the winter, stayed a few days to get drunk and work on ships, then disappeared again to help with the spring planting. Of our crew, Einarr and Asbrand, who were deeply involved with Boar-Rover, were the only ones in constant attendance.

As for me, I was expected to help with Boar-Rover, but was otherwise left to my own devices. Free to come and go as I pleased, I found myself spending more and more time with Ethelred. Time, as it turned out, that was of greater practical benefit than I ever expected.

I liked Ethelred, and we got along well together. He was unlike anyone I'd ever known. Most men I'd thought confident I found merely brash in comparison with him. Much of what I'd earlier taken for wisdom in lesser men I found in his light little more than pedantry. Ethelred was blind and he was ignorant of the outside world beyond the limits of the barbarian nations, and yet knew his own world supremely well. We conducted a mutual school, my knowledge for his, with the difference that I was little more than a chronicler, an encyclopedist of sorts, and he was a teacher.

How Ethelred brought the Northmen's gods to life! How, in the beginning, Ymir the Giant sprang from the water melted from the primordial ice during the conflict between

Heat and Cold, and how he fed off the milk of the cow that had sprung from the Heat. How the Aesir, the race of gods, was formed, and how they slew Ymir, from whose blood and bones they made the earth and heavens. (Dwarfs were made from the leftover remnants. They were wicked, spiteful, loved the dark and cold of caves, and were in nature more like the giants than the good Aesir!) How Odin and his brothers Hoenir and Red Loki crossed the rainbow bridge between heaven and earth and made the first man and woman from an ash and an elm.

On and on, the pantheon of gods and giants and dwarfs, so different from, and yet in many ways similar to, the Greek and Roman gods of antiquity, not to speak of the One Heavenly Father we worship. He told of Father Odin and his eight-legged horse, Sleipnir, and of his two ravens, Thought and Memory (which explained the Northmen's fascination with Amin), who flew out every day and brought him news of the world, and how, in exchange for one of his eyes, he obtained the giant Mimer's wisdom. He told the story of Valhalla, the Hall of the Heroes, with five hundred and forty gates, each wide enough for eight hundred men to march through abreast, and how Odin's nine warrior daughters, the Valkyries, waited on and poured the blessed mead for the brave warriors who'd died in battle on the earth below. He told the story of Kvasir's blood, and how the mighty fortress encircling Asgard, the home of the Aesir, was built. About Idun's apples, and how he who ate of them became young and strong again. About Red Loki, the Trickster, who caused so much trouble in his day, about Balder the Beautiful and Thor the Mighty. Of how Sindri the Dwarf overmatched the black elves' handiwork of golden hair, of Gungnir the Spear, that never missed its mark, and of Skidbadnir, the golden ship that could be folded and put into one's pocket, with wondrous gifts of his own, one of which was Thor's hammer. And of how Loki condemned Balder the Beautiful to death, and for that and his other crimes was himself condemned to be chained forever on a bed of sharp rocks where, with poison from a venomous snake dripping onto his face and driving him mad with pain and rage, he lies to this day.

How pale in comparison, it seemed, were my stories of the gentle Christ. And how Ethelred shook his head in wonder that a god would allow himself to be led like a sheep to an ignominious slaughter!

Ah, Ethelred! How I cherish the memory of that man! To this day, I need only close my eyes and I'm back in his hut where he sat across the fire like a living statue. Amin perched on his shoulder and hung, as did I, on his every word.

"Listen," he said. "Eyes lie. Your ears will tell you as much as you need to know." And he was right, because I learned to hear obstacles in front of me as I walked about in the utter blackness.

"Young men boast vaingloriously," he said. "With age, a man learns how vain glory may be." And, with a chuckle, "And an old man, like me, is too apt to glory vainly in his years. They mean little."

"If you trust a parsimonious man to protect your back, you are likely to find yourself fighting alone."

"Your god is jealous? Jealousy is greed's other face. If the world and all that's in it is his, what more could he possibly want?"

"It's useless to try to bend a strong man to your will. Appeal to the child inside him instead, and he will take your hand and follow you to the end of the earth."

Ethelred's maxims, like any others, could be turned on their heads, but I enjoyed listening to them, and observing the world through his sightless eyes.

Outside, in the meantime, that world continued.

The Geats resolved the problem of Boar-Rover's gender by resorting to the neuter.

A large hole was chopped in the ice and Boar-Rover was floated.

Hugleik, Thyri, and a small party left for two weeks to hold court and determine the blood-debt owed by a thane who had killed a freeman's son near the head of the fiord. Hervarth was left in charge, and two days later had the bad taste to appear at dinner wearing a royal armband. Whereupon Olaf the Silent removed his own warrior's armband and put it on his twelve-year-old son, who'd joined him the day before. Hervarth said nothing, but his face turned red. His arm was bare the next night, and from then on.

Einarr continued his regimen, and to it added twice daily swims in the open water around Boar-Rover.

I woke one night to an unearthly din of cracks and groans. The next morning, the ice on Knar's Fiord was widely fissured. A week of warm weather followed, at the end of which fishermen could work their way through the floes and bring in fresh fish. That night there was a celebration, and the next day runners were sent to summon the Sons of the Boar from home and field.

Spring was on us. Flowers peeped through the snow and the sap ran in the trees. Knar's Fiord thundered as ice-loosened rocks fell, as icicles and sheets of ice and snow tumbled from the heights, as streams filled with runoff and formed hundreds of large and small cataracts. Ships from farther inland called at Grend to take on trade goods and added provisions, and, in some cases, to flesh out their crews.

The folk-hall and Grend were very nearly bursting at the seams with men, all obviously happy to be released from their wintry prisons of home and family and eager to take the whale-road. Old friends renewed friendships, old enemies renewed feuds. Shouts, laughter, boasts, and challenges shook the rafters. Mead at that time of year was in short supply, but they made up the difference with keg after keg of freshly brewed beer. The slave girls were put to the test, and how any of them escaped that (or any other) spring orgy without getting pregnant was a miracle. (Actually, virtually all of them did get pregnant, and every year. Most, however, drank some sort of herbal tea and, in their second or third month or so, aborted painlessly. It was just as well. In the first place, Grend would otherwise be overrun with bastard children, and in the second, the whole lot, the next fall, would be too great with child to service the returning heroes, which, in their eyes, would have been an insufferable inconvenience.) And over and around the beer, sex, brawls, and work, the speculation about the Grundbur, Einarr's expedition, and Boar-Rover was a constant noise from which there was no escape.

As for the Grundbur and Einarr's expedition, not only I but the crew as well, who as Geats could ride a story to death, got so tired of talking about it they took themselves elsewhere when the subject came up. The endless discussions about Boar-Rover were less easily escaped. Everyone had an opinion. It was too wide in the beam. It carried too much mast and sail, and would heel and founder. It was too heavy to be hauled overland. The macabre boar's head insignia with its strange eyes was an affront to the sea, who would take her revenge. And, of course, who ever heard of a masculine ship, this last of which was approached rather more circumspectly after someone asked Ulfberth the Fair if he looked forward to slipping into and riding *him,* and very nearly paid for the jibe with his life. The tide began to turn in Boar-Rover's favor the first time they saw it sail—not one oar in the water—across the fiord in what was very nearly a crosswind, but the arguments persisted until, on its first day in the open sea, it left a half-dozen other ships far behind and then, a vision of awe-inspiring beauty for those who watched and talked about it for days to come, raced back along the coast, heeled over and trailing a long white wake.

I wasn't as much surprised that Boar-Rover worked as that it worked so well. We broke the first rudder and had to design and build a new one, which happily worked well. We cracked a mast, which likewise had to be replaced. Maintaining the correct angle on the sail was at first difficult, but Gurd devised a system of long sticks that helped stabilize the lower spar, and they worked well, with practice. Most of our problems, however, had more to do with the crew accustoming itself to a new type of craft and, indeed, a whole new way of sailing. The Sea-Geats lived up to their name, though, and learned—or taught themselves—rapidly. They were seldom surprised after they'd taken it out ten or twelve times.

One surprise, though, angered them and set their teeth on edge. Here is what happened. For all my experience with court intrigues, I'd decided not to meddle. I saw no point in another encounter with Hervarth, whatever he was up to, and had no desire to antagonize Hugleik. It's a wise winner who knows when not to play again, and I feared I might not be as fortunate the second time. I was an outsider, lacked Einarr's physical prowess, and certainly was no relative of the royal family. Whatever was in store, wisdom dictated that I keep a low profile and sail away when the sailing was good rather than provoke a second confrontation that I might very well lose. So while I understood the undercurrent of tension that prevailed at court, I stopped following the details as they developed day to day. They could go at each other with hammer and tongs, and I didn't care as long as Boar-Rover sailed with me on it. What happened after that was too far in the future to foresee.

The tension had increased when Boar-Rover turned out to be such a spectacular success. Hugleik had feigned a monumental indifference, but the closer our sailing and his burgeoning fear that Einarr could very well return covered with glory, the more his barely concealed antagonism and burgeoning fear for Hervarth's succession flared. As a result, and I was there when he did it, he at last let loose the rat he'd kept hidden in his sleeve. It was a trick designed to put pulling a coin out of a man's beard to shame.

It was a beautiful morning. A stiff wind blew out of the west and, although the fiord was relatively calm, we knew the sea would be choppy as the waves adjusted from the previous night's northern winds. We'd just the day before added Gurd's sail stiffeners, long ash sticks designed to keep the lower spar at the correct angle, and Gurd was explaining how he thought they'd work when Hugleik and Hervarth arrived. We were used to spectators and Hugleik had visited before, so no one took it amiss until we started to board and Hugleik strode forward.

Einarr was stiffly polite as he answered his king's questions. "Yes," he said. "We hope the sail stiffeners will help."

"No," he said, "it won't sail with the wind directly on the beam, but very nearly so, Sire."

"Yes, my lord," he said, "I wouldn't hesitate to take the open whale-road. I believe Boar-Rover would make the crossing from Denmark to the Spit in a day's sail. And from here to Hrothgeirr's domain? Who knows how fast?''

"Yes," he said. "My crew is the best. Stout-hearted and stern men, all."

"But only fourteen," Hugleik said, startling everyone in earshot.

Einarr looked puzzled. "I beg my sire's pardon," he said, "but we are fifteen."

Hugleik paused, raised an eyebrow, and looked us over as we stood there waiting. "I count only fourteen," he said. "And a dwarf."

A lesser man might have been incensed, but I understood immediately that the insult was no more than an excuse for what would follow. Surely Einarr saw, too, for his shoulders stiffened. "Musculus the Dwarf has proven himself as much a man as any other here, Sire," he said, and I credit him for taking my part.

"Oh?" Hugleik asked. "What battles has he fought? Who has he defeated in combat? Where does he hang his shield, and what is his sword's name?"

Einarr's tongue was slow, as I've reported, but even had he been as glib as an ambassador, how would he have answered satisfactorily?

"Who," Hugleik continued, not letting go the advantage, "is his father? What his lineage?"

He hadn't addressed me and I couldn't have answered him if he had, so I don't blame Einarr for remaining silent. Nor, since this contest of wills was between Hugleik and Einarr, could I blame Valgard or the others. In any case, it was evident Hugleik was determined to prevail. Evident, too, it would be foolish to press the issue with so many jealous thanes allied against us.

"It seems apparent to me and to many of these others, Nephew, that your crew lacks a man. Would it not be prudent, then, in the name of safety and good fortune, to add a man?"

Kings are known for using brazen artifices to get their way, but for a Geat to invoke prudence and safety was laughable. Nonetheless, no one laughed, and invoke them he had. Einarr was boxed in, as much by the jealous thanes who'd been excluded from his crew as by Hugleik's arguments. To defy him would be tantamount to revolt, for which Einarr did not have the stomach in the first place—the Battle of the Goose Leg notwithstanding—and knew he couldn't win in the second. His only choice, he told me later, was to try to limit his losses. "My lord sees farther than I," he said, his shoulders tense in anticipation of the name he'd hear. "Perhaps, with his vision, I could prevail upon him to suggest a suitable man to join us."

Hugleik played his role as well as any thespian. "Mmmm." His brow knotted as he considered the matter. "I've wanted for some time to send an emissary to my kinsman, Hrothgeirr, in order to propose a marriage cementing our houses' friendship and common good. Someone, then, who's a warrior and highly born . . ."

He paused to further humiliate Einarr by forcing him to say the name.

I could almost hear Einarr's teeth grind, but he saw it through. "Who better, then, Sire, than your son, Hervarth? He would be a suitable emissary, and could plead his own suit with Hrothgeirr's niece."

Hervarth, the little shit, actually smirked.

Hugleik's voice was iron. "An admirable choice, Nephew. One I perhaps should have thought of myself," he said and, having won, turned on his heel and stalked off.

And that, as they say, was that. The king, which should come as no surprise, had the last word. They very often do. Why else be king?

For wealth, yes, but as enjoyable as wealth is, it's spread and shared, and there are often men whose wealth exceeds their king's.

For power, yes, but as exhilarating as power is, it too is necessarily shared, and how often have the lowliest, through error or malice, brought the highest to grief?

For admiration, yes, but as much as kings love to be fawned over, many other men are admired, too, and a king is as often despised and, though he may be buried in marble and have statues erected in his name, sometimes reviled for generations.

No, the one simple pleasure that a king enjoys from day to day as long as life and power endure, the one perquisite of kingship that he can't afford to share, is the last word. Take away the last word, as Einarr did in the great Battle of the Goose Leg, and he'll fret, fume, and worry until he's debased, humiliated, and repaid your effrontery ten to one. Which is why I was careful not to remonstrate or argue. Who was I, after all, to deny a king his pleasure? If he could prevail over Einarr, who was as nearly his equal as anyone, he'd crush me like an ant. No, kings, like avalanches, are dangerous only when you get in their way. In any case, though the crew didn't see it that way, I didn't see what difference it made if Hervarth shared in the glory since everyone would know he hadn't earned it, so it didn't matter if he accompanied us in the first place, and I had my own pleasures in the second. And of those, I'll mention only one, because later it happened to save my life.

I mentioned Ethelred's great-grandson some time ago. I forget his name, but he was a pleasant lad who, like the novices who take care of me now, saw to Ethelred's creature needs. Happily, the boy admired his grandfather, and spent every moment he could with him. One of their great delights, when the weather was nice, was taking to the fiord in a small dory Egil and Gurd had built and given Ethelred a few years earlier. And when I had the time, they took me with them.

Ethelred, Sea-Geat to his bones, became a different man the second we pushed off from shore. A different man? More like a boy, really. His nostrils swelled, his eyes, I'd swear, twinkled! How he laughed! How he fell into deep, almost holy reveries when the tiny sail sent us sliding silently across the fiord! The water revitalized him, the more so when he took the oars himself. It was like watching a miracle. His sheepskin vest shed, his parchmentlike skin glowing in the sun, he laid into his task and sent us skimming rapidly across the water.

"Careful, careful!" he'd shout, grinning from ear to ear. "Whirlpool ahead! Hang on!" Whereupon he'd dig one oar into the water and, sculling furiously with the other, set us spinning in circles until, roaring he'd save us from a watery death, he straightened us out and continued, within a point or so, in our original direction and straight at the far bank. The first time, I thought we'd pile onto the rocks, but the boy began to beat on the side of the boat with a stick when we were some distance from shore, and Ethelred, by listening to the echoes, turned us away from destruction at the last moment. Then, his fun over, he relinquished the oars to the boy, pulled on his vest, and lay back in the sun, the very picture of contemplative repose.

And what of my fear of the water? I embarked as leerily as ever on our first expedition, as you may well imagine, but my fears were soon laid to rest. Simply being with Ethelred inspired trust. Soon I, too—how amused they were by my early efforts—learned to row straight and true, scull through imaginary whirlpools, charge the rocks, and turn aside at the last moment. Never in my wildest dreams had I thought I could have so much fun on the water, but I did.

Full of politics, practice, and play, the days wore on in their strange combination of frenzied preparation and waiting. Wear on they did, though. The valley greened, one laden ship after another sailed out of Grend, Boar-Rover was declared sea-ready, and so, Einarr announced one afternoon, were we.

The farewell feast that night was monumental, I was told. Told because I wasn't there when they ate, but took myself and Amin off for a last meal and visit with Ethelred. Amin on his shoulder, where he loved to perch, and I across the fire from him, we ate the food the boy brought us and then sat, in the dim light, content to let the silence speak for our friendship and love of one another.

I cherish those few, final hours. Ethelred's calm acceptance of what life offered and took away, his sure confidence in the correctness of fate and his enormous strength of will, filled the hut and instilled in me some small measure of those qualities, gifts I count beyond measurement. At one point, though, I realized he'd dozed off, and it was time to take my leave.

I didn't want to say good-bye. Good-bye was an end I didn't want to admit, or face. As silently as a butterfly landing on a flower, then, I gathered my woolen robe, climbed down from my bench, and started to steal out.

"You've forgotten Amin, Musculus."

I smiled to think those remarkable ears had heard in spite of my best intentions.

"No, my lord," I answered. "He's given himself to you, and so, now, do I."

"I require no gift, Musculus. You of all people should know that."

"So I do. But a gift required is no gift at all, and you of all people should know that."

He chuckled, and raised his hand to stroke Amin.

"So humor me, my lord, and accept this gift from one to whom you've given so many gifts. He'll be happier with you, I think."

"Happier sitting in a smoke-filled hut with an old man? No. He'll be happier soaring over Boar-Rover."

So saying, he touched Amin's legs and transferred him to his wrist. "Go with your master, my friend, and don't fail him," he said, and, with a slight push of his arm, propelled him toward me.

Amin flapped his wings once, landed on my shoulder, and, with a croak, turned to face Ethelred.

"Go, then, both of you," the old man said. "And may good luck on the whale-road, and beyond, be yours."

What remained to be said? Heavy of heart, and secretly determined to leave Amin behind when I left in the morning, I turned to leave the hut that had become almost a home.

"Musculus!"

I stopped in the doorway.

"Don't flaunt me in this, my friend. See that Amin goes with you, because I've seen he'll have need of him."

"He? You've seen?"

"Much. So I repeat: if you'd hear Beowulf's song sung, take Amin with you."

# 18. Of Einarr's New Name, Beowulf, and Our Journey to and Arrival in Denmark.

**1**'ve used the name Beowulf earlier in this narrative, but that night, with Ethelred, was the first time I'd heard it. This is why and how Einarr was also named Beowulf, according to Valgard Halfbeard, who was a young man on his first voyage at the time.

Eggther, Einarr's father, was killed when Einarr was two years old in a battle with the Wendels. At the time, Eggther was in the service of Beowulf (not the Beowulf of this account), the king of the Bright-Danes, and fighting side by side with Hrothgeirr, the old Beowulf's grandson and one-day-to-be king, who saw him slain. When the news reached Vastergottland, Hreithar, Hugleik's father, in honor of Eggther, who had been one of his most trusted and valiant warriors, adopted the young Einarr. Two years later, the ailing Hreithar charged his son, Hugleik, with Einarr's care, and shortly thereafter died. Hugleik took his charge seriously, and took the boy with him on his first state visit to the Bright-Danes. There, Einarr met Hrothgeirr, of course, and heard firsthand of his father's heroism, how he fought valiantly while surrounded, and at last was hacked to death. Old Beowulf, still the Bright-Danes' king, also took a liking to the precociously strong Einarr, perhaps because he saw a resemblance to his own son, Halfdan (Hrothgeirr's father), who was killed in the same battle as Eggther, and was distraught when Hugleik announced their departure. The night before they left, he bequeathed his name to Einarr, to be assumed, he instructed, when the time was ripe. He died not too long thereafter and Hrothgeirr took his throne. To end the story, Hugleik arrived home to find himself the father of a son—Hervarth—and, his jealousy taking instant root, began to disparage Einarr and frowned upon any reference to his other name.

There were, though, those who remembered, and the word spread rapidly when I asked its significance. Miraculously, to my eyes, Einarr became Beowulf, which name I'll use from now on, within hours. The next morning, when we sailed, he too had accepted it, and wore it as proudly as any king his crown.

We left quietly, with no fanfare, as was the custom. I awoke in the dark, dressed in the dark, and left my warm quarters without a backward glance. I thought I was early, but the hall was already bright with light and our crew was assembled. They greeted me quietly, as stern men will when they're preparing to set out on a venture. When the last, Hervarth, arrived, we sat down to a hurried meal. Hugleik entered as we finished and, charging us with delivery of a bundle of ceremonial rune-sticks and other royal gifts for Hrothgeirr, accompanied us down the hill to Boar-Rover.

A small party waited to see us off. Askil embraced his wife and son. Olvir Iron-glove, how poignantly, in retrospect, clasped his bride of two months to his bosom and bade her care well for the child she carried in her womb. One after another, we Sons of the Boar swore loyalty to Hugleik, and begged he remember us when we returned. One after another, we clasped hands with Egil and Gurd, who wished us luck. Their eyes said they wished they could accompany us in the new ship of which they were so rightfully proud, but they were builders, not warriors, and to others the glory for their handicraft.

The sun was still behind the mountains when we embarked and checked our gear, which we'd stowed the day before. What anticipation, then, for one who'd once been terrified of the water! What a thrill of adventures to come as the rowers took their seats and wet their oars and I, the uncounted sixteenth man, took my place in the prow beneath the proud arched-neck boar's head insignia as we pulled out onto Knar's Fiord.

From my perch above the others, I looked back, saw a thin figure in front of Ethelred's isolated and well-known hut, saw a black dot rise from its shoulder and ascend in a tight spiral, heard moments later the wild croak and the whistle of air in wings.

"Ho, lads!" Askil called from his place at the tiller abaft on the starboard rail and pointed. "Our luck is with us!"

The rowers turned in unison in time to see Amin spread his wings to slow his flight, and settle on our insignia.

"What?" Askil roared in good-humored fury. "You've never seen a black bird before? To the oars, you gelded shoats, you misbegotten sons of marsh-monsters and Wendel whores! Stroke! Now, stroke!"

Heads bent to the task, backs and legs strained, and Boar-Rover fairly leaped ahead.

What other send-off than the wind did we need? What other spectator than the sun, rising to pick out our white wake? Stone and pine to port, soft green meadows and valley fields to starboard, the peace and quiet of home that dulls and dries men's souls slipped past. Ahead, the narrow blue-green path of Knar's Fiord led to the sea, where men breathe deeply and come to life. Ahead, the whale-road, which led to adventure and heroic exploits.

I wax poetic and hyperbolic yet again. But, oh, quieted, dimmed, and slowed as I am by age, how that memory stirs my blood! Can any man who's been to sea in a good ship fail to yearn for a deck under his feet and the wind in his hair? Can any man who's sailed rid his nostrils and ears of sea smell and sound, his eyes of the lure of the horizon?

And what, then, shall I say of the moment we passed, like a babe from its mother's womb, out of the calm of Knar's Fiord and into the turbulent world of the open sea?

Grown men, we became, like Ethelred, children again. How we smiled when we found the wind more west than north! What cheers rose from our throats as we raised our sail, and the brisk wind drove us southward!

There, my friends, was a moment, indeed a whole morning! In any other ship, we'd have been forced to row, but Boar-Rover's keel, shallow as it was, resisted the quartering wind that tried to push us into dangerous shallows, onto sharp sea-bones. In any other ship, we'd have been lucky to make twenty miles in a day, but Boar-Rover spun off that many and more before the sun reached its zenith.

I think I've never seen sixteen men more pleased with a ship. The sail bellied stiffly, made pregnant by Niord. The walrus skin lines hummed a low sea-song. White foam spewed from our rudder and left our track across the whale-road. His hair streaming, the indomitable Beowulf stood in our bow and searched the way ahead. Stern-visaged Valgard, posted at his side, scanned the shore on our left where lesser chieftain's mead-halls brooded over the sea-lanes. Proud Askil, his thick legs planted on the steering platform, the tiller under his arm, held our course. Asbrand the Careful prowled fore and aft, called for this line to be tightened, that loosened.

No Geat ever made a faster journey. Preceded by the fierce-countenanced boar's head, watched over from above by Amin, we raced down the coast. We slept the first night on a sandy beach near the mouth of a fast stream, the second aboard Boar-Rover in a tiny, rock-bound cove. On the morning of the third day, the wind holding from the northwest, Askil decided to leave the coast and sail directly for Denmark. Any other navigator would have hugged the coast until he reached the mouth of the Ore Straits, which separated the southern edge of the Geatish lands and the Danish Isles. No other ship or crew would have attempted to cross fifty miles of open whale-road without dire need. Niord and luck were with us, though, and we cheered when, before the sun had fallen halfway down the western sky, purple headlands rose from the watery horizon and hailed our passage, welcomed us to our destination and fate.

Shortly thereafter, rested and eager, we paused to don our warlike gear and raise friendly pennants.

Our arrival did not go unnoticed. High on one of the guardian hills, the sea-watch sounded an early alarm. Again, the ram's horn sent its clear note of warning as we negotiated the narrow passage separating the whale-road from the salt-bay over which the Bright-Danes, the Scyld-ings, held sway. There, we sped across the pristine waters that lapped at the feet of low cliffs and verdant meadows statued with fat livestock. At our journey's end, Heorot lay nestled in the foothills and, high above, the gold-adorned feast-hall, famous in tales, shone on its promontory.

The *scop* who wasn't there recounted high-flown words between Beowulf and the watchman, but was wide of the mark. The truth—and I'm the first to admit it's no crime to bend the truth for art's sake in an epic poem—is that the simple encounter he depicted was in reality more nearly like a communal event with a cast of a couple of hundreds.

Heorot was larger than, but in other aspects much like, Grend. Fishing and merchant ships lay at anchor and docked at wharves to our right. Shipyards with boats and ships in various stages of construction and the usual iron smiths' and wood benders' fires, rope walks, and stacks of timbers lay to our left. An alien ship, especially one as strange as ours, was an event, and we could see laborers, craftsmen, and villagers alike running toward the beach, as well as flashes of sunlight on armor as a troop of horsemen rode down from the hills above. In the meantime, Valgard, who remembered the way, pointed out our landing spot to Askil, and on we sped, our wake boiling, until, at the last moment, Asbrand gave the command. Immediately, the sail-stiffeners were loosed, the lines slipped. A breath later, even as the sail fell, Boar-Rover's keel touched and we drove hard aground onto the sand.

What a babble awaited us, and what a welcome! Greet-ings, questions, and exclamations of wonder assailed us as we threw out our hawse lines. Men stared at the keel that caused Boar-Rover to lie at an awkward and unusual angle. Boys raced around excitedly. Women with children at their breasts and hiding behind their skirts gawked. One and all, they both admired and recoiled from the fierce boar's head with its outlandishly mismatched eyes, then fell back as one when Amin rose from my shoulder and, circling briefly, landed on it.

The crowd must have grown to two or three hundred by then. Beowulf, Valgard, Asbrand, and a few others including me leaped overboard and splashed through the shallows onto the beach. At the same time, the crowd parted to form an avenue for the troop of mail-shirted, visor-helmeted horsemen that emerged from a copse of ash, thundered across a plank bridge over a small stream, and bore down on us. The leader's left arm from the elbow down was missing, but he carried in his right an iron-tipped spear he wielded with authority. His horse was stirruped in the manner of the Mongol barbarians, and was fitted with a mail chest-protector. The high-stepping and arch-necked steed trotted straight toward us, and stopped a spear-length from Beowulf, who faced the beast's master with hands spread in peace.

"I'm the watchman of these Danish shores for our king and ring-giver, Hrothgeirr, son of Halfdan," Hrothgeirr's emissary began as ceremoniously as the *scop* indicated. "You land openly by day, so I don't think you've come to spy or raid, yet neither can I be sure you are friends. You look like and are dressed in the manner of the Wave-Geats, but I've never seen Geats, or any other men, in a ship like this. Speak, then, and tell me who you are and where you're from."

"My name is Einarr, also known as Beowulf, son of Eggther, who is remembered by men as a brave warrior, and who died honorably in the service of Old Beowulf, the Scyldings' onetime king and ring-giver."

An old man, a commoner, stepped forward. "I was Old Beowulf's serving man, and was there when he gave his name to Eggther's son. I remember that day, Beowulf, and I'm glad you've returned, for Hrothgeirr has need of you," he said.

The emissary glared at him for interrupting, but Beowulf held up a restraining hand. "Your memory is keen, old father," he said, stilling the murmuring crowd. "It's a powerful name, and I wear it proudly."

He continued, then, the proud Beowulf, spoke simply and to the point, as was his nature, of Boar-Rover, the fearful boar's head insignia, and the unlikely raven and dwarf that accompanied him. Finally, when the emissary, his troop, and some of the bystanders had asked their fill of questions, and Beowulf, Asbrand, and I, especially, had our fill of answering, Beowulf gently turned to the reason for our visit.

"We've heard, in our land and elsewhere, that a mighty warrior of the night stalks the Scyldings' land, and with slaughter and other bestial acts stains the wooden planks of your lord's folk-hall with the red gore of men. These accounts, which have been sworn to by brave and renowned warriors, make fine fare around a fire at night, but by day strain the imagination."

The emissary, that proud horseman, answered soberly. "The accounts are true, my friend. The vile deeds of the Grundbur—that's what we call him, we don't know what he calls himself—can't be exaggerated."

A smile of satisfaction, twin of the one I'd seen on the day we first sailed in Boar-Rover, crept across Beowulf's face. "Good," he said. "Let's tie up, then, men, gather our warlike gear, and climb the hill to Hrothgeirr's folk-hall, where, if he'll have us as allies, glory awaits us."

To our surprise, the crowd reacted with knowing smiles and the emissary laughed. Beowulf's smile turned into a scowl, and he stepped forward.

"Stay, my friend," Valgard said, quickly laying a hand on Beowulf's arm. "There's more to his laughter than meets the ear. I don't think he mocks you." His eye, the daunting eye of a warrior, took careful notice of the emissary. "Your age and wound, sir, mark you as a man of experience, so you ought to know not to taunt this man, and say what you mean straight out."

The emissary had stood his ground, a brave act when confronted by Beowulf. "I beg your pardon, sir," he told Beowulf. "Your compatriot is right. I wasn't ridiculing you. But how many bold warriors, though none as magnificent as you, I think, have disembarked on this same strand with similar intent? And how many fine ships, though, again, none as fine as yours, have sailed home half-emptied?''

Beowulf, the proud one, blackened with rage. ''You dare to put me, Beowulf, Eggther's son, on the same shelf as men who failed?''

''I'll be honest,'' the watchman said, his voice even. ''I've heard men in Oostergottland, whence I hail, repeat your name and recount your deeds, but hearing and seeing are as different as geldings and stallions. I haven't seen you in battle so I wouldn't taint your courage with unhappy predictions, but fate and luck doom a man, not I.'' He turned to me. ''They say you're wise, Dwarf. If so, perhaps these brave warriors will let your wisdom override their pride. If not, then I wish your companions well, and hope they become no more a meal for the dark and sullen eater of man-flesh,'' and at this, he held up his truncated left arm, ''than I.''

The crowd murmured and our crew shifted uneasily. It was one thing for a man to lose an arm in battle, quite another to hear it had been eaten as well, but Beowulf stood firmly resolved.

''Very well, then,'' the watchman continued with a wan smile. ''Since you're determined, Beowulf and you men, come along with me. Leave your ship, which on my word will be unmolested, and take your war-gear with you as befits honest and proud men. I, Eirik Stone-tooth, will vouch for you at the folk-hall. They'll know how to treat you there, and I think Hrothgeirr will welcome you.''

Eirik Stone-tooth meant nothing to me, but did to Beowulf and the others. Few men in those northern lands, it seemed, had a more illustrious lineage or had won greater renown in battle, and that he'd lost a hand and forearm to the Grundbur gave them pause to think. Not overly long, though, because the Geats, more than most, found it incomprehensible that other men's disasters might visit them, too, and the shining court-hall beckoned with its lure of gore-stained planks and lasting fame.

# 19. *Of a Royal Greeting, and the Ominous Pall that Overshadowed It.*

**M**any men are timid: they lack imagination or inspiration, and epitomize the mundane. They're buried when they die, and that's the end of them.

Some men are bold: they dream and dare, and embrace the unknown. Their songs live on after their deaths, and they are remembered.

What lure, for the dreamer, Hrothgeirr's gore-stained hall! Death lurked there, to be sure, but also life, adventure, and song. The timid had no business in that place.

From the look of most of it, the traveler might think Hrothgeirr's kingdom was one of the most peaceful spots on earth. The beaches were clean, the view around the bay serene. The stream we crossed ran fast and clear, and tinkled merrily. Heorot looked a veritable northern Eden with its neatly kept houses and shops, its verdant meadows and fecund gardens. The villagers following noisily in our wake were lively, cheerful, and boisterous. The Grundbur had neither visited nor caused them harm, but like villagers everywhere I've been they were consumed with curiosity and gossiped endlessly about the lives—and deaths—of the nobles who figuratively and literally lived above them, and ruled them.

We made a colorful procession. Beowulf on a borrowed warhorse and Eirik Stone-tooth on his huge gray stallion led the way. Mail corselets, embossed shields, and iron-tipped spears glinting in the afternoon sun, Boar-Rover's brave crew followed closely behind. In the wake, a quartet of young men carried Hugleik's gifts, and Eirik's troop brought up the rear.

The crowd fell away and its members returned to their daily tasks as our procession passed through Heorot and took the upward, stone-paved path through a kine and rune-stone spotted meadow. Soon we passed between a pair of ancient and holy oaks and into a trimmed forest much like the one guarding the approach to the Geats' folk-hall and at last emerged onto the long-sought promontory near whose apex stood the fabled hall.

The *scop* who described Hrothgeirr's court would probably describe an elephant, if he was ever lucky enough to see one, as large and gray, and let it go at that. I saw only a handful of mead-halls and only two at close hand, but I can't imagine any more splendid. Hugleik's certainly paled in comparison.

Hrothgeirr's was half again as tall and probably as much wider and longer than Hugleik's. The roof was sharply pitched, laid over with clinkered and caulked planks, much like ships' staves. Its frame was of massive, squared timbers set on boulders so they wouldn't rot from the bottom up. The sides were of heavy planking cut with rows of shuttered windows that were opened in good weather, and re-inforced at the corners with iron straps. A deep and faced eave supported by round wooden columns overhung the front. The facing was richly decorated with intricate designs wrought in gold, silver, and amber, and glowed in the light. Under the eave, three wide steps led up to a porch that stretched the width of the hall. The most remarkable of its features were the doors. Wider and taller than Hugleik's, they were made of massive tongue-and-groove oak planks further reinforced with iron bands, and decorated with deeply carved illustrations depicting the history of the

Scyldings in general and the exploits of their king, Hroth-geirr, in particular. There could be no doubt the troop-, feast-, folk-, gift-, and mead-hall was preeminently a monument to Hrothgeirr, who was respected both for his self and for his works.

We were expected, and the main doors were closed. A squad of armed and armored warriors, most too young to be battle-hardened or a deterrent to our experienced crew if we'd wished to force our way in, stood arrayed on the porch. In front of them, an older man wearing a wide gold armband waited to begin the ceremonies until Eirik and Beowulf dismounted.

Man, the laughing, story-telling, cruel, and ceremonial animal, to hark back to earlier descriptions. Mother Church carefully records her ceremonies so they'll be performed correctly and to the letter. The Northmen, though they re-lied on memory alone, were as meticulous. Thus Beowulf was formally greeted and reexamined (though briefly, for-tunately, since we'd have to repeat the whole process in-side) by Hrothgeirr's herald, Alreck the Frightener, who knew—Eirik had sent someone ahead—precisely who he was and why he was there. Thus, equally briefly, Beowulf begged (in a diplomatic sense: I never heard a Geat beg anything of anybody) Alreck tell the son of Halfdan that we came in peace, etc. Thus Alreck assured Beowulf he'd inform the ring-giver that great-hearted visitors carrying a forest of battle-shafts had arrived from far over the fish-field, etc., and return quickly with his answer. Thus, too, we sweated in our iron helmets (yes, I'd been given one) and heavy battle gear until he returned, bade us leave our spears, swords, and shields on the porch and enter wearing our helmets and mail, which latter was a gesture of respect and trust on Hrothgeirr's part. I needn't, I think, repeat the hyperbole that followed our entrance into Hrothgeirr's pres-ence. A court is a court, and royal ceremonies are much the same the world wide.

The Scyldings were lavishly munificent and gracious hosts. Hrothgeirr said he was delighted to meet Beowulf again, and was obviously impressed by the man the boy he'd known had become. He remembered Valgard Halfbeard favorably and (though he hadn't all of them, I'm sure) assured the others he was acquainted with their names and exploits in battle. (He most graciously stretched the case with Hervarth as a mark of respect for Hugleik.) He likewise, when he'd received Hugleik's presents and listened to his scribe read the rune-stick greetings and avowals of friendship, etc., expressed his deep gratitude and love for his brothers, the Sea-Geats, whom men and nations honored, respected, and feared above all others, etc. Finally, the formalities completed, we were invited to remove our helmets and mail vests and, a tainted blessing if I ever heard one, to make their hall our home as long as we wished to stay.

The Grundbur was on our minds, I'm sure, but decorum demanded that any discussion of him be delayed. I wasn't sure why at the time, but later decided it was because the Scyldings were so desperate, and had been disillusioned so many times before, that they simply wanted a few hours of pleasure before we got down to business.

"Tomorrow," Hrothgeirr said when Beowulf broached the subject. "Tomorrow, son of my friend, friend of my grandfather. Today, let us laugh and enjoy ourselves. Let us eat, drink, renew old friendships and make new friends, and for these few hours put our weary cares to rest. Don't worry, my stalwart warrior. There will be more than time enough. The Grundbur won't go away, and you'll have your chance to prove your strength and mettle against his might."

He was right, the wise Hrothgeirr. And the Geats, still blithely ignorant of exactly how ferocious and dangerous the Grundbur was—what enemy, after all, had a chance against even one, much less fifteen Geats?—and, as ever, ready for a party, were happy to oblige.

If the Geats expected a riotous, drunken orgy so typical of their own, they were to be disillusioned. Yes, there was mead, food, and laughter. Yes, the slave girls were there, but so was Urth, Hrothgeirr's queen, the wives of many of his advisors and friends, and the widows, their hair down in invitation, of too many who'd challenged and been defeated by the Grundbur. Yes, there were contests of strength—Beowulf handily, almost yawningly, put down the tenth as easily as he'd put down the first young man who challenged him at arm wrestling, and only Eirik made it a contest with the rest (Hervarth excepted) of the crew. Yes, new friends were made—Beowulf and Alreck the Frightener hit it off like father and son—and the banter and boasting ran as freely as the beer and mead. And yes, even as a slow, cold river of caution ran underneath and sent a chill through the resounding wood floor, I, too, enjoyed myself, though not, thank goodness, in the same way or to the extent I had upon my introduction to Hugleik's court.

Were the Scyldings, the Bright-Danes, more civilized, more sober and serious than the Geats? I wasn't there long enough to know, but it seemed to me that much of the braggadocio, so evident in the Geats, had been wrung out of them. Their best warriors had been slain, dispatched as easily as a man might break a rabbit's neck, and, to make matters worse, often without corpses to mourn or burn. The mightiest of their mighty had been as helpless as Ilgen's child staked out to bait a bear, and they were humbled, as we all may be when faced with an inexplicable and implacable evil. The Grundbur had tempered their enthusiasm and, forced onto a more philosophical path, they seemed more like Ethelred than Hugleik, more like Martina than Thyri.

Hrothgeirr and Urth both epitomized and symbolized the Bright-Danes. Hrothgeirr was perhaps ten years older than I, taller by two hands than anyone else in the folk-hall, and posed a strikingly regal figure with his full beard and long, graying blond hair. There was nothing hurried about him: his speech was measured and laconic, his movements fluid and confident. The questions he asked me were succinct and intelligent.

Hrothgeirr was known in his warring days as Madlaugher, and I was told brave men had shivered with fear when they heard his wild, maniacal laughter coming toward them in battle. He'd mellowed with age, but I sensed, under the gentle front he presented, a restrained wildness that could break out at any moment. Age had slowed him, but hadn't eroded his courage. He, too, had faced the fury of the Grundbur, and wore his sword, Blood-Song, broken on the impenetrable skin of the monster, as a reminder he wouldn't rest until the foe of foes was vanquished.

Urth was a natural queen. My age at least, and probably older, she was tall, thin but buxom, and still a great beauty. No Norse goddess, I think, could have vied with her regal splendor when Amin, whose friends were previously limited to Ethelred, Valgard, and me, perched of his own accord on her shoulder and, as black as night, made her piled hair glow in contrast like spun gold. Gracious and soft-spoken, she complemented Hrothgeirr perfectly, and I think he would have been at a great loss without her.

Much has been made of the pedestals men raise for women. Urth was a woman made for a pedestal, and a tall one at that. She greeted Hervarth as if he were a man tested in battle, and brought out the best of whatever there was in him. She immediately donned the heavy silver and amber bead necklace Thyri had sent her, and wondered aloud how she should match such a beautiful and precious gift. She complimented Beowulf without making any of his crew feel a lesser man, and bestowed a cordial welcome on each of us as we bent our knees to her. A special favor, she held Valgard's hand in both of hers while she admonished him for staying away so long, and she drew from both Olaf the Silent and Ulfberth the Fair, those men whose souls and hearts were as cold and hard as ice, what very nearly passed for blushing smiles. And need I say she won a dwarf's heart? Credit where credit is due: I was, in her presence and as we talked, as tall, fair, and handsome a man as any other. Smitten, I elevated her to a pedestal as high as Ilgen's, where she remains to this day.

The sun was in Cancer and the days nearly as long as the nights had been in the dead of winter. Busy at the high table—a dwarf who kept a pet raven and who came from a distant land of which they'd heard only rumors was a rare bird in Denmark—I'd talked more than listened, and had little time for myself. Eventually, though, I excused myself to visit the urine vats, which were kept outside during the warm months, and, when I was finished, walked alone toward the edge of the promontory.

Behind me, the folk-hall glittered in the slanting evening sunlight. Far below, a lone fisherman rowed across the dusk-purpled water, cut an arrow into the green-circled bay that lay as placid as a mountain lake. The sky in the east was the dull gray of old, wet leather, and from the west, streaming almost to the zenith, long feathered clouds glowed the dull red of a blacksmith's forge.

How could a Grundbur, be he man or monster, stalk a place of such pristine beauty? Hrothgeirr's vanity was monumental, but in a land where vanity wasn't counted a sin and, indeed, was as ubiquitous as trees, I saw no reason why his kingdom should be singled out. On the contrary. I heard no one fault him, save for his bad luck. He was considered a good and wise king. He was unyielding in the tributes owed him by other rulers, but was generous to his own people and ruled with an even hand. He and his thanes were no more (or less) bloodthirsty than any of the other Northmen. His freemen prospered and his slaves were well treated, with the exception of the few he'd sacrificed (mercifully, by the account I heard) in an attempt to placate whatever evil being had visited the Grundbur's wrath on the Scyldings, and to restore their good fortune and luck.

Puzzled, I made my way back to the folk-hall, where I stood on a bench, propped my elbows on a windowsill, and read the book that lay before my eyes. There were few surprises. Servants bustled through the hall with trays of food and drink. Hrothgeirr's sons (I forget their names), as is ever the case with a strong king's sons, regarded Beowulf with deep suspicion and, though they'd never have dared to do so to his face, made derogatory remarks about him to each other. His niece, Gytha, a vacuous, cow-eyed girl of perhaps fifteen, appeared suitably impressed by Hervarth, who actually, as unnecessary as it was, appeared to be courting her, though I couldn't imagine why anyone would want to. Beowulf, his massive shoulders being massaged by one of the young and beautiful widows, was deep in conversation with Alreck. The rest of the crew, eager for fresh conquests, had chosen willing companions for the evening, much to the disgust of Hrothgeirr's young nobles, who until then had the widows to themselves. And above

the fray, perched on a wheellike candelabrum that hung
from a high beam below the hall roof, Amin looked as if
he'd been sent by Father Odin to watch over the proceedings.

He looked, too, disturbed, bothered by the gathering he
watched so closely. First on one foot, then the other, he
shifted his weight back and forth. His head jerked nervously from side to side, not so much watching as, I could
tell, listening. Immediately on guard, I became even more
suspicious when he failed to heed my hand signal to come,
and noticed and obeyed me only after I whistled.

"What's wrong?" I asked, once he'd landed on my
shoulder.

His croak was a raven's whisper, and he didn't hone his
beak on my hair.

"Is there danger?"

Neither positive nor negative, he shifted his weight,
looked over his shoulder into the gathering dusk, and back
to the crowded feast-hall.

Nothing was wrong, something was wrong, and I hadn't
an emperor's back to read. Everything looked normal. Head
to head, Hrothgeirr and Urth conversed privately. Hervarth
still wooed. Egil Blackbeard threw back his head and roared
with laughter. Beowulf stood, picked up a bench with one
hand, and held it at arm's length. The young nobles snorted,
but said nothing. And Amin, wise bird, croaked again,
touched my eye, and with that touch brought back Ethelred's sage advice.

"Listen. Eyes lie. Your ears will tell you as much as you
need to know."

How right he was! Unencumbered by the mask of sight,
my ears heard a great division of humors. The Wave-Geats,
my noble companions, were feast-happy. Their laughter
rang true, their smiles were carefree. They drank their mead
as men should, blithely and with gusto. Those who had
found a slave girl or enthusiastic widow had taken her outside in order not to offend the refined Urth, but all had
returned, for hearing and seeing, as Eirik had said, were as
different as stallions and geldings and, having yet to face
the unknown, they believed themselves indomitable.

The Scyldings, on the other hand, were ridden with fear and tension. Their laughter was brittle and edged, and rang with hollow falsity. The young thanes were sullen, their voices thick with anger and frustration, with conspiratorial mutterings against Hrothgeirr and the other old men, whom they blamed for the ill luck that lay like a pall over their lives. The unrest and simmering discontent was as visually evident when, informed by my ears, I reopened my eyes. The Scyldings' smiles looked like comedic masks worn by actors. Their movements were jerky, like stringed puppets. Their eyes darted nervously from window to corner as the shadows lengthened and deepened. They looked over their shoulders. Their backs were stiff. Their legs and arms were taut, as if they were ready to push away from their tables, leap over their benches, and flee. The victims of monumentally bad luck, they looked more like captives than free men, prisoners taken after a battle and penned tightly, unsure what the next moment would bring—death, dismemberment, terrible wounds that would never heal.

What relief, then, washed over their faces when a horn sounded and Hrothgeirr rose. Immediately, the folk-hall stilled, and faces turned to the high table.

"The long shadows darken the land, friends, and it is time to quit this luck-stricken hall. As always, let the shutters remain open and the doors wide, so whatever visitor comes by can see the folk-hall is empty." The Sea-Geats couldn't conceal their astonishment at the unheard-of curtailment of the festivities, and Hrothgeirr raised a hand to still their murmurs.

"Time enough for explanations tomorrow, you brave guests from across the white-flecked fish-field. For tonight, we invite you to shed travel-weariness and be merry and carefree. Take your weapons and your armor, and go one and one with the long-haired woman of your choice. Each, in the safe haven of our outer houses, which are well supplied with food and mead, will be courteous and generous."

The words were spoken gently, but weighted with urgency and dark warning. The response was outside my experience. Couples left precipitously. Servants ran about collecting plates, cups, and platters, and spirited them away.

Not sure of what to think of the aura of fear that enveloped the hall, my travel-companions stood as if struck, and then, suddenly infected themselves, hurriedly moved to gather their weapons, and allowed their companions for the night to lead them out.

I vaulted into the folk-hall and made my way to Beowulf, where he stood looking defiantly around him. "Take her and your weapons and go, my lord," I said. "He means what he says."

"That Sea-Geats should hide in women's beds?" he asked scornfully.

A widow I'd talked to earlier approached. "It isn't for a woman to tell you," she said, moving aside some rushes to uncover a dark stain on the plank floor, "but please, lord, see you all that's left of a man who scorned to know his enemy before he lay in wait for him."

Beowulf bridled, but I stayed him. "Perhaps our host, and this woman," I said, "speak wisely." Amin croaked loudly from the windowsill, rose into the air, and flew to me. "He, too, is nervous. There's more to this than meets the eye."

"You think I'm afraid to face him now, tonight?"

The woman, whose name was Bera, I now recall, was as bold as she was beautiful. "It's said, Beowulf, that an opponent who leaves behind no more of his enemy than a stain on a floor deserves even the sternest warrior's respect."

Beowulf's face grew thoughtful as he stared at the gorestains. When he looked up, his and Bera's eyes met. "Perhaps you're right," he said. Then, in a quizzical, almost shy tone, he noted, "Your hair is down."

Bera's smile was a secret waiting to be told. "As is the custom, my lord."

Tentatively, like a boy, he who was accustomed to taking whatever woman caught his fancy offered her his arm. "Will I go with you, then?"

Bera hesitated, then, with downcast eyes and in all modesty, laid her hand on his arm. "If it pleases you, my lord Beowulf."

Ah, Beowulf the courtly gallant! Love's *scald*, his defiance cooled by ardor, he gathered his tools of war and allowed himself to be led away.

Hrothgeirr breathed a sigh of relief. So, too, did I as Urth stood and laid her hand on his arm. "Quickly, now, friends," he said, turning to escort his queen out, "before lamps are needed, and attract the unfriendly one."

"Unfriendly but not unsought," Beowulf said, pausing in the doorway for a last look at the rapidly emptying feast-hall. And a last word. "For when we meet, we'll see whose arm is strongest, and whose blood stains the hall floor."

# 20. Of Burned Steel, Slaughter Detailed, and the Skeptical Geats Convinced of the Grundbur's Ferocity.

We met in solemn conclave early the next forenoon. The hall was cleaned, but otherwise unchanged from the night before. Servants carried platters from the outside summer kitchens and dispensed the morning meal. Hrothgeirr's young thanes ate silently and hurriedly, then gathered in small knots to mutter and grumble. Our crew, some still half-asleep, sat together and compared bedmates while they ate. Beowulf alone, of the fifteen, was moody and pensive. Silent and withdrawn, introspective, he dabbled at his food and avoided conversation. As did I, and not only because I'm not given to describing what I've done in bed with a woman or comparing the one I had to another's, but rather because the Scyldings' home, after the excitement of our welcome, had drawn my interest and I took that time to inspect the feast-hall more closely than I had the evening before.

The interior was, if anything, more resplendent than the exterior. Deeply carved and lushly painted scenes from the lives of the Northmen's gods decorated the walls. Among others, Odin received the draught of wisdom, paid for with one eye, from the wise giant, Mimer. Thor hurled his hammer at a cowering foe, while the lovely Frea bestowed an apple of youth on an aging god. The Fenris wolf struggled against his dwarf-crafted bonds—and Red Loki, bound eternally to his sharp bed of rocks, writhed in indescribable agony.

The effect, though, was flawed. Here and there, the wood was newer, the paint brighter, and the carving less detailed. Whole boards had been replaced, giving a skewed, out-of-joint appearance to many scenes. I didn't have to look far to find other repairs. One of the five candelabra was new, two more had been rebuilt. Three or four tables were virtually new, as were fully half the benches. Some of the wall sconces differed from the majority. The iron hinges and many of the bands reinforcing the doors showed shiny spots where they'd been reforged. The overall impression was of patched opulence, as if the manifestations of Hrothgeirr's wealth had been attacked—beaten, broken, smashed.

Had Beowulf or any of the others noticed? Would they have cared if they had? I doubted they had, or would. Similar repairs were necessary as a matter of course at the Geats' feast-hall, so they in all likelihood shrugged off the damage. Which made sense, to a point, but the extent of the damage, especially to the hinges and iron reinforcing straps, indicated violence on an order of magnitude greater than that which could be attributed to boisterous rowdiness. Any possibility that my reasoning was flawed was laid to rest when Hrothgeirr and his councilors entered and bade us join them at a long table, at the head of which he stationed himself.

"You were treated courteously and slept well, I trust, friends, so we'll put these courtly niceties aside. We have serious business to discuss, and we'll be open and honest with you, and answer your questions to the best of our ability. Alreck will speak."

Hrothgeirr's second-in-command, Alreck the Frightener, was a formidable man. Nearly Hrothgeirr's age, I'd guess from his graying hair and gnarled and scarred hands, he was shorter than most of the men there, but built as sturdily as a boulder. His voice was as deep as any I've heard, and rumbled like distant thunder in his cavernous chest. Of note, a new scar lined his head and face from where his left ear should have been to the corner of his mouth.

"Stories of the Grundbur have brought you here. Eirik Stone-tooth has told you these stories are true, but truth, as you know, comes in many shapes and faces." He stopped as Beowulf stood and glowered at him. "Our friend, Beowulf, wishes to speak?"

"Words," Beowulf sputtered, at a loss for them. "Words!"

"The noble Beowulf, son of Eggther," Valgard said, rising to explain his friend's frustration, "means we slept well on soft benches last night, and have no desire to be put to sleep on these hard benches by droning words. You are famous warriors whose arms speak plainly. Let your words be as to the point as your swords."

A diplomat as well as a frightener, Alreck took no umbrage. "The Sea-Geats are din-hasteners, a noble trait. Very well, then. The Bone-muncher we call Grundbur, he who harries and attacks us at night, first came here five half-years ago."

He went on, the rumbler, the noble Alreck, and though I don't recall his exact words, no man who heard him could possibly forget his harrowing message.

Two and a half years earlier, as he said, on midwinter's night, the folk-hall was ablaze with light and mead flowed freely. Then there were bright eyes and bawdy laughter, for fate and luck, as they supposed, smiled on them. They had harried well on the continent that year, and returned home rich with silver, goods, and slaves. Their king and ring-giver had extracted tributes from many chieftains and, with his coffers overflowing, was unstinting with gifts.

They discovered fate had turned on them and their luck had changed when, that night, without warning from man or dogs, the doors burst on their iron hinges, an icy, foul-smelling wind extinguished the lamps and candles, and, in the darkness, men and women screamed and died. The Grundbur had come into their midst, and when he left, the lamps they lit illuminated a grisly scene. No trace of two men and a woman could be found, of one man, only his

head remained, five more were dead, seven were grievously
wounded and would soon die, and another half-score were
wounded seriously.

"One against a hallful?" I recall Valgard asking in
astonishment. "No one fought back?"

"We, at the time, as do the Geats at home to this day,
hung our swords and knives, our spears and axes, on the
wall behind the high table." Alreck's shrug was eloquent.
"The sudden darkness, the stink of rotted flesh, the bone-
chilling wind, the thunderous battle-roar, louder than any
man's, and the choking, eye-stinging cloud of ashes from
the fire caught us unprepared. There was consternation.
Men sought their weapons, but tripped on benches and ran
into tables, into women trying to flee. Then the unmistakable spray of blood, the death cries, the ugly voice that was
no voice! One man alone, one whom we never saw again,
whose bones we never found, reached a sword. We found
it after the foe left: the blade was black and twisted, no
longer a blade but a useless, brittle piece of burned iron."

The tale of the Grundbur—what tale wasn't exaggerated
by the Northmen?—while we huddled under the sheltering
Spume-Spear, and during the long winter months of preparation for the journey to Denmark, was plausible enough,
but an account from the mouth of a man who'd survived
the carnage was as incomprehensible to us as the attack
itself must have been to the Scyldings. Some said they must
have been attacked by a raiding party, but when they lit
torches and ventured outside, they found only a single set
of footprints in the snow. Then there was indeed consternation, and fear, too, for the prints were of unshod feet
unlike any they'd seen before.

There was no sleep that night. The missing were
mourned. The dead were examined. One had died of a broken skull, but the others were horribly maimed—one dis-
embowled, others with faces ripped away, huge gouges
bitten out of their flesh, appendages torn from them, strips
of flesh dangling. Two more died before dawn, one a
woman whose time had come when, rather than lose the
child, too, they cut it from her womb. Five hovered on the
brink of death.

Everything about the onslaught was, and remained, a mystery. No one knew who the foe was, or where he came from. His spoor—readily visible and accompanied by a trail of blood—led to a deep mountain lake named Grund. Prior to the foe's arrival, Grund had been known for its beauty and sleek, fat trout. Since then, the trees at its edge had sickened, and some had died. Cold mists lingered there year-round, men caught a chill in their bones if they ventured too close, the evil smell of rotting flesh permeated the air, and animals—deer, horses, dogs, and birds—refused to go near it. Rumors about the lake abounded. In the early days before Grund was well known as a luckless place, a wanderer had camped on its shore one night, and swore he'd seen a creature dive into it and disappear. Another said he'd seen monstrous snakes and other unknown creatures swimming in it. Like any other lake, it froze over solid in the winter in the old days, but from Gyrth's Mount, where it could be observed from a safe distance when the mist lifted, it was seen to have waves year-round, and not to freeze.

Details about the creature were virtually nonexistent. Its name, if it had one, was unknown, so they called it Grund-bur, which meant Grund-dweller, and appended Bone-muncher, Blood-drinker, Night-stalker, and a variety of other names. Neither could anyone say what it looked like because it always attacked at night and the wind that accompanied it blew out the lamps and candles and raised a cloud of dust. Sentries were posted to watch for it after the first attack, but the practice was discontinued when it either made its way past them unseen or slaughtered them. Most people thought it was large, but an obstinate few swore it was quite small and compact. Some said it was furred, others scaled or armored. One woman, who lived on an outlying farm where a cow was taken in the only known attack outside Hrothgeirr's feast-hall, swore it looked like a giant dwarf (!) and was accompanied by a companion she took to be a female from its swollen belly and dugs, which she'd seen in profile as she cowered in the snow.

The questions and answers went on well after the sun reached its zenith. No, it wasn't known what had happened to the sword, but from that and other incidents, the Grund-bur was known to be impervious to metal weapons. No, it wore no armor—some said it went naked, like an animal—and it used no weapons other than teeth and claws. No, one couldn't predict when it would come: it sometimes appeared as often as twice a week, and sometimes stayed away for two or three months. Yes, men of renown, warriors known for their bravery and prowess in battle, had come to Heorot and climbed the hill to contend with the foe. We'd seen Eirik Stone-tooth's shortened arm, and he was only one of many. Rorik Double-ax, Starketh the Devastator, Ottar People-mower: they and more had pronounced their boasts, kept lamps lit and stern vigil, only to meet the same fate as so many lesser men.

Dejection was written on the Danes' faces. Hrothgeirr looked tired and worn. The proud Alreck the Frightener's shoulders slumped. Eirik Stone-tooth's stump was a silent, grisly testimony as it rested on the table. Quiet, the Sea-Geats looked from one to another, none wishing to voice the growing skepticism that gnawed at his breast.

"We, as do you, see the world as it is and take that which is given us for good or ill," Alreck finally said to break the silence. "We, as are you, are reasonable men, but there are black arts that reach beyond sight and reason." He paused and looked angrily at me. "The wise dwarf smirks. You disagree, Dwarf?"

I was courteous. "You speak of magic, my lord," I said, rising. I walked to the head of the table. "What's this?" I asked, pulling a piece of cheese from Hrothgeirr's beard. "And this?" I asked, startling Eirik by producing a coin from his ear.

"Tricks," I said, "that the uneducated think are magic. I don't believe in magic, because all the magic I've ever seen has sooner or later been revealed as nothing more than the sly productions of clever men."

"And you'd deny, too, there are creatures of darkness that are not our kind?" Alreck asked.

"I would," Beowulf spoke up. "We speak of elves and goblins, of gnomes and witches, but who has seen one? I've heard tales of trolls and monsters all my life, but al-

ways from *skalds* and old women late at night around dying
fires. I believed them, but believed, too, they were stories
of an earlier time when gods and giants walked the earth,
because no one I knew had ever seen or battled such a
creature. Every man I know has fought only other men—
perhaps a bear or a wolf, now and then. Some men were
larger, stronger, faster, angrier, or more ruthless, daring, or
clever, but each was indisputably a man. Cleave him with
a sword, pierce him with a spear, hew him with an ax, he
bleeds, he falls, he dies.''

Hrothgeirr's eyes, pale gray and fierce under bushy white
eyebrows, glared at Beowulf, burned with anger at the challenge, the implied accusation of exaggerations and lies.
''You think a *skald*'s song stains a floor with blood? That
a toothless old woman's tongue can bite off and eat a man's
arm? That we're babes to run from any mere man?''

Beowulf stood his ground. ''I don't accuse,'' he said, his
words slow and considered. ''I wonder.''

Hrothgeirr's elder son stood and moved to his father's
side. ''And I wonder,'' he said with a sneer, ''if your wonder is fear.''

The blood drained from Beowulf's face, but he con-
trolled his fury. ''I spare your life out of respect to your
father, who's a gracious host. But never again say Beowulf
fears. Anything or anybody.''

The young man was brash. ''I've heard, Beowulf, that
during the spring flood two half-years ago, you spurned
Brykk Roar-speeder's wager to race the swollen Vistula
because it was too dangerous, and he alone breasted the
flood.''

''That is true,'' Beowulf answered. ''And Brykk himself
discovered how dangerous when he dove in and tried to
swim across. Not twenty paces from shore, a floe struck his
head, and he sank. He would have drowned, too, if this
man you don't dare openly call a coward, this man who
knows the difference between courage and stupidity, hadn't
braved those frigid, racing waters, dove deep to find him
in the murk, and hauled him to safety and life.''

Hrothgeirr's son's face reddened. ''Brykk himself said—''

"Brykk Roar-speeder is a liar," Beowulf interrupted, "and in proof, hear my boast. The next time I see him, I'll take the life I saved that day in the Vistula, for he's no longer a friend of mine, and his lies have made him my enemy."

"That would be a fight to see," Alreck rumbled. "A live man against a dead one." He went on to answer Beowulf's unasked question. "He arrived here just before last winter's first snow, Beowulf, widely proclaimed his boasts, and perhaps his lies, and—"

"There's no perhaps," Valgard interjected. "I was there, climbed down the bank, and tied a rope around the half-drowned liar when Beowulf pulled him to shore."

"And Askil and I hauled him, like a dead pig, up the embankment," Asbrand added.

Alreck nodded. "Very well. Widely proclaimed his boasts and his lies, and died the next night. We found his half-eaten body discarded halfway between here and Grund Lake."

A heavy silence lay over the folk-hall. "Eaten?" someone finally asked, his voice uncharacteristically thready.

"His body-cave emptied—heart, liver, intestines gone—at which point we suppose the creature was sated, for he'd carried off four more the same night."

"And none of them fought him?" Beowulf asked.

"All fought," Alreck rumbled. He pointed to the side of his head and face. "That was the night he gave me the hate-bite that took my ear and tore my face."

"Fought him with what?" someone asked.

"Everything we had," the Frightener answered as Hrothgeirr nodded assent. "Armed to the teeth, we lay in ambush for him, and our weapons, all of them, were turned." His voice grew bitter. "We might as well have asked a girl to piss out a forest fire."

Beowulf leaned to Asbrand and Askil. Ulfberth and Olaf conversed intently. The feast-hall buzzed, and in the buzzing, Hervarth alone had the wit to stand and ask, "And may we, my lords, see those weapons?"

"Of course," Hrothgeirr said, gesturing with a raised hand. Immediately, two boys standing behind him ran out, and a moment later returned with a chest they set on the table.

"Look, then, you skeptical Sea-Geats. What say you when you see"—and here he opened and upended the chest on the table—"the remains of Scyldings'-Song, Bear-Slayer, Skull-Cleaver, Elves'-Magic . . ."

The litany of names—ten, twenty, I don't remember—of famous swords continued while we stared at the burned, the charred, twisted, and blackened remains. In that moment and with that sight, seeds of doubt sprouted in me, because I couldn't conceive of a trick clever enough to produce that ruination. The Geats' skepticism, I could tell, shriveled apace. The Grundbur, whatever he—or it—was, may well have belonged to a time when gods and giants walked the earth, but also belonged to our time. And in that knowledge, the first tendrils of fear began to wrap themselves around our hearts.

# 21. *Of a Mighty Battle, and a Grundbur Defeated.*

Lowering clouds, raging winds, an impending storm would have more suitably matched my mood. Having pushed Beowulf and his companions to seek out the Grundbur—albeit he and they probably would have anyway—seemed in hindsight to be absolute folly. I smelled and tasted doom. Amin had been nervous that morning, and had since disappeared. My stomach was sour, my bowels loose. I'd dreamed badly during the night, and was plagued by recurring images of black destruction. Everything I'd seen and heard since our arrival in Denmark led me to believe my machinations and manipulations—Musculus the malicious Wasp God, on a broader scale—would lead to disaster. No amount of courage could overcome my stupidity.

The Geats, had I expressed these fears, would have disagreed loudly, at length, and derisively. Not that some of them didn't fear, because I'm sure they did. The Geats, as all Northmen, believed in trolls, ogres, marsh-monsters, and dragons the way Christians believe in Satan and demons, which is to say they assumed and accepted their existence, but never suspected they'd come face-to-face with one in the flesh. The distinct possibility that they soon might was a daunting prospect to be considered with no small degree of trepidation. But heaven forbid one of them should voice or otherwise express such an emotion! Oh, yes, they put on a brave front, but I, if no one else, heard the fear behind their boasts.

"The only defense is absence!" one laughed. "Have the Danes become women?"

Did I detect a wistful yearning to be absent? I think so.

"His battle-roars turn the blood to ice. Pfaugh!" another sneered. "Are the Wave-Geats to run from a noise?"

Not run from, perhaps, but worry about, I could tell, because if men like Eirik Stone-tooth and Alreck openly admitted they'd been frightened, there must have been some substance to the matter.

"We should have come last spring or the spring before," a third lamented. "Think of how many more men would be alive to sing the praises of the indomitable Sea-Geats!"

Perhaps. But perhaps, too, the hollow tone I heard behind the fulsome words masked a sigh of relief that he'd been elsewhere—and might prefer to be elsewhere again.

More troublesome were those who clearly relished the challenge set before them, for one man's foolish courage is often a more cautious man's death. Asbrand, Askil, and Valgard, among others, had the good sense to realize that what they'd asssumed was only smoke was instead a raging fire, and tempered their boasts. Ulfberth the Fair and Olaf the Silent, though, were ready, even eager, to place themselves in harm's way, and would wade into battle with the Grundbur without hesitation. And the others—Hervarth especially—were dragged along by their cocksure belligerence, and their fear of being thought cowards.

One, of course, needed no dragging. One surpassed the others in his readiness to meet and contest the foe. One had staked his good name on his ability to defeat the one no other could defeat. No longer would he have to fear the innuendoes of slowness, of clumsiness and ineptitude. That night, the next night—soon. Soon, the moment would come when he could bask in song and glory.

The sun, high in the sky, beat down on our bare torsos,

beaded us with sweat. A zephyr high in the trees rustled the leaves, murmured soothingly, counseled rest against the long night coming. Far below, diamonds sprinkled the blue bay in which a trio of dolphin-specks leaped and cavorted, at whose northern end lay access to the wide world, the whale-road where I wished I was spearing the waves in Boar-Rover.

Not a cloud in the sky. No deadly omens crying to take heed, warn caution, foretell disaster. Only, with a rush, Amin slipping through the trees and landing at my side, rousing me from my torpor.

"Where have you been?" I asked.

He bobbed his head, hopped toward me, then away.

"Is there danger?"

He spread his wings, looked over his shoulder in the direction of Grund Lake, and did not hone his beak on my hair.

I sat up. "The Grundbur?" I asked in a whisper.

He didn't answer, of course. Instead, he hopped onto my shoulder and, pressing himself close against my head, stared intently at Beowulf. Beowulf the Bold, also called the Clutcher, his mighty torso gleaming white in the green grass, his features composed as he slept and, no doubt, dreamed of the coming battle.

Did the wind blowing down from the highlands bear the stench of rotted flesh, or was it my imagination? The day had dragged on interminably with its eerie combination of torpor underlaid with tension and anticipation. Hrothgeirr and Urth, with their councilors and thanes, had gathered with us for the evening meal. The mead flowed sparingly, voices were hushed. Beowulf, with Bera at his side, talked quietly with Alreck. His voice rumbling like an ancient volcano, Alreck told tales of the old days of his youth when he was nearly as strong as Beowulf. Listened, too, as Beowulf talked, uncommonly frankly, about his demon.

"You're right," Alreck said when his young friend finished. "They'll whisper no longer. But keep in mind your distinction between courage and stupidity. You believe greatly in yourself, as a man should, but I tell you the difference between the two is slight when it comes to the Grundbur.''

''And no difference at all once the fight starts,'' Beowulf said, ''for the man who thinks and fights at the same time, dies.''

Alreck shook his head knowingly. ''Exactly. Save in years, you and I are much alike.''

''Then the years will make the difference,'' Beowulf said, his belief unshaken.

''I hope so,'' Alreck said. ''But keep in mind, too, he did this in a wink,'' he added, touching his ravaged face. ''I know a man fights his own fight, but listen to me. Don't let those hands near you. They're more dangerous—he's a mightier foe—than you can imagine before you've faced him.''

Beowulf chewed on the thought. ''I've spoken my boast,'' he said at last. ''If the Grundbur's a greater warrior than I, so be it. There'll be no shame.''

''None,'' Alreck agreed. ''But some sorrow, I think.''

Beowulf met Bera's gaze, put his arm around her, and pulled her to him. ''Lucky the man who is mourned by a beautiful woman,'' he said.

''True,'' Alreck agreed again. ''But luckier by far for her to have no need to mourn.'' He extended his hand. ''And with this, may all the luck be yours.''

Their hands clasped in friendship.

Beowulf smiled. ''Musculus, here, says a man makes his own luck.''

''And so he does, if he's stern enough, and determined.'' His face creased, and laughter rumbled out of him. ''Ah, Beowulf, we should have been born of a time, and on the same side. Alreck the Frightener and Beowulf the Clutcher. That would've been a pair! Side by side, we'd have hastened a din or two, eh? Plowed a swathe, eh?''

No doubt they would have, I thought, half listening, half keeping my mind on the rest of the hall. They went on, the Frightener and the Clutcher, until the sheer black silk of shadows slipped silently through the open windows and, a slowly rising veil, masked the last rays of the setting sun.

Night, with its somber duty, was on us. Urth herself, a

queenly gesture, passed among us with a large cup, and when we'd drunk, she and the other women—how poised and dignified, the fearful Bera—took their leave. Soon after, the horn sounded and the solemn Hrothgeirr rose, and king and thanes alike passed among us to clasp our hands in solemn ceremony, and withdrew. The time had come for boasts to be fulfilled.

We hadn't wasted the entire day basking in the sun, and were not without plan or weapons. We piled the tables along the wall opposite the door so we wouldn't stumble on them in the dark. We set the benches along the walls, cleared the floor of anything someone might trip over. Thorfinn laid a fresh fire in the cleaned and scrubbed fireplace, and lit the pot of oil he'd prepared. We removed metal armbands and necklaces, and donned heavy oxleather corsets and leggings, hot though they were. As the last light faded, we bolted the great doors and, with the exception of Thorfinn, who would keep the watch, armed ourselves with clubs, nooses, and fire-hardened ash spears and daggers, and lay down to get what rest we could.

The nights were short at that time of year, and I woke with sun in my eyes. The Grundbur hadn't come. And so, with a combination of disappointment and relief, we waited out another day—and one after another, four more uneventful nights until, during the heart of the fifth, the foe struck.

We were, having become accustomed to our vigil, sound asleep when, with a suddenness that took the breath and set the heart racing, the great doors splintered, an icy, fetid wind swirled through the hall and extinguished the lamps and candles, and the foe was among us with a beastly, deafening roar.

Instantly awake, the first thing I saw was Thorfinn pouring his burning oil on the laid fire. Just as the tinder caught, the foe's battle-roar was punctuated by a man's shriek, and a heartbeat later, something—Olvir Iron-glove's head, as it turned out—flew through the air and struck Thorfinn with such force that he pitched torso down on the first licking flames and smothered them.

What followed was as confusing as Ilgen's fight with the bear, or any other battle I've seen, so the account I render is a combination of what I saw, heard, and felt, and what others later said.

As he'd requested, the men had given Beowulf the honor of first engagement and, ready for battle, his cry vying with the foe's and ringing off the rafters, he took the middle of the floor and bellowed his challenge. Fleetingly, silhouetted against a window, a massive manlike shadow lurched forward to meet and grapple with the hero, Beowulf the Clutcher.

Beowulf had met his match at last, for the first time had found a worthy foe. So, too, the Grundbur, I believe, for when else, by all accounts, had any mere man held him for longer than a heartbeat? Never, I think, has the world seen such a struggle as theirs. The advantage went first to the Grundbur, by reason of his forward rush, but was lost when Beowulf caught his arm, stepped to one side, and twisted the arm behind his back. That advantage, too, went for naught, for the foe was fast and, spinning free, caught Beowulf's wrist.

Face-to-face, hand-to-wrist and hand-to-wrist, the two titans were locked in a death grip, neither able to move the other. Their breaths whistled, their feet were planted firmly as if rooted in the floor. Circling them, crouching, ready to leap, we kept our distance, waited for the leader's word.

"Valgard!"

That one word, that break in concentration, gave the foe the advantage. Pressing forward, he pushed Beowulf back, his arms high. But to no avail, for Valgard was already charging with his ash spear leveled, felt it strike and bite the foe's side. Howling, the Grundbur let go Beowulf's wrist, swung with his free arm, and with that mighty clubbed fist smashed Valgard's shoulder and sent him spinning across the floor and into a wall.

Valgard was wounded, incapable of continuing, but he'd turned the tide. The advantage regained, Beowulf caught the foe's right wrist with both hands, jerked it down, and pulled his arm behind his back at the same time as the rest of us joined the battle.

"I've got his arm!" someone yelled, and for his effort was flung into the rafters.

Somehow, I forced my way through the press of bodies, swung my club at what I thought was the creature's leg, and felt the shock, as if I'd hit a boulder, clear up my arms and into my back.

Askil, in the meantime, had managed to get a noose around the creature's left arm, and he, Olaf, and one other were holding on for dear life while being whipped back and forth.

"Get his feet!" Beowulf roared. Low as I was, I grabbed a leg and hung on with my left arm while stabbing what I hoped was his Achilles tendon with my wooden dagger.

The hall rang with the shouts of men and the foe's anguish and battle-cries. How describe the sounds he made? Not words, as we know them, but dark, foul utterances, the precursors of words. Unformed curses, evil bellowings, spewed hatred, vile and loathsome, that, as Alreck had said, curdled the blood and sent raw fear coursing in veins and bowels.

But we persisted, even began to make sense out of chaos, for Thorfinn had recovered and, with remarkable presence of mind and selflessness—any Geat's instinct would have been to join the battle—had somehow rekindled the fire.

Beowulf's feet were planted again, his hands gripped the Grundbur's wrist, and, muscles bulging, he had pulled its right arm back and ever higher. "His feet!" he yelled again over the tumult. "Get his feet!"

Still busy on his left leg, I caught a glimpse of Egil Blackbeard struggling to tie a rope around the Grundbur's right ankle. Successful, he passed the long free end over his shoulder and, standing, ran away as fast as he could and jerked the Grundbur's leg out from under him.

Everyone except Beowulf, it seemed, fell in a heap. The Grundbur crashed facefirst onto the floor. Egil, as the Grundbur's leg came out from under him, likewise fell in the opposite direction and, I later learned, knocked himself unconscious. Momentarily pinned by the left leg—I was suddenly aware of how hairy he was as his thigh ground me into the floor—I wormed my way out from underneath him.

Askil and the others kept hold of the line on the foe's left arm and, though being thrown about, generally rendered that arm ineffective while Ulfberth beat its shoulder with his club. Beowulf towered over the creature, held its wrist in a death grip, and slowly pushed its straightened arm upward over its head. And though its strength was phenomenal, nothing could have withstood the pressure when I leaped on the foe's back and plunged my wood dagger under the upraised shoulder bone.

What iron wouldn't do, wood accomplished. Once the muscle tore, however slightly, Beowulf's power was enough to spread the damage. Bone cracking, tendons, cartilage, and muscles tearing, Beowulf forced the arm straight forward onto the floor. Kneeling, then rolling over his own shoulder and standing again, he twisted the arm in a full circle, and, thrice repeating this process, tore the arm out of its socket. The skin and flesh twisted into a thick rope. Blood flew, the creature roared in agony. Then, his own battle-cry ringing in the rafters, Beowulf pulled straight up on the arm, leaped into the air, and slammed his feet into the creature's back. Two more turns, and the flesh shredded and popped, and the arm was torn completely off.

Was any creature ever so enraged, so maddened by pain and the knowledge of imminent death? Formidable almost beyond belief from the moment he'd entered the folk-hall, the Grundbur's howls of fear and fury were as painful as blows to the head. Thrashing wildly, a creature uncontrolled, he bit into Ulfberth's leg and stood and hurled Askil and his helper tumbling like wind-driven leaves across the floor and into the wall.

I fell off his back when he stood, grabbed his leg, held on as he lurched away from his tormentors and ran drunkenly toward the door, and was finally knocked off him by the splintered remains of the door frame.

The battle was over. And though I was unconscious for some time, they said they could hear the creature's screams of agony reverberating through the hills as he fled toward Grund Lake, and his certain death.

# 22. Of Celebration, and Unexpected Vengeance.

We'd earned the celebration that followed. The Scyldings, from Hrothgeirr and Urth to the most miserable *thrall*, poured into the killing-hall. I revived on a table. My head pillowed on a widow's lap, I lay on a soft sheepskin. My ox-hide armor had been removed, and willing hands bathed my scratched and battered face and the deep bruises covering my torso. Lamps and candles, hundreds it seemed, brightly illuminated the scene, and I heard laughter, praise, and boasting as I sat up and tried to make sense of my surroundings.

The hall was a shambles. One of the chandeliers had been turned into kindling. A hole gaped in one wall, and a ceiling timber dangled. Blood spattered the benches, tables, and floor. Quickly, I asked the fate of my companions.

Olvir Iron-glove was dead. Decapitated, his bloodless torso, missing an arm, too, lay reunited with his head on a table in a place of honor. Next to him, also dead, lay the noble Asbrand, my friend, who'd been thrown through the wall.

Valgard Halfbeard's arm and shoulder were shattered.

The breaks had been impossible to set properly, pieces of bone had pierced the flesh, and he'd lost a great deal of blood. His condition was precarious, and he'd been taken to one of the outbuildings where the Scyldings' healer, an old lady, was attending him.

Thorfinn, entering the fight late, had had a finger bitten off.

Egil Blackbeard broke his nose and one cheekbone when the Grundbur and he fell in opposite directions, and looked as if he was wearing a black mask to go with his black beard.

Olaf the Silent had gotten the creature's blood in his good eye and was blinded, we hoped not permanently.

Ulfberth's leg was broken and had a chunk bitten out of it. Splinted and bandaged, he was weak as a child from a loss of blood.

The rest of us were battered, bruised, scratched, and burned, evidently from the creature's blood. Beowulf alone was unscathed save for a deep bruise circling his right wrist where the creature had gripped him, and a series of smaller and odd bruises on his hands and arms where, in his effort, small veins had burst.

As for the Grundbur—ah, the Grundbur! A trail of black blood darkened the porch and grass where he'd fled toward his home beneath the waters of Grund Lake, it was supposed. And in the agony of his flight, hung from a beam where all might view it, left behind his right arm.

Olvir Iron-glove and Asbrand were mourned, but they'd died warriors' deaths, and honorably. Even as dawn broke, stonecutters from Heorot had been set to work carving their commemorative rune-stones, and boys sent to fetch wood for their pyres, which Hrothgeirr had ordered heaped with furs, metal vessels, weapons, silver pieces, and, on each man, a gold-beaded necklace, suitable honors for valiant, esteemed warriors to carry and wear as they strode proudly through the wide, welcoming portals of Valhalla.

The *scop,* I think, might have given more credit to these men, as well as made more of the celebration that commenced with dawn and continued the day long. Every man, woman, and child—free and slave—from Heorot was in-

vited to enter, praise the heroes, and gaze upon the mighty
Beowulf and the awesome, fear-inspiring arm of the Grundbur.

And oh, how they stared, how they shuffled forward for
a better look, backed away in alarm, as if the horned claws
at the end of that mighty arm still held powers they didn't
trust, and might strike them, tear their flesh! And who could
blame them? I, myself, though I'd clutched the foe's leg
and drawn his blood, avoided it as I would have a plague.
The arm hung from a noose at the end of a leather rope.
At the shoulder end, stiffening shreds of skin, muscle, and
sinew were black with dried blood. The arm was more than
a match for Beowulf's. The upper part was as thick as a
man's thigh, the lower long in proportion to a normal
man's, and knotted with muscle. The skin, during the day,
changed from the pale gray of fine wheat flour to very
nearly black, and was thickly endowed with coarse black
hair that, according to those who dared touch it, was nearly
as thick as pig bristles. The hand was the most impressive
I've seen in my life. Twice the size of any other—even
Beowulf's—it was like and unlike a human hand, like and
unlike (I've seen them, so I know) an ape's hand. Its fingers
were long, the knuckles prominent, and the nails thick and
horny, claws but not claws. Perhaps, as was commonly
thought, it was a troll's, but I wasn't then and still am not
prepared to agree or disagree. Suffice to say it was unlike
any other I've seen, and remains, to this day, one of the
unsolved mysteries in a long life.

The celebration, however, like an ellipse, had two cen-
ters, and if one was the Grundbur's arm and hand, the other
was Beowulf, who deserved the gifts, praise, and adulation
heaped on him. The Grundbur was as fearsome a creature
as the world has known, and that Beowulf stood grip to
grip with it and held his own testifies to his courage and
heart, to his unflinching will and strength of character as
much as to his phenomenal grip and power. And if that
weren't enough, I add the observation that it takes a strong
man who knows what he's doing to sever an arm the size
of the Grundbur's: that Beowulf actually ripped it from his
body defies belief. Interestingly, I thought he'd boast, strut,

and play the hero, but he was subdued, modest, and more attentive to Bera, who virtually glowed with pride and love, than to the accolades heaped on him.

We all received gifts: the grateful Hrothgeirr opened wide his treasure chests. Silver in abundance, in exquisitely crafted coffers, was allotted to the slain men, to be returned to their families. To fourteen of us, then, appropriate largesse: finely wrought weaponry; rings, armbands, necklaces of gold and silver, intricately carved amber, and precious jewels; saddles and bridles; furs and bolts of fine cloth; and sundry other items. Even Amin was given a gift for being one of us: a bowl of mackerel eyes, which, to shouts of approval, he attacked with gusto before, sated, he carried away the last few to hoard somewhere in the rafters.

But of all the gifts, Beowulf's were deservedly the most lavish. The *scop* who sang of the ring-giver's munificence mostly erred, but did mention a helmet with a wire-bound rim that was exceedingly strong, and horses. And oh, such horses! The best the Danes had to offer, one was a match of the fabled Bucephalus, a proud stallion named War-Strider with flashing eyes and a high step, massively well proportioned, a steed fit for the greatest of warriors. (How we were to transport them in Boar-Rover was a mystery to me, but Askil assured me we would.) Urth herself placed on his arm an ancient armband she said once belonged to Ing, a legendary early king of the Danes from whom they derived one of their tribal names, Scyldings, or friends of Ing.

How Hrothgeirr's court was revivified as a result of our victory! The creature—didn't that grotesque hand prove it must have been a troll or other unnatural being?—was dead. The black arts, in whose relentless spell the Scyldings had been gripped, were thwarted. Good luck had replaced bad, and their world was a better, brighter place than it had been for five half-years. Cheer replaced doom. Not a frown could be found. The young thanes, relieved of their gloomy life and the prospect of unsung death, put aside their surly faces and sullen conspiracies, and gazed with unstinting, openmouthed awe at Beowulf and his Geats, and even me.

Oh, that was an afternoon to remember in this, the December of my life! Mead flowed like water from an artesian spring. Venison, whole roast boar, and great slabs of whale meat oiled the tables, greased our hands and chins. Forgotten the sidelong, cautious appraisal of the dwarf who, for that day at least, was as much a hero as the others. How many times did I recount my role—hacking at the foe's leg, climbing his back and driving my dagger under his shoulder bone, the hot blood stinging my hands and arms—to the blonde, busty, and willing maidens and widows who lavished me with the gift of caresses.

Beowulf and Bera left to be alone. As for the rest of us, when Urth and the noble ladies obligingly retired to private quarters, who were the ravishers, who the ravished? To the victors go the fair, and I played a willing role in the frenzied orgy that followed, but that I forbear describing in detail. Enough to say that sexual frenzy seems to feed itself, and we partook until we were limp with exhaustion. How the day ended for the others, I don't know, but the last I recall is being carried off by two women, being bathed in a large tub of cool water, then being carried into another building and laid on a bed.

I awoke sometime later to battle-shouts and cries of alarm. Groggy and disoriented, still somewhat drunk probably, I struggled out from between the two women, ran outside, and joined the dim figures, armed and as naked as I, running through the starlight.

The folk-hall was a scene of confusion. Naked, mead-touched thanes and women wandered about in a daze. What had happened unfolded piecemeal, and when the pieces were assembled, they told a grim story.

The Grundbur's female (we supposed) had entered the hall and attacked them. Not as ferocious as the Grundbur, she was nonetheless formidable. Men had seized weapons to attack her, but she was as swift and deadly as they were drunk and disorganized. And before they could stop her, two young thanes lay severely wounded, and she had fled. Not, though, without wreaking a full measure of vengeance. For missing too, carried off and not to be found, were Alreck the Frightener and the Grundbur's arm.

# 23. *Of Alreck's Return, the Scyldings' Utter Demoralization, a Dwarf's Contempt, and Beowulf's Struggle with Himself.*

**A**lreck greeted us when we approached the narrow defile between a pair of large boulders choking the pass to Grund Lake. Not in words, to be sure, nor in his entirety. His head alone, facing us, had been driven onto a stake. His eyes were wide, his lips pulled back in a sneer, and the familiar scar turned from red to white as snow.

Hrothgeirr and Beowulf, side by side on their mounts, stared at it in silence while the rest of us closed ranks and reined to a halt. "We'll take him back with us when we return," Hrothgeirr said, showing no emotion. "Let's go."

We were willing, but the horses plunged, reared, and tried to turn back, so we at last tied them and set out on foot. The path descended sharply and into a cold mist that, as related, chilled us to the bone and hid, that day, the surface of the lake until we were very nearly at water's edge.

What is there about a place that engenders fear? I've wandered battlefields on which the dead lay as thick as ripe and rotting olives under an untended tree, and the moans and cries of the wounded and dying stirred a wind on the still night air, and not been affected. I've groped my way alone through, and eaten my lunch in, ancient catacombs filled with bones under the streets of Rome and thought none the more of it. I've slept soundly in passage graves where the souls of the dead are said to linger.

Grund Lake, on the surface, differed little from any other lake I've seen. The air was cold, true, but we were in a mountain depression that received scant direct sunlight. The water was a little less blue than normal, perhaps, but blue enough, and unmarred by the twisting backs of serpents or other monsters. I saw, contrary to earlier reports, no dead trees. The air was still—no birds relieved the heavy atmosphere with bright songs—but Amin seemed unconcerned, even bored. Yet the horses had refused to approach, and I, as the others, from their nervous glances, sensed a maleficence that weighed on the soul.

"Grund Lake," Hrothgeirr said, as if we needed to be told. "No man knows how deep it is."

Depth alone is meaningless. A dwarf can drown in a puddle.

"They swim down to their home?" Beowulf asked, though we'd been told so.

"So it's reported," Hrothgeirr said. "Some animals have underwater entrances to their homes. Would you risk it?"

Beowulf sat pensively. I nudged Amin, and pointed. Immediately, he lifted off my shoulder and soared low above the water across and around the lake. Our mouths wide, as if we expected a hand to emerge and snatch him from the air, we watched in silence. Soon enough, a quick tour sufficed, he reclaimed his perch on my shoulder and honed his beak on my hair.

"His signal that all is safe," I told Hrothgeirr, and added, heeding the nameless fear in my gut, "at present."

Heraclius could be devious. There came to him, on occasion, certain important prisoners of state who were too stubborn to be broken by torture. These he imprisoned under trying conditions in isolated cells, from which they were taken at unpredictable times, subjected to prolonged but not life-threatening torture, and then returned. One day, for no apparent reason, these men were unchained, given a small purse of silver for their trouble, and released. Invariably, they exulted in their freedom and rushed to home, concubine, the baths, whatever. In a few days, however, just as they began to slough their cares and believe in their good fortune, a squad of soldiers descended on them, summarily executed someone—anyone would do—near and dear to them, and removed them to a court of interrogators who accused them of abusing the emperor's clemency, and sentenced them to harsher conditions than those under which they'd earlier suffered. One and all, in anticipation of the same horrors they had previously withstood so stoically, they were unmanned, and broke like dry twigs rolled over by a cart wheel.

So it was, I mused after we returned to the Folk-hall with the sorry trophy of Alreck's head, with the Scyldings. Suddenly and unexpectedly relieved of the horror that had stalked their lives for five half-years, and that they'd confronted courageously and stoically, they exulted in their freedom. The lines of fear and worry that creased their faces were smoothed, and smiles and laughter replaced frowns and sullen grumbling. Their luck was restored, their future bright. They cavorted like colts, ate and drank without heed for the morrow, lay with whoever would have them as often as physically possible, and, with self-satisfied sighs of contentment, flopped down to sleep in their own folk-hall instead of ignominiously creeping off to women's beds in outer buildings. Their nightmare was over—and no sooner did they sleep than it descended on them anew.

Heraclius would have smiled knowingly at what followed. The Scyldings, predictably, had I thought to predict, were utterly demoralized. Not sure which way to turn, they walked around in aimless circles or simply stared into the distance. Of them all, only Hrothgeirr (and, of course, Urth) and Eirik Stone-tooth rose to the occasion with calm counsel and measured responses to the disheartened young thanes, but even they, I could tell, were shaken to the core after the grisly discovery of Alreck's head.

The Geats, too, were more frightened than I thought they'd be. Only one of them had seen her, but that one was

Sigtrygg, who was noted for his keen eye and sound judgement. His description, which in the Geats' minds super-
seded a half-score widely varying ones given by the young
thanes and the women, lacked the slightest hint of exaggeration. He'd been drunk like everyone else, he said, and,
upon waking, had gone outside to use one of the urine vats
when the female entered the folk-hall. He'd heard a guttural
roar, like that of a bear, perhaps, which was followed by a
scream, then a series of confused shouts amid general
clamor. Naked, half-asleep, mead-befuddled, and caught in
midstream, he'd staggered to a window to see what was
happening.

He thought, at first, the Grundbur had returned, had
somehow grown a new arm, for the creature inside the hall
stood with its back to him, its arms outstretched, and each
hand holding a man in midair. "I thought I was dreaming,"
I recall him saying, "caught in a web of elf-magic. Until,
suddenly, she brought her arms together and crushed both
men head to head, then, with a howl, leaped into the air
and tore the arm from its high mooring."

She landed facing him, and if, the night before, he'd been
too busy fighting the Grundbur to be frightened, such
wasn't the case with the female.

"She was terrible to behold," he said, his speech halting,
as if he found it difficult to believe his own words.
"There's no doubt she was a female. Her dugs were heavy
and sagged deeply over her distended belly. Her skin was
dark—not black, but not fair, like that of our women. Her
hair was long and matted, like seaweed caught on an oar.
She wore no clothes, but she was covered, I think—I
couldn't be sure—with dark hair. Her face, though . . ."

Pausing, he shuddered, and avoided our eyes. "Perhaps
she is a troll, or worse. Her face was hideous. Her nose
was large and hooked like a crone's, and I'd take my oath
she had fangs like a sow's that she bared when she saw me
staring at her. The worst, though, were her eyes. Her eyes
. . . glowed . . . like . . ." He faltered, the precisely spoken
Sigtrygg, unable to finish the sentence. "Never before have
I felt such hatred," he finally said in a near whisper.
"Never before such . . . fear."

No one moved or said a word. Each looked within himself, kept his own counsel. None admitted it as such, but I could smell the aroma of their fear over that of my own.

Hrothgeirr's intrusion into our circle was a welcome diversion, at first. Accompanied by Eirik Stone-tooth, who supported him with a hand under his arm, his face was ashen, and he had aged. He sat heavily, the troubled king, and announced he hadn't slept. "I'm weary," he said. "I've laughed scornfully at fear all my life, but now I'm troubled, and fear, like a devouring worm, coils inside my body-cave and sucks the life-force from me."

The Northmen, so disdainful of fear, were stricken by an epidemic of it. Like a plague, fear was no respecter of the brave, and infected the most highly born and courageous of them. The Geats were no less susceptible than the Scyldings: once one of them succumbed—actually said the dread word aloud—the disease raced through the rest and, because they were ashamed, they averted their eyes from Hrothgeirr.

The silence grew. Beowulf and his Geats were Hrothgeirr's only hope, but to ask for their help, I could tell, would be to plead, and plead he could not. At last, he pushed himself to his feet. "Half my hoard," he announced brusquely, his voice choking with shame. "Half my treasure-hoard of silver and gold, of weapons, jewels, and women, to those who rid my kingdom of this scourge."

No mention of fame, as he stalked off. No mention of reputations to be won, of boasts unquestionable, of respect, of awe, of songs sung by *skalds* for years to come.

"We have silver and gold," one Geat said.

"And weapons, jewels, and women," another added.

Ulfberth shifted, arranged his splinted leg more comfortably. "Two dead, one blind, and who knows if Valgard Halfbeard will ever fight again," the subdued one said.

"Four out of sixteen," Egil Blackbeard reckoned. "And two more useless for battle until they heal."

Askil stood, pounded the table. "A man! Any man, any men! But these are creatures from Niflheim's icy pit, I tell you!"

Hervarth spoke, he who would be king. "And how many

more in their cave under the lake?'' His voice was smooth, flowed like warm mead. ''Must we share the dead ones' bad luck? This is Hrothgeirr's fight. We overcame the Grundbur's magic. We fought bravely, and were victorious. What more can be asked of men? I say our fates are ours to decide, not Hrothgeirr's. If he and his people have offended the gods, let the punishment meted out by the gods be theirs. We've done our duty. Any more would be to confuse courage and stupidity. I say we mourn our dead, and sail for home.''

He was clever, the scion Hervarth. I'll give him that much. His ''we,'' that elicited nods of agreement. His inclusion of magic, that set my blood boiling. How cleverly he parroted Beowulf's distinction between courage and stupidity, how adroitly included the gods in his rhetorical equation! How kinglike—oh, yes, I give him that, as well— to sense and voice what others thought, to give them an excuse to act badly when it served his interest.

Forgotten my misgivings about leading the Geats to disaster. Forgotten my resolve not to antagonize the son of the crown. Angrily, I stood and signaled to Amin, who dove from his perch in the rafters and landed on my shoulder. ''Alreck the Frightener, a warrior worthy of his name, and a friend,'' I said, my voice choked with contempt. ''Asbrand and Olvir, renowned warriors and our table- and ship-, our battle- and mead-companions. Haven't I been told it's better to avenge a friend than mourn him? I didn't think I'd ever hear words of such shame from a Geat's mouth, or that it would be a dwarf's duty to say as much.''

Hervarth's face, I saw as I turned to leave the folk-hall, turned white as chalk. Later, I heard that Askil had stayed him when he started after me, for which I was sorry, because my hand was on the hilt of my dagger—the good steel one, not the wood—and I'd have welcomed the opportunity to humble him further with his own blood.

Beowulf found me sometime later at my favorite spot, where I'd taken to sitting and, that high noon, at least, thinking how much I wished Ethelred was there to share his wisdom with us. ''What are you doing here?'' I asked, echoing another time when one of us joined the other over-looking another, bleaker vista.

He lay down beside me on his belly, rested his chin on his hands, and gazed out over the bay. "You were right," he said, "and shamed us with your words."

"Then I shouldn't have, because I'm as frightened of the female as anyone else," I admitted. "The truth is, I was angry. I don't like Hervarth, and like less his slick words. They're half-truths, easily spoken, and turn my stomach."

"Perhaps so. But the fact remains, it's better to avenge than to mourn."

"Forget it. You have a woman, now. Enjoy her for a while."

"I want to. But how?"

"Just do it. The others won't help, and if the Grundburs are trolls, it'll take more than one man to kill her."

"That's my opinion, too." Beowulf shook his head. "I don't know what to think, Musculus. We were very lucky with the male. Now he's taught her, and she'll be prepared for us."

"Taught her?"

"If he went as far as we followed his spoor, surely he gained the safety of their lair before he died."

"She could have found him dead, and carried him."

"We would have seen that. No. He returned alive." That was likely enough, when all was said and done, but Beowulf had more on his mind. "The eyes," he said, abruptly changing the subject. "Sigtrygg was right. The eyes were the worst part." He actually shuddered, the indomitable Beowulf. "Hot and cold at the same time. Like ice, like a glowing auger, drilling hatred into a man's soul and kindling fear. I matched him grip for grip, but his eyes . . ."

Astonished, I thought for a moment that Beowulf, of all men, might actually weep. Hardly daring, yet compelled to, I prompted him. "His eyes?"

He spoke carefully. "We speak of good and bad men. The good we praise and call companions. The bad we hunt down and kill. But he, and the female, from Sigtrygg's words, are more than merely bad. They are . . ." He searched for a word, and settled for a helpless gesture.

"Evil," I said, using the Latin because I knew no word in their language for evil.

He looked questioningly at me.

"A badness that exists of itself," I explained poorly. "Utter corruption that hates and would destroy anything good or beautiful, and soils everything it touches."

Beowulf chewed on the thought. "I've never known anything like that," he said at last. "Have you?"

I had to think about it. "No," I finally decided. "But I've known men and women in whom evil resided, who took evil as their consorts, so to speak."

"So have I." He rolled onto his back and squinted into the sky. "Tell me, Musculus. Do you think they're this . . . evil you speak of?"

"I don't know," I said. "For all my fine words, I don't know if that's possible."

Agitated, he rolled back, sat cross-legged, reached to one side, and plucked a long piece of grass. "If this much of the grass were evil," he said, holding it so only the tip was exposed, "would you destroy it?"

"No," I answered.

"Because then you'd have to destroy all grass, as you'd have to destroy all men. And this much?" he asked, revealing a quarter part of the blade.

"Probably not."

He went on to a half. "And this?"

"How would you know what was half? It would depend."

"And this? Would it, too, depend?"

The grass, held by the end of the stem so virtually all of it hung free, swayed in the light breeze spilling over the cliff from below. "No," I said. "But it would take a true hero to face such a one."

"Yes," Beowulf agreed. "I think so."

Pensive, he chewed on the grass. Pensive, too, I pondered the difficulties faced by philosophy when it's stuffed into an all-too-real sack of practicality. Evil is one thing when discussed in cloisters by gentle men, quite another when a Grundbur's female lurks beneath a nearby lake.

Beowulf the Clutcher, awkward in his role as a thinker,

mused. "If a man wins an arm-wrestling match, is he said to be a hero? No. If he defeats another in combat, is he? Often, yes. But what's the difference? The fear of death? Yes; but what if he doesn't fear? And why should he, since Valhalla waits?

"A man enjoys lying with women, and he enjoys battle. Is he a hero for lying with women? No. Is he a hero for enjoying battle? Often, yes. But if he enjoys both equally, why is he a hero for one and not the other? I don't know." He fixed me with his eyes, the brow-furrowed one. "You're wise, Musculus. What's the answer?"

"I don't know, Clutcher. I've never been a hero."

Beowulf shrugged. "You were when you helped defeat the Grundbur, so perhaps it's easier than you think. But even though men will tell you I stood face-to-face with him, and held him, and tore his arm from him, I'll know I had help, that the arm first tore with the bite of your wooden dagger. When all is said and done, I won an arm-wrestling match, without fear, and for reward. Do you know what I think, Musculus?"

"What?"

"I sought fame all my life. I wanted to be counted the equal, the better, of my father, Starketh, old Beowulf, the legendary Ing himself. Now I will be, and now I know what old Beowulf meant when he told me a man becomes a real hero only when he stands face-to-face, soberly, with his fear, and stares it down without thought of riches, fame, or the eternal delights of Valhalla."

What should I have said? That old Beowulf was a wise man? That he was a windbag, and Beowulf would be better off forgetting such oft-repeated platitudes?

"I'm frightened, Musculus. My blood runs cold with fear. Am I man enough to stare down this fear? To confront this . . . evil?"

He wanted an answer, the querying Beowulf, but I equivocated. "Many men are man enough in the light of day overlooking a blue bay," I said, "but few, I think, are, in a Grundbur's lair."

"Yes." Beowulf rose, turned his back to the bay, and peered upward into the hills and toward the place where his destiny awaited him. "And you?" he asked.

Thank God he didn't look at me, for I couldn't have faced him. "I?" My face, I'm sure, reddened with shame, but no fool, I, and no hero, either. "I'm one of the many, my lord. Only one of the many."

Silence, for the longest time. At last, Beowulf sighed and shuddered, as if awakening from a trance. "Very well, Musculus," he said.

Did I hear sorrow in his voice? Disappointment, rather, that echoed my shame.

"Tonight we honor our dead friends, and send them on their way to Valhalla. Tomorrow, then, I'll go alone," he announced, starting back to the folk-hall. "Tomorrow, to the Grundbur's lair, where my fear waits for me."

# 24. *Of the Grundbur's Deep Lair, and a Mighty Battle.*

The sun was high when they arrived. They rode in silence. Beowulf, flanked to his right by Hrothgeirr, to his left by Eirik Stone-tooth, trailed by his wounded and sullen thanes who'd refused to go the final step with him (Ulfberth and Olaf would have, but couldn't), led the way on War-Strider. Purposefully, looking neither to left nor right, up nor down, the fear-seeker rode, urged his mount upward to the crest, beyond which, nestled malevolently in its deep depression, lay Grund Lake.

No, I didn't accompany them. I was neither welcome nor comfortable in their midst after the Geats, the day before, had blamed me for Beowulf's imprudence. Even Hrothgeirr, when he learned the hero would go alone, paled and looked askance at me. Never mind that Beowulf had insisted the decision had been his alone: I was out of favor once again and, wisdom being the better part of valor (no Geat, I), I ate in solitude and silence, slipped out of the folk-hall, and, with a small jug of mead and Amin my only companions, took refuge for the night in a tack room next to the stables. There I slept and reconsidered, and was up and gone, unseen, before first light.

They stopped at the defile. Unable to see them from where I lay hidden, and not caring what they had to say, I slipped silently downhill, signaled Amin to join me, and took a position behind a tree where I could see but not be seen. I didn't have to wait long. Soon enough, the distinctive clink of mail wove through wind sound, and Beowulf appeared alone on foot.

How noble, in his isolation, he appeared as he strode to the water's edge. He wore leather boots, the thongs wrapped around his calves. An ox-hide shirt and skirt overlaid with dull gray ringed mail covered him from neck to midcalf, and protected his arms. He wore, too, the boar-crested helmet with the brass nose-guard Hrothgeirr had given him, so his eyes, cheeks, and hands alone were exposed. At his belt he wore daggers, both of wood and double-edged steel, a club of hardwood burl and a double-bladed, short-handled ax. At his side, the ancient sword, Bone-Bane, said to have been forged by the Black Dwarfs and once wielded by Ing himself, hung sheathed in fine leather intricately worked with a confusion of intertwined foxes and ravens, bears and boars, and dragons, too, with fiery breath.

He was, I saw immediately, in a quandary. How, after all, should he (who, remember, had boasted of swimming heavily laden a hundred miles in a storm-tossed sea) swim laden with that armor and those weapons, but how face the unknown without them? Hesitant, then his decision made, he'd just begun to remove his weapons belt when I stepped out of hiding.

"No need to swim, my lord, for that isn't the way."

Like a statue, he stared at me, the astonished Beowulf. "Ah," he finally said. He tightened his belt. "I wondered where you'd gone."

"But didn't think here."

"I'm sorry," he said, the apology as rare as virtue in a slave woman. "No."

"I don't blame you," I told him. "I astonish myself." I pointed across the lake, touched Amin's breast. "Ethelred said you'd have need of him, and he was right. Amin found the entrance. Over there, in a jumble of boulders. Come. I'll show you.''

Bright sun came and went with the clouds as we walked north along the narrow and pebbled beach toward a deadfall of trees that masked a low but vertical cliff. ''People thought he swam down because he entered the water here,'' I explained, doing the same. ''There's a shallow ledge, though, that leads around this cliff. Careful. It's slippery.''

Slippery, indeed, but passable, as I'd discovered earlier with the help of Amin's keen eye. In file and hugging the cliff, we sidestepped—hip deep for me, calf deep for Beowulf—through the cold water. At cliff's end, we stepped into momentarily deeper, then rapidly shallowing water, emerged on land once again, and sat on a log.

''And your fear?'' Beowulf asked as the water dripped off us.

''Oh, it's here,'' I assured him, touching my belly. ''Healthy as a horse. I'm surprised you didn't smell it. I've shit four times already this morning. Three of them within a hundred paces of where you stood at the water's edge.''

Beowulf nodded. ''Fear shit smells the worst.''

I smiled in spite of myself. ''You said you'd never feared.''

''I lied,'' he admitted. ''Only a fool never fears.'' He stood abruptly. ''Let's go.''

My knees, under the burden of fear, wet ox-hide, and my weapons—I was glad I'd left my mail behind—fared badly, and we moved slowly along the beach through a copse of young summer-green black alder, and up a west-rising slope, at the top of which I motioned us to earth. Below us lay the boulders I'd mentioned and, barely discernible in a puzzle of shapes, one shadow darker than the others.

''The entrance,'' I whispered, pointing it out. ''An ancient barrow grave, fitting for a Grundbur's death spoor, and at its end, the opening to what looks like an old mine shaft.''

''You've been in there?'' Beowulf asked, looking at me with new respect.

"Not for long. It isn't a place for a man to be alone. Over here."

Crawling, I led the way to a fallen tree, beneath whose trunk I'd earlier built a fire. "The wind comes out of the cave, so I thought she wouldn't smell it," I explained. I lay some dry twigs on the ashes, blew the fire into life, and added two crude pine knot torches I'd fashioned before he arrived.

"You've been busy," Beowulf observed.

"Busy is easier than waiting." One knot, then the other, caught, and I motioned Amin into a tree to wait for my return. If, of course, I did. "Well?"

The barrow grave was perhaps twenty of my paces long, so low Beowulf had to stoop, and narrow enough that I could touch both walls with my outstretched hands. Black blood smeared the right-hand, rune-scratched rock wall, and a slow but steady cold exhalation emerged from the open shaft that led underground. Bone-Bane drawn, though he could at best stab within those confines, Beowulf led the way.

In a long life, and including those interminable hours in Azak's bloodthirsty company, I don't believe I've ever been so abjectly, totally terrified. Our torchlight, with the shadows it cast, was a prelude to the flickering fires of hell. The soft clank and creak of our armor and weapons was one moment magnified out of all proportion by the narrow passageway, the next fading, eerily reminiscent of fell engines of destruction advancing unseen through the night. The wind moaned like souls in agony, a promise of the end awaiting me.

I thought my knees would fail me. My heart beat in wild rhythms, and I swallowed nearly as much air as I breathed, and consequently belched painfully. I'd entered the barrow grave alone, true, but never in a score of lifetimes would I have descended that mine shaft alone, or with any other man in the world, I think, than Beowulf.

Looking back, I wonder if I dreamed such a magnificence of resolve. He was glad of my company, I'm sure, but I'm equally sure he'd have entered the terrifying depths alone. It wasn't easy, either. Always stooped and at times having to slide through narrow openings sideways or on hands and knees, he was defenseless against a child, much less a Grundbur. He no more than I knew where the way led, or what lay at its end. If any man ever in the world faced and stared down his fear, it was Beowulf. I will admire him to my dying day for that passage alone, and then, if I be allowed, will earnestly beg my dear Christ to relieve him of the agonies imposed on him for his disbelief.

I don't know how far we descended or how long our passage took, but at length we rounded a bend and found the shaft enlarged. His joints aching, Beowulf stretched and limbered himself. Ahead, a pale glimmer seemed to play on the ceiling, and we heard the frail whisper of what we later learned was an underground stream running over a low fall. Most telling, a sickly sweet aroma that had tickled our noses for some time swelled into a nauseous stench, one we had known from another night.

Beowulf's face was pale, but his hand on Bone-Bane was steady as he leaned to whisper in my ear. "I'll leave my torch here. Keep yours, stay close, and cover my back if there's more than one of them. Otherwise, bare hands, steel, or wood, she's mine."

His torch extinguished, the wire-wound hilt of the broad Bone-Bane firmly gripped, Beowulf edged forward to the final bend in the shaft. My torch held behind me in order to cast as little light as possible, we stopped and peered carefully around a sharp-edged corner. The cavern was large, dimly lit by fire. The high ceiling and the walls lay in darkness. The stream, a low curtain of falling water catching the light, lay to our left. Ahead of us, silhouetted by the fire, the iniquitous one crouched with her back to us, at feed, from her movements and the loathsome sounds coming from her.

She wasn't expecting us. What living man, after all, had ever come to call in the deep lair? I'd have sneaked up on her, surprised her with a killing blow, if possible, but that wasn't Beowulf's way. Rather, his ringed mail announcing his presence, he strode forward purposefully and loosed his battle-cry, sent it roaring and echoing wildly through the chamber of death.

She wasn't frightened. Her own hate-cry joining Beowulf's, she leaped up without hesitation and sprang to meet him.

Never have I seen a battle more frightening for its ferocity. I recall the first blow, the glint of firelight on swinging steel, the hag's arm raised to protect her neck, and the blade, striking bone, breaking—unthinkable that the famous sword's bane should be a bone!—and the shattered pieces flying. I recall the second, her good hand, claws like spikes, cuffing his head, sending him reeling. I recall the third, with which, a rock in her hand, she leaped on him. Then, as they rolled and tumbled, locked in confusing embraces, my vision blurs and, as usual, I recall no more than details, threads picked from a tapestry.

Beowulf drew his ax, but she struck it from his hand—a mighty blow, that!—before he could raise it. The hag clawed at his face, but he evaded her grasp. He tried repeatedly to catch her arm, but she was slippery and fast.

I don't know how long they might have gone on. Beowulf was tiring, though, I could tell, for suddenly he was on his back and she was straddling him, her great weight and ponderous bulk pressing him to the bone-strewn earth. Somehow, she had gotten his dagger, and held it poised, point down, over his face, stayed only by the waning power in his arms.

And what was Musculus the Dwarf—who was not at all, as the Northmen believed, meant for the darkness of caves—doing all this time? Anything more useful than shouting encouragement to Beowulf, scurrying about to keep out of their way? Not much, to be sure. O, yes, I did keep an eye out for others of the Grundbur's kind. I was, also, when I saw Beowulf weaken, about to intervene, was positioning myself to strike her in the face with the torch, when Beowulf suddenly appeared to lose heart, and the hag cackled—obscene glee, the echoing laughter of the Evil One exulting in the writhing anguish of the damned.

She thought she'd prevailed, the foul one, thought the victory was hers, and exulted too soon. Faster than the eye could discern, as adroitly as a dwarf plucking an egg from between a woman's breasts, Beowulf turned the blade and drove it upward, deep into her throat.

Rarely has a contest turned more abruptly or completely. Blood spewed, gushed out the gaping hate-bite. The hag's laughter became a choked plea for air. Unrelenting, Beowulf pushed the hilt from side to side, twisting the thrusting blade like a cruel auger before throwing her off him.

She landed on her side at my feet. Terrified, the torch held before me to ward her off, I stumbled backward but, and I don't know how, retained my footing. Her eyes, as she struggled to her hands and knees, burned with the hatred of her kind for ours, and I knew, in that moment, that evil was no more a philosopher's construction than was a sword, and that it could wound as surely, and as deeply.

I watched her, then, through the torchlight, and observed evil manifested, as clearly delineated as the line of ink that emerges from my pen and lays its trail across the skin I write on. She attempted to approach, but when she felt the heat on her face, she backed off and, her elbows buckling, fell onto her face and, as I supposed, expired.

# 25. Of Beowulf's Wounds, My Discoveries, Both Revolting and Troubling, and Our Ascent from the Deep Lair.

**W**as she, as the Northmen thought, a troll? I don't believe in trolls, but if she was, if they exist, I've seen one. Was she a spawn of Satan, evil personified, as one friend, who's a priest, suggested? I don't know. There are some things that men, perhaps, were never meant to know.

Whatever she was, Beowulf had killed her. The lifeless hulk of the foul one lay at my feet. The nails of one clawed hand dug into the layer of detritus covering the floor. Her head was canted sideways, her red glowing eyes were rolled back in her head, her lips pulled back to reveal the short, sowlike fangs Sigtrygg had mentioned. I stood, both mute and paralytic, until, at last, I emerged from my daze and looked for Beowulf.

He was nowhere to be seen, the victorious one. Not where they had rolled over each other, not by the fire. I realized he'd made his way to the stream only when I heard a moan from that direction, followed by a large splash.

He was lying unconscious, his head submerged, when I reached his side. Luckily, he coughed and sputtered the moment I rolled him onto his back, and shortly thereafter sat up.

"Where is she?" he asked, his eyes closed, gasping for breath.

"On the far side of the fire. Dead. You prevailed."

"It doesn't feel like it." He moaned. "By Loki's torment, but her blood burns!"

I planted my torch, stripped off my helmet, and removed the rag I'd tied around my head to make the helmet fit tightly. "This way," I ordered, helping him to lean toward the water. There, laving his eyes, rinsing the rag in the clear, flowing water, and repeating the process time and time again, we finally relieved the pain somewhat and he announced he could see again, however dimly.

"A close call, Musculus. Now I know how, in combat, the lesser man feels. The next time I have the upper hand, I'll more carefully beware the desperate move."

He'd been no further than a whisker from dying and, giving no thought to his mortality, concentrated on the lesson learned. "You'll be lucky to have a next time, with those eyes," I pointed out.

"Yes. And this," he added, raising his left arm. "She very nearly gutted me."

I hadn't noticed, but she'd ripped through the chain mail and the ox-hide shirt, and blood oozed through the tear. Quickly, I helped him shed mail, ox-hide, and linen undergarment. Two nails had raked his ribs, had torn the skin and flesh to the bone, but luckily had not invaded his body-cave.

I set to work again immediately. Beowulf sat stoically as I scrubbed away the clotting blood and used my dagger to debride the shredded skin and pick out the filth left behind by her nails. "It's the best I can do for now," I said once clean blood flowed freely. I tore strips from his linen and bound the wound. "You'll need a better healer than I, though. At least we had clean water."

Beowulf cupped his hands, drank, and leaned against a large rock. "It's the only clean thing in here." He closed his eyes. "I'm going to rest. Wake me in a while, and we'll leave."

He was asleep immediately, a phenomenon I've seen often among men who've fought for their lives. Not having much else to do, I made him a pillow of his mail, covered him with his ox-hide shirt to protect him from the chill, dank air, and set out to explore.

The cave was a chamber of multiple horrors, I discovered soon after I built up the fire and extinguished my torch to save it for our return to the earth's surface. First and foremost, which almost made me vomit, was the half-eaten body of the Grundbur, on which, evidently, the female had been feeding when we surprised her. Yes, I know some men are cannibals, which has never ceased to amaze and sicken me, but that any creature could stomach not only its uncooked mate but as foul and corrosively fleshed a beast as the Grundbur was revolting beyond belief.

As for anything after that, I was so stunned as to be inured. Their larder was the floor. Rotting meat and bones, most of them human remains, I thought, and certainly split-open skulls, were scattered haphazardly. No thought had been given to the isolation of bodily wastes, which everywhere lay uncovered and walked through. (In one pile—I left it untouched—a silver finger-ring gleamed in the dull light of the burning brand I carried.) I saw no utensils or any other artifact of civilization for their use other than the fire, and saw no indication of how they kindled it. Their treasure-hoard, alone, was clean. There, two piles of rings, necklaces, clasps, bracelets, silver, jewels and amber, swords and unattached hilts, daggers, silver cheek-plates and nose-protectors from helmets, and other costly and precious wares had been arranged to make a pair of low, nest-like structures in which, it appeared, they made their beds.

I'd seen enough, and Beowulf had slept long enough. But on my way back to wake him, I passed the female and received, if I hadn't already, the fright of my life, which lives with me to this day.

She hadn't been dead! Somehow, and silently, a shadow amid the shadows, she'd rolled over. Her head had fallen back and the wound in her throat gaped like a second mouth. But the epitome of horror lay farther down, for, when I inspected her corpse, I saw her belly had deflated and a spreading pool of steaming blood lay between her spread legs where she'd given birth. And from there, over her leg and disappearing into the darkness, led a damp trail that, as I followed it with drawn sword, changed from the slither of a serpent to hands and knees and then feet alone, whereupon it dimmed and failed.

Was it possible? Would I have believed, a year earlier, that any of this tale turned true could be possible? I was quaking, I admit, but my heart nearly stopped when a dark figure no taller than a yearling goat leaped from behind a boulder, darted past me, and, before I could move, ran into a fissure in the cave wall and disappeared. A moment later, the blood beating like a tabor in my ears, I was sure I heard a weak mewing sound, a cry of distress, echoing faintly from the opening, and then silence once again enshrouded me.

How long did I stand there, struck as mute as stone? I don't know. Only that, eventually, I once again became aware of the sound of water. I'd sunk to my knees, and was trembling violently with the enormity of what I'd witnessed. Evil had spawned after death—I'd been certain she was dead!—and reproduced itself, propagated its kind to inhabit the earth, in whose bowels it would live and on whose surface it would emerge, one day, to take its unending toll. A Grundbur was dead, as was its female, and long would live the Grundbur.

I didn't tell Beowulf. Instead, I rolled the female onto her belly and kicked dirt and offal over the slime of her offspring. Then I woke Beowulf, who, though the wound in his side ached fiercely, said he felt refreshed. I showed him the Grundbur, whose gnawed corpse he viewed impassively. I took him to the treasure nests, from which he took a sword and some other pieces to present to Hrothgeirr. Finally, we stopped at the female, whose head he laboriously severed with his new sword, and gave me to carry by its hair. That done, we relit our torches and made our way back up the long and tortuous passage, through the barrow grave, and into light and the sweetest, freshest air I've ever smelled, where Amin greeted us with unalloyed joy.

I'll add here only that Beowulf was so tired by then that he could barely walk, the sun was deep in the western sky, and his dispirited thanes had kept their listless vigil at the boulder. The rest I'll save for a new day, and the final chapter of my account.

# 26. *Of Beowulf's Death, and of My Arrest and Escape.*

And so, as the reader can tell from the few pages remaining, I near the end of the account that has spanned so many half-years and includes so many adventures.

Jubilation marked our arrival at the defile above Grund Lake and our return to the folk-hall. However fatigued, Beowulf held up well that first night, graciously received the Scyldings' accolades and gratitude, and equally graciously shared them with me for obvious reasons. There seemed no end to the honors heaped on him by Hrothgeirr, who, true to his word, presented him with fully half his treasure-hoard (minus the women, to Bera's relief) as itemized by his councilor charged with its care. The young thanes gazed on him with unconcealed awe, and listened—as did even Hrothgeirr's sons—with rapt attention to the hero's account of the battle and the female Grundbur's death, as proved by the head, which took the place of her mate's arm. All wasn't well, though, as was evident to me, at least, from his restraint at table—he ate sparingly and drank only a taste—and the beginning flush of fever on his cheeks.

But who was I, the voice of reason in the midst of wild

euphoria, to say? I told Hrothgeirr, Urth, Eirik, and the Geats that Beowulf's wound was serious and needed attention, but the truth is, too, I didn't press as hard as I might have because I was seduced by their questions and attention. Giving Amin full credit for finding the entrance, I played the Geat in descriptive narratives that I didn't have to exaggerate much at all to convey the horrors found in the Grundburs' lair. The only part I omitted was the birth and, as far as I knew or know, the survival of their progeny, for sufficient unto the morrow are the horrors thereof, and the Scyldings had suffered enough and deserved their happiness.

The merriment came to an abrupt halt near first light when Beowulf suddenly keeled over in midsentence and fell heavily. Great consternation ensued. In the confusion, one man on each limb and Bera and I at his head, we carried him to the healer's room and laid him on a bench near Valgard Halfbeard.

Valgard had attended the festivities earlier the evening before but, still very weak and in great pain, had returned to his bed after a short stay. As badly injured as he was, though, his blood would replenish itself and his broken bones would knit, however crookedly. Beowulf, I feared, was in greater danger. His breath was fast and shallow, his pulse weak and fluttering. His face was flushed, and he burned to the touch. The cause was evident the moment the old woman who was the Scyldings' chief healer removed the bandages I'd improvised hours earlier and we saw how badly infected the deep scratch inflicted by the Grundbur had become.

Might the infection have been thwarted had we recleaned the wound upon our arrival? Who knows, given the notoriety of carnivores' claws and teeth for the infections they cause. This one had festered faster than most. The skin was puffed and red, hot to the touch. Pus oozed from its length. Chiding us for letting the wound go untended for as long as it had, the healer declared extreme measures necessary, and directed us to carry Beowulf to the stream that ran nearby the folk-hall and lay him in the water. Not too long thereafter—the sun had yet to rise—once the water had cooled his fever, the healer cleansed the wound anew and applied a dressing soaked with herbal medications.

The news of Beowulf's precarious condition raced through the royal grounds like wildfire and rapidly spread to Heorot. A crowd of well-wishers and the worried gathered outside the healer's building. And as I could and should have predicted, had I not been so concerned myself, I, who at dusk was a hero, by dawn was a goat. To wit:

I'd prodded Beowulf to ignore the Geats' consensus that we should sail for home as heroes at best, or at worst waylay the female as we had the male and by our numbers overwhelm her with no harm to ourselves. Never mind that the consensus was mostly silent acquiescence to Hervarth's oily speech, and that two of our number were dead and three out of commission, which could as easily have been the result of a group encounter with the female.

I and my bird found the barrow grave and mine shaft that led to the Grundburs' lair, and Beowulf came to harm through our meddling.

I wasn't there when Beowulf invited those who were physically able to accompany him, but it was for some reason my fault they refused. I never did understand why.

Never mind Beowulf ordered me not to interfere until asked to—an order they all obeyed the night of the first fight—which he told them. As far as they were concerned, I'd stayed aloof in a cowardly manner, and Beowulf probably wouldn't have been hurt if I'd done my part.

Never mind who knows what else, but they rapidly concluded I was to blame for everything that had gone wrong, and should pay for my errors. Hrothgeirr's objections notwithstanding—the Geats reminded him I was under their jurisdiction, which seems to have been a law in the far north—I was manacled in the same chains we'd brought to bind the Grundbur, and told that if Beowulf died I'd be burned—alive—with him on his pyre. You can imagine my relief when Beowulf took a turn for the better, pronounced himself fit to return to the folk-hall, and, upon seeing me in chains, angrily and emphatically ordered my release.

Beowulf and everyone else knew his time had come to be separated from the living. Knew but, outwardly at least, pretended his wound was a minor scratch and that he'd be back to his normal self and up and about in no time. As hard as everyone tried, though, they could disguise their feelings only so much, and a funereal pall hung over the folk-hall.

One or more of the surviving Geats were at his side constantly, ready to fulfil his every wish. Bera attended him as devotedly as a wife, and cheered him with tender touches and brave smiles. Hrothgeirr and Urth visited often, as did Eirik. The young thanes, careful not to disturb his rest, spoke in hushed whispers. Beowulf himself acted almost embarrassed by, and grasped every opportunity to make light of, his predicament. He also, and perhaps not as uncharacteristically as I thought at the time, was tender and solicitous with Bera, with whom he was now openly and obviously deeply in love. He was also, I'm sure, aware of and troubled by the Geats' animosity toward me, and did what he could to protect me then and later.

He thanked me publicly and more than once for showing him the entrance to the deep lair. He noted how I alone had dared accompany him (which, I fear, only made them more jealous of me), and recited how I'd saved his life and helped him return to the surface. He recalled our unlikely meeting in the forest, and laughed again (oil on fire) as he retold the story of the comb I stuck in Hervarth's armpit. He publicly bestowed a quarter of his new riches on me, to do with as I pleased and without hindrance. He directed me, on my return to Hugleik's court, to give certain of his newly acquired treasures to Hugleik, and also to seek out the two boys he knew for a fact were his sons, to pass some of his wealth on to them and see to their futures. And, in one rare moment of solemnity, he directed that I was to be one of those who beat the drums as the flames on his pyre rose, which was a signal honor.

It was apparent to Hrothgeirr and his court that I was highly esteemed by Beowulf, and Beowulf himself seemed convinced the Geats understood and would comply with his wishes, but it was evident to me, at least, that they had no intention of doing so. Two of them might have turned the tide, but one, Asbrand, was dead, and the other, Valgard

Halfbeard, was isolated in his sickroom and too weak to protest, if, indeed, he was aware of the plans afoot.

And what could I do to protect myself? I might, I suppose, have prevailed upon Hrothgeirr or Eirik—they saw as plainly as I what was happening, and were opposed—to spirit me away before it was too late, but I would no more abandon Beowulf on his deathbed than I had Heraclius on his five years earlier.

From Beowulf the Clutcher to Beowulf very nearly the Babe, it was painful to watch his deterioration. Better by far to suffer Asbrand's, Olvir's, or Alreck's fate than Beowulf's. Every effort was bent to arrest his downward slide. Bera worked herself to exhaustion. His thanes comforted him as best they could. Hrothgeirr sacrificed a pair of *thralls* by throwing them into a bog. The healer was in constant attendance, washed and redressed his wound frequently, and gave him nourishing draughts to drink. The infection was insidiously tenacious, though, and when it got inside him, it attacked with a ferocity matching the Grundbur's in her lair.

All too soon, he could hold no food in his stomach and was reduced to sips of water mildly sweetened with honey. His face thinned, and his incredible physique wasted perceptibly as his muscles melted away. As a result of the intense fevers that raged in his poor ravaged body, and that were quelled only by immersion in the swiftly flowing cold stream nearby the folk-hall, he was seized with convulsions. He was at first lucid between these fever-bouts, but more and more often confused and disoriented.

The end came none too soon, given the pitiable creature he'd become. The fever tearing at him, he clutched Bera's hand, then raised his right arm and, with clenched fist—a ghost of the fist that could squeeze the juice from a raw onion—uttered his final war-cry and, convulsing, died. At last, he was separated from the living, and the living were the poorer for that separation.

How doleful the sweet, mellow tones of the silver-bound *lurs* that announced his death to the wide world! How exquisite the liquid notes that reverberated like life itself through the folk-hall, that floated like bereaved souls over village and bay! Geats and Scyldings alike, all men and women, free and slave, who heard, were stunned. Beowulf, though they'd watched his decline, was in their eyes indestructible, immune to the commonality of death. His death, though they saw, washed, and laid out his corpse, was incomprehensible. Other men died: not Beowulf.

Stunned incomprehension gave way to grief in the Scyldings, and outrage in the Geats. The Scyldings, that is to say, mourned, and the Geats sought revenge. And though the head of the Grundbur who'd killed Beowulf hung in plain sight, I was of course their target. One or two would have killed me then and there, but the voice of reason in the person of Hervarth—oh, what an expensive joke that comb in the armpit turned out to be!—prevailed. Once again, I was manacled, and thus saved to be burned on Beowulf's pyre.

Hrothgeirr and his court were displeased and pled my cause, but Hervarth—kingly material, he—was eloquent, and his legal arguments and implied threats—Hrothgeirr was vulnerable, and knew it—won the day. My trial, if that's what you'd call it, was over in short order. Judged and sentenced, I was carried to a room behind Valgard's, tied to a bench, and locked in with a guard at the door, there to remain until Beowulf's immolation.

Beowulf died shortly after sunrise. His corpse, according to custom for a warrior of his stature, would the next afternoon be placed on a pyre made out of a ship and burned that night. If the Geats had their way, I'd be led to the pyre shortly before it was lit and tied next to Beowulf's corpse, there to wait, surrounded by seal-oil–drenched cedar billets and the throb of funeral drums, for the heat and flames. As is perfectly evident, their intent was foiled. Here is what happened.

I wasn't, needless to say, sanguine about my prospects. How many times, after all, could I expect to escape certain death? I had friends and allies, though, not the least of whom, ironically, were the Geats themselves, for they all got so drunk they were unaware of the intrigues hatched to free me. The others, whom I'm more than pleased to thank as effusively as I can, were Valgard Halfbeard, Bera, Hrothgeirr, Eirik, and evidently some others whose names I never learned.

The plot began to unfold the next afternoon as the sun sank toward the horizon. Resigned to my fate, as I recall, I was considering the state of my soul when I heard a scratching sound and, after what seemed an eternity—though wasn't, in comparison to the real thing—saw a shaft of light from Valgard's room enter my cell. Moments later, Bera wiggled through a gap they'd made by loosening a log and untied me, whereupon we enlarged the hole and escaped into Valgard's room.

"They won't like this," I warned Valgard once we'd replaced the chunk of log we'd removed.

Valgard was exhausted by his labors, in great pain, and barely able to speak. "Beowulf didn't like their plans for you," he whispered.

"This was his idea?" I asked.

"He said you were the one man who stood by him when he needed help, and he'd ask no more of a friend and fellow warrior."

"He flattered me, Valgard," I replied, deeply honored. "You'd have stood by him, too, if you could have."

"I want to think so," Valgard agreed. He added, with a droll smile, "He also said, 'Besides, think how they'd laugh at me if I appeared at Valhalla's gates with a dwarf in tow!' So don't let your head swell too much."

Pity the man, even in Valhalla, who laughed at Beowulf!

Valgard's voice was faint. "To think. The one joke I ever heard him tell, Musculus, was on his deathbed. We should all die so bravely." He paused, wiped the cold sweat from his brow, and winced with the effort. "And now get out of here, Flat-face. You have little time. She"—he nodded at Bera—"will take you to a boat that's waiting for you."

Bera handed me a light cloak and a belt with a sheathed dagger. "You'll see to Amin for me?" I asked, tying on the belt.

"I will if I can."

"Good. He'll go to you, I think. Take him back and give him to Ethelred."

"And say?"

I considered a message, but couldn't think of anything to say that Ethelred wouldn't know without my saying it. "Amin will be message enough," I said. I wrapped the cloak around me, stepped to him, and took his hand. "You've been a good friend, Valgard. I thank you, and will remember what you've done for me."

"Only what a friend would do. Good luck, Musculus!"

Bera shouldered a small bag of provisions, opened the door, and checked outside.

"I'll make the best I can," I said and, at the door, slapping my ass, "and keep an eye and ear peeled."

If nothing else, I left him smiling.


The shadows were long as Bera and I slipped into the forest. We kept away from the path through the sacred oak trees, made our way swiftly downhill, and skirted Heorot. Still unseen, we ducked behind the hulk of a ship through whose broken body-beams I could see Beowulf's pyre.

"Boar-Rover!"

"I'm told everyone agreed it was fitting," Bera said.

Fitting, perhaps, but also lamentable, even if, as I knew, Egil and Gurd could build a new one. The proud ship lay in a cradle at the water's edge, with the fierce boar's head insignia facing the bay and, beyond, the sea. Pennants flew from the mast, prow, and stern. The sail, decorated with brightly colored pieces of cloth, was set perpendicular to the wind and fluttered like a thing alive. On board, a newly constructed high deck, his bier, was canopied with rich fabric in which gold and silver threads had been woven. Cedar billets that I knew had been drenched in seal oil and would burn fast and hot were visible above the freeboard. "Not a good way to die," I said, with a shiver of relief.

"There are worse, Dwarf," Bera announced. "It will be an honor."

I hadn't known, and looked at her in a new light. "You?" I asked, amazed.

"Gladly!" With what fervor she spoke! "Our souls will fly upward together in the sparks! But now you and I must hurry."

I don't want to sound cynical but, better her than me, I was easily persuaded. We kept to the shadows of sheds, partially completed hulls, and cannibalized derelicts, passed as quietly as whispers into a copse of young trees, and emerged shortly thereafter at the edge of a small cove, where a dory much like Ethelred's waited.

"Eirik Stone-tooth said to tell you he arranged for this with Hrothgeirr's consent and help," she told me. She threw the bag of provisions aboard and pointed across the bay. "There are weapons and enough food for a week aboard, and silver and jewels for your use as you need them. Row openly, as if you have every right to do so, to that spit, then hug the shore to the entrance of the bay. No alarm will sound." She handed me an oiled skin bag. "This is a map and a safe-conduct from Hrothgeirr. Once on the open water, bear west. I must go."

"Bera!"

Already on her way, she paused at the edge of the copse. "Why?"

Did she smile? I think so. "Why did you accompany him into the deep lair?"

I didn't know why, and my answer sounded lame. "He was my friend. I couldn't let him go alone."

Without a doubt, she smiled, then turned and melted into the shadows. And all that remained of her was her voice, filtering through the trees, which I can still hear as plainly as if I were there again.

"Just so, Dwarf," she said. "Just so."

# Epilogue

**I** rowed openly to the spit, hugged the shore to the bay's entrance, and, once upon open water, bore west. Then, unable not to, I pulled my boat well above the high-tide mark and, no easy task, in the growing dark, began to climb. Once at the summit, I pulled myself into a tree and climbed again, and very near the top wrapped my arms around the trunk and waited.

The sky was cloudless. A rising full moon streaked the bay with a path of light—the sea calling someone to her bosom. Sometime later, points of light like very slowly falling stars descended the far hillside, flickered as the funeral procession wound down from the heights. Soon, as I knew they must, the orange stars gathered in a knot around Boar-Rover, which had carried Beowulf to his death, and would, in moments, carry him beyond his death.

Were they angry? No doubt. Did Bera climb aboard of her own free will, lie next to her lord, and peacefully await their consummation? I hope for her sake they let her, but didn't—don't—know. I knew only that one of the stars detached itself from the others, and with its fire lit another greater than itself.

Soon, with the flames leaping, Boar-Rover was unleashed, and as it slipped into the water, a storm of sparks, each with its bit of soul attached, streamed into the sky. And when, at last, the wind brought me the throb of drums, I loosed my hold and climbed down.

It was done with. No reason to remain, every reason to leave, I scrambled down the hill, pushed my boat into the water, set my sail, and bore west.

And as the wind pushed me, I beat my fist on the side of my boat. Beat slowly and with respect, and love, for Einarr, Beowulf, Clutcher, my friend and a hero, who'd lived honorably and died bravely.

For himself, that is true, but as I've known since that night, with one's self is the only place one can begin when Grundburs stalk.

Hail, Beowulf, whose song is sung!

# Available by mail from

## PEOPLE OF THE LIGHTNING • Kathleen O'Neal Gear and

### W. Michael Gear
The next novel in the First North American series by best-selling authors Kathleen O'Neal Gear and W. Michael Gear.

## RELIC • Douglas Preston and Lincoln Child
*Alien* meets *Jurassic Park* in New York City!

## DRAGONFLY • John Farris
Preying on every woman's worst fears, the critically acclaimed author of *Sacrifice* has once again crafted a chilling novel of psychological terror.

## THE FOREVER KING • Molly Cochran and Warren Murphy
"I found *The Forever King* to be one of the most original things I've read in years. Books like this don't come along very often."
—Marion Zimmer Bradley, author of *The Mists of Avalon*

## STEROID BLUES • Richard La Plante
"Mr. La Plante tells the story skillfully, creating tension and a mounting feeling of horror as he peers into some very sick minds."—*The New York Times Book Review*

## SPOOKER • Dean Ing
It took the government a long time to figure out that someone was killing agents for their spookers—until that someone made one fatal mistake.

**Available by mail from**

TOR  FORGE®

TOR  FORGE  TOR®

---

## DEATHRIGHT • Dev Stryker
"Two bestselling authors combine forces to write a fast-paced and exciting terrorist thriller. Readers will want to stay the course."—*Booklist*

## RED CARD • Richard Hoyt
"A brave smart shot...heaps of soccer lore....Hoyt manages to educate as he entertains."—*Publishers Weekly*

## DEAD OF WINTER • David Poyer
A thrilling novel of revenge by the bestselling author of *The Only Thing to Fear*.

## FALSE PROMISES • Ralph Arnote
"Guaranteed to please all fans of non-stop, cliffhanger suspense novels!"
—*Mystery Scene*

## CUTTING HOURS • Julia Grice
"Readers will find this hard to put down. Love, hate, and a mother's determination to save her daughter make for a ten

## WINNER TAKE ALL• Sean Flannery
"Flannery is a major find."—Dean Koontz

## ULTIMATUM • R.J. Pineiro
"The purest thriller I've seen in years. This book may define the genre."
—Stephen Coonts

## OTTO'S BOY • Walter Wager
"New York City's subway becomes a deathtrap in Wager's taut thriller."—*Library Journal*

---